"THIS AIN'T NOTHING BUT A CATHOUSE ON A MUDBALL PLANET."

The man from Startraders took an aggressive stance. "Why should you care?"

"I like my friends to be left alone." Rader started to add, "I like my planet to be left alone," when the man interrupted with a sneer.

"You have whores for friends, then?" The man tensed, then drew his gun.

Rader was faster. The ruby beam from his laser struck just below the sternum, cut up through the heart in millisecond pulses, and split the man open. The corpse fell back with a clatter, his unfired laser spinning through the splatters of blood.

The war for Zikkala had begun.

THE FAR FRONTIER

WILLIAM ROTSLER

PLAYBOY PRESS
PAPERBACKS

THE FAR FRONTIER

Copyright © 1980 by William Rotsler

Cover illustration copyright © 1980 by PEI Books, Inc.

Published simultaneously in the United States and Canada by Play-boy Press Paperbacks, New York, New York. Printed in the United States of America. Library of Congress Catalog Card Number: 79-90926. First edition.

Books are available at quantity discounts for promotional and industrial use. For further information, write our sales promotion agency: Ventura Associates, 40 East 49th Street, New York, New York 10017.

ISBN: 0-872-16633-3

First printing April 1980.

for Steve Langley

In the deepest chamber of the Old Place, ten young males and ten young females stood before a glowing sphere of light. The sphere pulsed slowly, growing and shrinking, changing colors and floating unsupported over the rock floor worn smooth by countless feet.

In the minds of each, a voice was heard.

I am Kaleen-ka, Mother of broods, Father of the nest. You have reached the age of testing, the time of host survival, the time of proving. You must test yourselves as no one else can. The time of the nest awaits you. Shir-ka-kaloon, my father, my son, mother of us all, will be with you. Go, and be tested.

The sphere of light expanded, splashing vivid colors over the bare bodies, pulsating so rapidly that the ones who watched were blinded. A wordless fire burned briefly in their minds; then the sphere of light sank into the rock and disappeared.

The chamber was dim, lit only by torches in the passage outside. The twenty filed out, silent, apprehensive, involved in themselves and their worthiness, but their twin hearts were eager.

The time of testing was upon them, and they rejoiced. For they were the fortunate ones, the first full generation to face the supreme testers—the new ones on the surface who called themselves human.

"Where are they?" Wolf Briggs muttered angrily, his breath stirring up the dust as he lay on his stomach among the ragged, gray rocks. His blue eyes nervously watched the rocks below in a frantic search for the Kaleen warriors that had downed both his horses and sent him scurrying for shelter under a hail of sling-propelled rocks.

His palms were sweating; he pried loose his stiffened right hand from the grip of the laser and wiped it dry on his dusty shirt. He slithered to another opening between

7

the boulders and got another angle on the downslope. His breath came in short gasps as he wiped his beardless face with his free hand.

"Damn," he said softly, his eyes stopping on the still forms of Penny and Nickle, his two dead mounts. Sometime during the furor Nickle's pack had been taken, and there were marks in the sand where it had been dragged into the brush. They had been good mounts, both of them, Penny the mare and Nickle the stallion, grown from frozen sperm and ova that had come out on the early ships and trained by the scarred trappers back at Shamrock.

Wolfgang Amadeus Mozart Briggs shifted again, wiping the sweat from his eyes and silently cursing his luck. He should have listened to the men back at Shamrock. *But no,* he thought bitterly, *I had to be the brave trapper, going out when the more experienced hands were saying stay in, at least until late summer, then go out with the others.* "Damn," he whispered again, condemning himself for the hundredth time since the Kaleen ambush. *Just had to play it tougher-than-thou, didn't you?* He castigated himself mercilessly. *Know-it-all. Cleanboot.*

He saw a movement and thrust the laser through the cleft in the rocks to fire a ruby-beam into the brush. The bushes caught fire, but only after a hail of rocks came whistling out of nowhere to strike him and his frugal shelter. He yanked himself back, a stinging cut on his cheek and another, from a ricochet, on his right arm. Then just as quickly, he rolled to the left and aimed around the other side of the rock. He was panting, wide-eyed and scared, but he fired twice and had the satisfaction of seeing movement stop suddenly.

Wolf Briggs rolled over and looked up the low hill behind him. It was too barren to afford much camouflage, just dirt and rocks that gave shelter only if you were flat on your face behind them. He rolled back, thirsty, his throat clogged with dust and fear.

What's it like to die? he wondered. *Do the Kaleen kill fast or slowly, given the choice? Where do you go when you die, or do you just stop?* He blinked his gritty eyes and glanced at the sky. *Hours until dark,* he thought bitterly. *Probably more day than life left.*

He moved again, trying not to stir up dust, his brown

hair falling limply over his sweaty forehead, the cut beginning to throb. There was another movement in the brush, but he was far too slow to react. *Closer each time,* he thought.

He looked at the horses again. At least they didn't seem to suffer, not for long, anyway. Would he have that same merciful death, sudden and eternal?

Wolf Briggs gulped and looked around for a pebble to put into his mouth, something which, he had read, often helped. He almost picked up a tiny, armored beetle before he found a stone of suitable size. He brushed it off against his sleeve and popped it into his mouth. It rattled against his teeth, and he held it firm with his tongue. It tasted salty and bitter.

Briggs checked the tiny ready-light on his laser. About five good bolts were left. His eyes went to his saddle on the dead Penny, where extra batteries were cached in the bags.

Five bolts, he thought. Would that mean five dead Kaleen? He doubted it. So far, he had barely seen them—only flashes of brown skin, of strong muscular arms spinning slings and glimpses of dark hair.

I'm too young to die, he thought, then laughed at himself. What would his brother say? "You're too ugly to die," Aram would say; or maybe, "You're too dumb to die." Nothing very original—but with most of his meaning lying below the words, in the tone and context. "I wish you were here," Briggs muttered to his brother, then immediately changed his mind. "No, stay there. Take care of Frédéric and Mum." He blinked away the sweat in his eyes, suddenly frantic. There had been movement, and he hadn't reacted at all. They'd think him dead and come at once.

Briggs edged around the short barrier of rocks, letting dust rise, then backtracked toward his original position, letting the dust cover his movements.

The sun was hot. A summer day on Zikkala, way out at the end of the Orion spur of the Perseus arm, umpteen light-years from Gauguin III, his home planet of Matisse. A distance not long in time, subjective-time, he realized. Less than seven months, with all but seconds of it involved in running in and out of a system to where the null-space drive could operate. But back on Matisse, hundreds of years had passed. Frédéric Chopin, Aram Khachaturian, his mother Ermine, even Handy, the pet Moloch—all dead.

Briggs blinked away the sweat and tears and prepared to die—and to take some of his killers with him.

Rader stopped his horse just below the edge of the rusty stone ridge and stood up in the saddle. His eyes moved in a swift search pattern from the near to the far, from the foothills of the Redpaws just ahead to the green savannah around Shamrock's domes, and glimpsed through the passes. Beyond were the blue-gray Marble Mountains and the blue sky above, cloudless and powerfully azure.

The big, dark-haired man took his time, standing easily in the stirrups of the tawny animal. Everything seemed quiet, but Rader had not lived on the vast Marengo continent of untamed Zikkala for almost four years without being very cautious, very smart—and very fast. He kept his hand on the butt of his laser now at rest in its well-worn holster, for it was certain that between him and the fortress trading post of Shamrock, at least one party of Kaleen waited to attack.

Rader directed his steed to a higher location on the ridge and sat down in the big command saddle, his eyes still scanning back and forth, probing and seeking. He shifted his weight in the stirrups and felt the comforting bulk of the laser rifle in its saddle scabbard. The sensation of it against his leg brought a grim smile to his lips. Early every summer, in the domes and bars of Blackbull and Shamrock, and over in Nuevo Monterey, they kidded themselves ruthlessly and self-consciously about injuns and cowboys and the winning of the Out. But beneath the jibes and laughter, beneath the repeated jokes and oft-told tales, there was the very real knowledge that living on Zikkala was not a job for the slow, the stupid, or the cleanboot. Wearing lasers and carrying knives were not picaresque, outdated customs to delight the tourist trade, like the fancied-up pirates of Hammurabi or the dragonshirts on Zinzir. For one thing, there was no tourist trade on Loki IV. It was hundreds of light-years to Coronation and even further to

Terra-Sol, back along the Perseus arm of the Milky Way galaxy. Even with n-drive, which sent ships through null-space in subjective nano-seconds, there was a terrible price to pay not only in centuries but in social disorientation.

To the passengers on an n-drive ship, they seemed to leap light-years instantaneously, but to the outside observer —if there could be such a creature—it took the ship 24.8 standard-years per light-year. A ten light-year jump to a planet and back brought the ship home five hundred years after departure, but to the subjective experience of the passengers and crew it had been only moments.

Thus only a few trader ships arrived at Zikkala, one or two a year, sometimes more, depending upon the faith of the ship's owners, who gambled that, hundreds of years after they dispatched a vessel, it would return with a payload that would make it worthwhile. Thus governments— planetary, regional, great federations of starworlds, or guilds—were the only ones that traveled the stars for profit. These few ships were Zikkala's only contact with other inhabited worlds, as inadequate as they were.

Rader turned in his saddle and looked back down the dusty trail at Liana and Korda, who were sitting patiently on their mounts at either ends of the pack train, scanning the brush and the back trail with restless eyes. He signaled them to wait, slid off his mount, and crept to the ridge. He was a dark tall lean man in soft, leather clothes and a wide-brimmed black hat, well armed and cautious.

He saw a plume of dust, faint and gone in an instant. He narrowed his eyes, saw the two distant lumps that were dead horses, and cursed, silently. He lay motionless for several minutes, well hidden behind a dark *scrit* bush, his sharp eyes picking out the probable routes of attack and the probable hiding places of the Kaleen blades. Then he moved back, raising no dust, until he could get to his feet. His face was grim as he motioned Korda and Liana forward with a warning sign. As they rose cautiously toward him, Rader thought about the situation, his eyes still searching the brush around them.

Rader had no desire to meet any war party of Kaleen, and he bore several scars to prove that he had met them before. The tough Kaleen were formidable warriors, and Rader knew them to be complex entities, with much of their lives kept very hidden from the byworlders who had come there.

"Ambush?" Korda said, his deep voice rumbling.

Rader nodded and pointed at their pack animals.

"Liana, you guard the treasure and—"

"God-*dammit,* Rader!" The slant-eyed, honey-skinned woman snapped at him. Korda laughed, a deep, slow chuckle, and she punched him in a beefy black shoulder. "Stop that, you bonehead! I'm tired of people with testicles expecting those without to be helpless." There was a lot of suppressed fury in her voice, and Rader's grin faded.

"There's someone out there, pinned down," he said. "Just one pack horse, so either he or she lost them earlier or it's some tourist." The last word dripped with sarcasm. None of those who put their lives on the line for the way they lived had much concern about sightseers, usually spacers off a Guild ship who were contemptuous of any danger that didn't take place in a vacuum.

"So?" Liana said, bristling. The big black man started to speak, and her eyes flared at him. "If you say one more time that I'm beautiful when I'm angry, I'll make you a eunuch!"

Rader looked at Korda, and they both shrugged. "All right," he said mildly. "Korda, you get the train together and ready to run at my signal. We may have to make an ungraceful exit from this bit of territory." He looked at the beautiful oriental woman. "That better?"

"It'll be better when you learn to think of me first, not after a little persuasion!" She drew her handlaser with expert smoothness, checked the ready-light at full, and put it back, all in one swift movement. "Do we go in on foot or ahorse, noble leader?"

"Horse, I think. If that's a cleanboot out there, he might not recognize us as friends until the burial." He looked at Korda and scratched his jaw. "Maybe we should all go in noisy as hell, except we detour toward the rocks and—"

"What rocks?" the burly, black man asked.

Rader knelt and quickly drew a map in the sand. "He, she, or it—is here. The Kaleen are probably here and along here. Korda, you go this way, as if you were circling, but actually you just ride like hell to reconnect to the trail here. No use waiting for us, just keep on going to Shamrock."

"We go this way?" Liana asked. "Sweep through here, collect the cleanboot, and join up with m'man here."

"Uh-huh," Rader said, grinning. "Not exactly book generalship, but it will do. Mount up," he said, but Liana was already swinging into her saddle, the *taba*-cloth loin-covering whipping in the wind of her passage. She settled the equipment-belt on her hips, tugged at her short vest of soft leather, and touched the long knife at her left hip.

Rader and Korda exchanged another look, and there was a stern warning in the black man's eyes. Normally Korda was gentle, except when decided ungentleness was needed to survive; and as Rader had learned on several worlds, Korda was a survival type. In his way he was reminding his friend Rader of Liana's impetuousness, which more than once had gotten her in trouble.

"Come on, let's do it," Liana said.

Rader shrugged and swung aboard his mount. Stroking the neck of his horse, he looked around, then walked the horse to where he could again survey the land on the other side.

Nothing much had changed. Just then, a rock unexpectedly arched up from the brush and plinked against a boulder, but there was no answering fire. Either the person trapped was dead or dying—or was conserving his bolts. The rock rolled back down the slope and came to rest. Rader looked over at Liana, nodded, and dug his heels into his horse's flanks.

The animal lunged forward, and Rader pulled the heavy Excalibur laser rifle from the boot and thumbed it on. He rose in the saddle as they went down the slope and put a series of millisecond pulses into the brush where the last rock had come from, sweeping it in a figure-eight pattern.

Liana let out a terrifying scream, her bloodthirsty battle cry, and fired several times into likely hiding places. Rader quickly shifted the long, powerful weapon across the saddle and fired in the other direction, aiming not from the shoulder but by instinct. Something thrashed in the brush; an arm went up, whirling a sling, and let fly a shot as Rader brought the ruby-beam sweeping across the gray-green Zikkala *scrit*. The sling's stone thumped against the horse's neck even before the severed arm hit the sand.

Rader's horse bucked but straightened out and galloped

on. The ruby-sword of the Excalibur flamed again, slicing through a half-grown *pungi* tree and two Kaleen blades that had leaped up. They fell back with strangled cries, spurting blood. The brush was set ablaze in several places, and thick, oily smoke billowed up from the fire-swept vegetation. Another Kaleen charged through the smoke, brandishing a polished spear, throwing it while Rader was engaged in shifting the heavy weapon back across the saddle. But Liana acted, cutting the Kaleen down, and the victors' horses thundered on.

Rader ducked some stones and thrust the heavy-duty laser back into its scabbard, drawing his hand-weapon quickly. Another of the red-brown humanoids leaped up, his muscular tail slapping the thick *scrit* as he leaped toward Rader, a long knife in his bony hand. Rader fired point-blank into his face, and the headless body fell away.

Looking back, Rader saw Liana firing and Korda whooping and waving as the pack train came over the ridge. There were screams and smoke, the acrid odor of burning *pungi*, dust and sweat. Liana veered toward him, pounding by upon her steed, low over her saddle, firing coolly. Her ruby-beam sliced a long, low swath through the *pungi* and *scrit*. Splatters of thick red fluid plopped and slithered to the ground from severed body parts as the beginning of a Kaleen battle cry was cut off in midscream.

Rader galloped out of the last of the thick brush, and the horse slowed as they went up the rocky hillside. Rader saw movement behind the rocks and cried out to the figure, "Climb aboard!"

A slender figure jumped up, half fell over the rocks and ran toward Rader's horse. The dark-haired man in the saddle looked quickly around, saw a ruby-beam blink from behind some rocks, and Liana's horse stumbled and fell, screaming shrilly, his front legs gone, pumping blood in sudden amputation. Rader's laser splashed flame over the rock, then suddenly stopped. Cursing, he thrust it back into his holster and stuck his hand into the saddle bags, groping for the extra batteries.

The ambush victim cried out and clawed at Rader, trying to get aboard—and almost caused him to drop the battery. He pulled the slender youth on behind him, then drew his laser again and quickly replaced the battery as they started down the hill.

Liana was on her feet, running toward Korda and the last of the pack animals. Rader stood in his stirrups and fired quickly into the several likely spots. He galloped into the brush, forcing his animal to get between Liana and where he thought the Kaleen were. She was dusty and unkempt, but her dark eyes flashed wickedly, her laser readied.

Rader grinned through the sweat and fear. Liana ran like a cat, leaping, dodging. She caught up to the last of the pack animals and holstered her weapon long enough to slash the straps on its bulky load, letting it thump into the dust. Then she leaped lithely astride and whooped at the horse to move.

The rest of the pack train shied at the noise and sudden movements and were straining to break loose from the tough plastic line that held them together. Liana rode to the middle of the train, reached out and grabbed the ear of a rearing animal and twisted it. Almost at once, the animal calmed and the train started moving again.

"Hawww!" Liana yelled, and it was echoed by Korda at the head of the line.

Rader rode hard, the youth holding on behind, until he had caught up to Korda. He stopped, shouting at the extra rider to get off. "Jump on that second horse! Don't drop the pack unless you start falling behind!" The stranger staggered on weak legs until he had caught the animal and pulled himself up.

Rader was already galloping ahead, hearing Liana cursing at the pack train in four languages to keep them on the trail. But his attention was keen for the next potential ambush point, the spot where the Kaleen would attempt to cut down the panicked trappers running from the fight, scrambling toward the safety of the Shamrock guns.

That grove there, he thought and fired the Excalibur into it. A tree slowly toppled as a flight of startled *chandthruts* winged into the air. Two of the ancient trees burst into flame. Rader looked back, saw Korda and Liana bringing up the string of frightened animals and the stranger swaying as he clung awkwardly to the pack.

Ahead of them was Kilometer Rock. The Kaleen ambushers rarely went beyond it, for that was too close to the telescope-equipped weapons mounted in the watch towers. The lasers were backed by the pile beneath Dome One and could far outdistance anything portable. Rader felt their safety from the long-tailed ambushers was almost at hand.

A flicker of movement at the base of the red-stone monolith caused the Excalibur to swing to target. His finger hit the firing stud as three more Kaleen rose up. Two were swinging slings, but the third was aiming a weapon, with both hands. In a second, Kilometer Rock had another black melting-scar as it became the grave for three more of the Zikkala natives.

Rader swung his mount around, pointing the laser to where he looked as he searched the underbrush. The pack train galloped past, and Rader fired at another clump of brush. Then he kicked his heels into the horse and went galloping up the loose talus slope toward Kilometer Rock. He jumped off long enough to yank the partially melted needle-gun from the grip of a dead Kaleen, then swung onto his horse again and rode like hell down the trail toward Shamrock.

They slowed down a couple of hundred meters out, entering the cleared zone of the fort. They could see the guards in the towers, hunched over their long-range sights. Rader waved, and one of them waved back.

He rode up alongside Liana and looked at her. "I'm all right," she said, her face grim. "But I lost Moonglow, dammit." Her head swung toward the youth clinging erratically to the pack animal ahead. "Cleanboot. Not worth a good horse to save."

Rader agreed with a nod and rode on ahead. He looked at the teen-age youth for the first time. The boy was pale but composed, very dusty and with hairline rivulets of blood trickling down his face. He managed a weak grin and tried to wave at Rader, but his uncomfortable roost on the pack was endangered, so he nodded, smiling a little foolishly.

Turning in his saddle, Rader looked at their back trail.

It was all quiet. He rode up to Korda, who said, "Too bad about Moonglow."

"Yeah," agreed Rader, "but animals are secondary to people."

Korda grinned. "Don't let her hear you say that. The last time, she put a knife into the tree by your head. Remember?"

"Your woman is beautiful," Rader said, "a great cook, a person of worth and delight—but a horse is not as important as a man. Especially if me or mine are endangered."

Korda laughed, a throaty rumble of delight. "Just remember about that knife, Rader." He slapped his horse's sweat-foamed neck, then rubbed it affectionately. "Sorry to lose that pack, too. Unless you want to go back for it?"

"Forget it." He aimed a thumb over his shoulder at the pack train. "We have more than enough *shoka* furs for anything we need."

"Oh? And what if the winter ship brought in a whole new library? Or some better kinda weapon? Or—" Korda left the thought open.

"We'll get by," Rader said. He turned in the saddle and looked at the boy still clinging to the pack animal. "I wonder who he is? A novice, of course, but why didn't they make him stay in Shamrock until he got some smarts?"

Korda shrugged his great broad shoulders. "We'll bill him for the horse, saddle, and a percentage of the pack. Only fair."

"Uh-huh. Suppose he doesn't have anything?"

"We'll have him work it off."

"Oh, no. Not out at the cave, uh-uh. No cleanboot like that. No, sir."

"Oh, what the hell, Rader, we were all cleanboots once."

Rader looked back again, glowering. "I don't think I was ever that much of a novice, and I know you weren't. So what are we, charities?" He made a rude noise and turned again to look at the rock-melt walls of Zikkala's main outpost of civilization.

"Hey, isn't that a new tower over there on the left?" Korda asked. "And look there," he said, pointing.

Rader saw the cluster of domes that loomed over the walls. "New one, eh?"

Liana rode up to them, the pack train calmed and

walking along behind her, dusty but obedient. "Alena Petrovna has her dome up," she said, giving Rader a knowing look.

He grinned but otherwise ignored her. "Isn't that Konstantin and Gastoni up in the gate tower?" He waved, and they waved back, then turned to disappear down the inner steps. Rader shifted in the saddle of his slow-walking animal and looked back along the pack train at the several fires they had started. Already the smoke was lessening as the fires died out in the tough, green growth of the early summer.

The massive gate, made of thick *pungi* timbers, scarred and blackened, swung open, and Gastoni ran out, smiling through his thick beard and waving a bottle of Old Dragonblood, the local whiskey.

"Rader, you old bastard! Korda, you black *shoka!* Made it again!" He grinned at Liana with unconcealed delight and ran his eyes over her lush, taut body. "Goddamn," he said in an awed and happy voice. "She's back again."

Liana laughed merrily and looked up brightly at the gate. Then her smile died as Konstantin limped out through the thick rock-melt walls. He had no right foot.

Rader's jaws clenched. He jerked his head at the empty end of the man's worn leather trousers and raised his eyebrows.

"Kaleen, o'course," Konstantin said, balancing on his good foot and waving his carved *pungi* crutch. "Dan Coquillon killed Usi, that Kaleen blade that chopped Zavioskii last year, but the rest of them bastards got a thunderbolt." He shrugged and waggled the loose trousers leg. "I found out about it when Usi's nest-brother—or whatever they call themselves—when he came huntin' me right after the first snow. The only thing that saved my bum was that he didn't know how to thumb it off maximum pulse. It gave me a chance to get him before the damn thing charged up again."

Rader swung off his horse, his face serious and stern. A footless trapper was in heavy trouble, and a jobless trapper would die of boredom. The crippled were usually given administrative or guard duties by the guilds. An equity in a guild was the nearest thing they had to security on Zikkala or any other pioneer world.

"I'll buy you a drink," he said to Konstantin.

"This one first," Gastoni said with a whiskery grin. He held the bottle up to Liana, who burst into a smile, abandoning her somber look. She knew when to be a mothering type and when to be a tiger cat, as well as when to be herself. She leaned over farther than she needed to and gave both Konstantin and Gastoni a good look into her short vest. They cackled happily as she took the bottle and tilted her head back for a long swallow.

"Who's the cleanboot we picked up?" Rader asked.

"Some blank that came in on the winter ship," Gastoni answered. "Impatient 'boot. Drove us crazy for a coupla weeks, then took his kit and went out adventurin'."

"Why didn't the guild starbuck stop him?" Liana asked, handing back the bottle.

Gastoni snorted and handed the whiskey up to Korda. "Here ya are, you black dinosaur—the first drink all summer!" Korda gulped some and leaned way out of the saddle to give it to Rader.

"Tastes like melted nails," he grumbled.

Rader took a couple of short swallows as Gastoni went on about the novice. "He weren't a guild member, that's why. Little bastard jumped ship! The *Lee De Forest,* it was, out of Sargon, bound for Lao-tzu. About a day after it lifted and was punching in the n-drive, the little scrote crawled out of the west supply dome. Bright as a new stellar and dumb as horsepucky. Wanted to go out and find his fortune right then." He turned to glower back at the youth, still dazed and blinking.

The pack train crept past the slowly walking men, and Liana was approaching the walls first. Men were calling down to her. "Let's see 'em again, beautiful!"

"Don't you do that, Liana," Gastoni said protectively. "That cleanboot would just fall right off the tower and get himself busted up, and I'd have to train myself a new partner. You just wait until I get off duty before you show 'em off!"

Rader squinted against the sky, looking up at the men on the walls and those gathered around the gate in greeting. He knew most of them and saw only four new faces. He didn't listen to the words they shouted to Liana, only the tone, and not one man spoke disrespectfully, not even the new ones. First of all, Liana took nothing from no one, though she was inclined to be generous. Secondly, no one wanted Korda mad at them, and they knew that after Korda, came Rader. The humor was rough but not crude, and everyone seemed genuinely pleased to have them back.

"I guess Liana is still popular," Rader said.

"Yup," Konstantin said. It obviously took a lot of effort for him to walk, and he hadn't said much. To give him a rest Rader stopped, touching his arm, and pointed at the boy on the pack horse as he went by.

"He cost us a horse, saddle and pack of furs."

Konstantin chuckled, resetting the crutch under his arm. "Hah. He's not a guilder, and I think everything he had he walked out of here with. Good luck collecting."

Rader shrugged and sighed. "Oh, well, that's what we get for hero-ing."

Wolfgang Briggs was only then beginning to catch his breath. The shouts and screams had brought him out of a lurid, sweaty dream of death. The tall, tanned stranger on the rearing horse, the beautiful oriental riding and firing like a centauress, the big black brute running the string of pack animals—they had all appeared out of no-where and saved his skin. But the reaction of relief and cessation of fear had not yet set in. He felt in a limbo, awkwardly jogging in a dream, confused and blinking. *I am saved, aren't I?* he thought, and felt foolish for the thought. He looked at the men on the walls and the rough, tough men waiting at the gate. He saw one of the guilds' starbucks who had told him to stay inside until the fall, when he had learned more. Wolf Briggs felt embarrassed, and guilty, and very naive and impotent.

What do I do now? he asked himself gravely. *I'm broke.*

"Farplanet ship it was," Konstantin said, referring to the winter starship. "Some contract wives were taken off, and Alena signed up another one for her place." His eyes slipped over to Rader's face, but he could read nothing, which in itself told him something.

"Sounds like civilization's a'coming," Rader muttered. "Hi, there, Aaron!" he called out, waving.

"Remember Joan?" Konstantin said, hobbling along. "Her contract with Alena ran out 'bout a month back, and she moved in with Greg Laguna. And Shultz blew every credit in his guild account to go to Lao-tzu and get a new arm grown on."

"That's something we could get here," Korda said from his saddle. "A DNA recharger, dammit."

"Yeah, then what's next?" Rader grumbled. "Aerial freeways and coin machines and taxes on Old Dragonblood?"

"Hah!" Konstantin snorted. "You may not be far from wrong. There was some kinda blackcoat who came all the way from Terra to here!" Rader looked at him in mild amazement. "Yeah, came in on the *De Forest*. Acted official as hell. Wanted to civilize us with rule books!"

"Who shot him?" Rader asked, then waved to another familiar face. "Hey, Johnny! Levesque, you look fine! That *shoka* bite heal up all right? Great!"

"I thought no one ever would," Konstantin grumbled. "He was right pretty, with his fine, fancy United System Patrol dress uniform and everything." He saw the expression on Rader's face, and he laughed. "No, honest. He tried to arrest Zaiman for something, don't know what. Maybe he thought he was going to take him back to Terra for trial."

They all laughed. Even by going along with the supply ships and making the great loop back to the central worlds, it would take several subjective-years and hundreds of thousands of objective-years. There might not even *be* an Earth when they got back.

"Waldstein, you've grown a beard!" Korda yelled. "You turn Orthodox?"

"No, Korda, my lamb. Still Buddhist. But I see Liana is still as fine as ever." They were almost to the gate, and Rader didn't have to shout very loud to make himself heard.

"So is Korda," he said, and Waldstein held up his hands in surrender, laughing. There were a lot of faces grinning over the wall at them as they went through, and several slapped Rader on the back. Someone dropped a white flower to Liana, who stuck it in her cleavage, grinning impishly. There were groans and laughs, and Levesque made a loud imitation of a *shoka* mating cry.

They curved past Dome Three, going toward the Tiger Guild corrals, and Konstantin fell further behind on his ornately carved crutch, the product of long, winter nights. Rader let them all go on ahead, and he stayed walking with the old trapper.

"What did Zaiman do? Shoot the blackcoat?"

"No, the marshal did."

"Clem shot the Patrolman?" Rader stopped and stared, then broke into laughter. "Really?"

"Yup. Said Zikkala wasn't signator to any system pact, and the blackcoat had no goddamn business here disturbing the populace. The stupid bastard tried to outshoot Clem right in the Dragon Guild hall. Would have sliced through half the membership if Clem hadn't blown his head off." Konstantin snorted loudly. "Arrogant grubber had no respect for life, waving a weapon around like that."

Rader shook his head. Just as there was a proper tool for every job, there was a weapon for every task. Unless you wanted to kill a lot of people, a crowded room was not the place for a duel with lasers. Even needle-guns, with their 500-round magazines and limited range, were better for those conditions. Each weapon, each tool, had advantages and disadvantages, and worked differently in the hands of different people.

"Charlotte put him on the passenger list when the *De Forest* lifted, and as far as anyone knows, he was a blackcoat who died of some dreadful disease. They fed him to the converter."

Grinning, Rader unfastened a pack on the last horse and threw it up on the rock-melt dock, where Gastoni was sitting, finishing off the whiskey. Rader, taller and leaner than the other trappers, jumped up on the dock, exchanged greetings with the one-armed clerk and signed in his loads. He looked at the rescued youth as he signed, lowering his estimate of the boy's age by another couple of years, and then crooking a finger at him as Korda thumped the last pack down.

"What's your name, son?"

"Uh . . . Wolf Briggs."

"Wolf, huh?" Rader smiled.

Briggs blinked, trying to regain some of his shattered dignity. "Yeah. Wolfgang Amadeus Mozart Briggs. From Matisse, Gauguin III. I'm . . . I mean, I was a ship's records and supply clerk. Now I'm a trapper."

"Now you're an *ex*-trapper," sighed Rader. "Call me Rader. That big guy is Korda. That's Liana Chang. You hungry?"

"You bet! I mean, yes, that would be nice, but . . . uh . . ."

"It's on us. Come on, we gotta walk these beasts and cool 'em off."

"Sure, yeah, let me help." Briggs hopped down from the dock and trotted after the horses.

"You going to the hostel?" Konstantin asked, and Rader nodded. The crippled trapper waved a hand and headed that way. "I'll see you over there, all right?"

"Sure." Rader looked at Gastoni. "How's he doing?"

"Better'n me, probably, if I was in that spot. We're hoping the next ship'll have a DNA gadget aboard. Oughta."

"How's the clan doing?" Rader asked.

"Pretty fair. The tithe to our guild will be a touch less this year. He shrugged and grimaced. "But dammit, somehow those resupply ships never quite have everything a man wants."

Rader chuckled. "You mean, enough women so that you'll contract one? Listen, be glad we have ships that can go through null-space at all, or we'd still be on sleeper ships, huffing and puffing out of Earth toward Zeta Reticuli and Centauri and Tau Ceti."

Gastoni made a rumbling sound in his throat and stumped along the well-trod ground for a few meters, gloomy and quiet. Then his head came up and his natural good spirits came back. "Oh, to hell with that. The Guild-authorized traders are fair enough, I guess, and they do stock a lot of good stuff." He smiled as Liana, then Korda, caught up to them.

"What are you two talking about?" Liana said. She glanced back at Wolf Briggs and gestured for him to catch up. In a few moments they were all in a group, trailing the horses behind them.

"Aw, we was just complaining about the stuff that comes in on the supply ships," Gastoni said.

"I came in on a supply ship," blurted Briggs. "I was a clerk. I—I jumped ship to strike it rich."

Gastoni sighed loudly. "Just what are riches, boy?"

"Why, uh, stellars and uh . . . you know, a good credit balance."

Gastoni shook his head and spat again. "Huh. Dumb cleanboot. Riches are . . . are . . ." He waved his arm as he formed the words. "They're good air and something fine and wide to look at. Music. Women that like you for you, not for your credit. Food that makes the mouth dance. Dancing, dammit, unless you've got two left feet." He stopped to laugh and said, "Heard a DNA regrowth gave a fella on Sargon two left feet." He laughed again, shaking his head at the wonders of life. "Don't believe it, but it sounds right, anyway. No, young fella, riches aren't stellars or whatever metal or obligation each planet worships. Uh-uh. No, sir. We're rich, right here on ol' Zikkala. Damned rich. Look around you. Prettiest planet in the whole damn spur, I bet."

"Uh, that was one of the reasons I . . . I decided to jump ship here," Briggs said.

Gastoni nodded. "Get rich here just looking at sunsets, or the stars, or Destiny Mesa, or whatever." He waved his hand around, and Briggs nodded.

"Yes, sir," he agreed. "I can see that, but you still need, you know, things—weapons, seed, traps, chemicals . . ."

"Uh-huh," Gastoni said, looking sideways at Rader. "You'll need that all right. But not being in a guild you can't get 'em on credit. You'll need some help. Maybe some trapper will come through for you, boy. Maybe one that is responsible for ya, now."

"Hey, wait a minute!" Rader said, turning toward Gastoni.

"It's an ancient oriental belief," Liana said, smiling. "You saved his life."

"But I'm not oriental, and neither is he," Rader complained.

"You're rich enough to afford it," Gastoni said. "Just a basic rig to get the boy started."

"Rich?" Liana asked. "Are we rich?"

Gastoni grinned at her in obvious admiration and with some satisfaction. "Well, you ain't poor. The Guild'll get a good price for everyone's *shoka* and other stuff."

"Good," Liana said with vast satisfaction. She looked at Rader, then at Korda. "Can we get those big pans, and the medikit, if they still have them in stock?"

Korda put his arm around her and smiled hugely. "Anything, anything, m'love. You can order a corset from Farplanet and pick up a set of fancy underwear from Bizarre Outfitters and—*oof!*"

With a serene smile Liana strode ahead of them, leaving Korda rubing a hard stomach where her elbow had struck. But he was smiling.

They turned in their saddles to the one-handed wrangler, and Rader asked him to look around for a couple of new ones, a mare and a good stallion. The horses used on Zikkala and on most of the frontier planets were mixtures of originally Terran breeds: Arabians for intelligence and stamina, Morgans for endurance and even dispositions, Clydesdales for size and power in heavy-gravity situations and for hauling power, and mustangs for trail ability and the random factors of personality and decision-making. This mixture of breeds had proved out on many planets and had been exported throughout the perimeter of man's territory—along with the incubators and support equipment—as frozen sperm and ova. They were cheaper and faster than setting up a technology to support machines; they were self-reproducing, which was considerably more than landers, flyers, and ground vehicles could do; and a lot of people found them infinitely more interesting than machines. On worlds that had little or no grass, or where transplanted grasses just wouldn't take, a little genetic tinkering enabled horses to digest native vegetation. The horse, with all its overtones of the prespaceflight days, was an integral part of interstellar development.

"And look for a riding horse for the boy here," Rader added.

"I'm not a boy," Wolf Briggs said, a little testily. "And I'll pay you back."

"Damn right you'll pay me back," Rader said. He pointed

toward a rock-melt structure beyond the corrals. "Go over there tomorrow and have Bleek fit you for a saddle, too. Get one that's really comfortable 'cause you'll be spending a lot of time in it."

"Not like that rental you lost," Liana said, shaking her head. "Get Bleek to spend some time adjusting the fitting pads. Tell him Rader will check him out." She looked at the dark-haired Rader, who was walking along, his eyes veiled and his mouth set. She smiled, knowing he wasn't really angry, just mildly annoyed.

They went up the steps into the big dome, pockmarked with dents in the hard foam from rocks thrown by the Kaleen. They greeted some of the hunters and travelers lounging in the semi-circular lobby, many of whom were on the first drunk of the summer. The man at the desk waved an arm-stub and said, "Same as last time, boys. I saved it for ya."

"For Liana, you mean," Gastoni said, laughing. He slapped Briggs on the back. "Use my room, son. Two-ten. Door's open. There's a trunk under the bed—use anything you find there."

Liana ran ahead up the curving stairs, and by the time Korda, Rader, and Gastoni got there, Liana was already in the bath. Her vest, boots, hair-thong and loincloth were strewn in a trail from the hall door to the bathroom door. Her gun-belt and knife, they all knew, would be on a peg next to the tub. Survival habits kept one alive, and they expected nothing else.

Konstantin came limping up the central, spiral staircase and joined them as Korda and Rader stripped off their clothes. He fell onto one of the two beds, and Gastoni handed him a bottle from the table. "Here, have a drink on the house."

"Hey in there. You want a drink?" Rader yelled at the closed door.

"Later," Liana said through the panel. "Leave me alone to soak, will you?"

"Bathroom hog," muttered Korda. There was a splash, and everyone was quiet a moment as they put a picture to the sound of Liana in her bath.

"Come on down to my room," Gastoni said. "You can sluice that crud off you there."

Rader and Korda took turns getting washed up, while Wolf Briggs got dressed in some castoff clothing of Gastoni's. When the two hunters emerged and began pulling on their town clothes, they found Gastoni and Konstantin educating Briggs.

"Yeah, some of these boneheads around here call the Kaleen injuns and grubs—and worse," Konstantin said. "But they're a lot deeper than that, and you'd be wrong to think of them as primitives."

"But they have tails and use rocks 'n' live in caves," Briggs protested.

Gastoni sighed. "Yeah, the visible part of their society is primitive. The part we see. Or simple, maybe, depending upon your point of view. But don't forget, from what little we know of them—and that's mostly from the Firsters here, thirty years ago—they have achieved seven points on the intelligent entity guidelines to legal status."

"They are beings of pride and honor," Rader said. "They don't have our technology, but I think it's because they don't want it." He shrugged. "We really don't know too much about them. But they know and understand bravery, fighting ability and most of the skills of individual combat —including, using that tail of theirs like a third fist!" He looked somberly at the youth. "They are to be respected."

"But you killed so many—"

"Yeah, and I'll probably have to kill more of them, too. We're the invaders here, remember."

"But I read up on the history, over in the Tiger Guild hall," Briggs said. "Peoplekind got a contract with them, years ago, for three trading posts: here, Nuevo Monterey and Blackbull. All legal. They knew what they were signing."

Rader nodded, pulling on a white shirt with full sleeves. "And the Kaleen had a reason for signing. For about twenty-nine and a half years the Kaleen have been fighting us, and each year they are tougher to whip. They used to fight each other, tribe against tribe, clan against clan. But they found out there was more glory attached to killing a human."

"We're their destiny," Konstantin muttered.

"We're their testers," Korda said, stomping his feet into clean boots. "They have to survive us to go on to the next level of enlightenment."

"Survival of the fittest?" Briggs asked, unsure, and Rader nodded.

"Come on, let's go see if Liana is ready." To Briggs he said, "That's exactly right. They're complex. Approached in the proper manner and in the right season, they can be gracious hosts."

"And will try to ambush you on the way home," Konstantin muttered.

"They like a good fight," Gastoni added. "More, they need a good fight—or at least a worthy opponent. There used to be a species of, well, I guess you'd call them dragons. The Kaleen exterminated them centuries ago, strictly as a test of their counterforce. They honor them—you oughta see the murals and stuff—but they killed them all."

Korda opened the door to their room and went in. The others filed in behind and dropped onto beds and chairs. "Y'see, son," Gastoni continued, "they need us for their own enlightenment. So they ambush us going and coming."

"I know," Wolf Briggs said gloomily. "I didn't get very far, did I?" He shot a wounded look at Rader.

"Hell, you can't be all bad," the big hunter said. "You didn't go down, and you were holding them off all right when we arrived."

"Luck," Briggs said, making a face. "Pure luck. When Penny went down, I fell right into some rocks." He rubbed his bruises tenderly. "That stopped their stones and gave me a chance to get up to where you found me."

"Aw, forget it," Konstantin said. "Better men than you have been taken by the Kaleen."

The bathroom door slid back, and everyone looked toward it to watch Liana make an entrance.

Her long black hair was piled up on her head, and there were still beads of water here and there on her magnificent body. None of the men made a sound, but Konstantin's drink splashed quietly in his shaking hand.

"I'm clean!" she exclaimed. "Clean!" She shook out her thick mane of hair and set it swirling around her bronzed shoulders. She stood gracefully, smiling, letting them get a good look, unselfconscious and proud. Quite audibly they all heard Gastoni gulp.

"Rader," Korda said.

"Yeah?"

"Is there more than one type of that shimmercloth?"

There was a pause, and a droplet fell from her nipple to the floor.

"I don't know, but let's get some of each."

"Jesus and Mary," Gastoni said hollowly. "I'd forgotten. I thought I'd never forget, but I'd forgotten how great she looks."

Liana laughed and went to her trunk and pulled out a scarlet garment and shook it free of wrinkles. Her skin was more golden than ever, and all the men felt hairy and bony and ill-proportioned. Wolf Briggs stared, then swallowed air.

"Why don't you go down to the bar?" Liana suggested, bending over again to rummage through the compartments of the trunk. "This will take awhile. I want to really dress up."

Gastoni stared at her buttocks and was very silent.

Konstantin sighed deeply and looked very sad. His stump hurt.

Liana went back into the steamy bathroom, and Korda got up, waving them all toward the door. He had to slap Wolf on the arm to break the spell.

They were silent all the way down to the bar—and until they held filled glasses in their hands.

"To her," Gastoni said.

"Yeah," everyone answered and drained their glasses.

Korda sighed, waved at the bartender, and asked what else had been going on.

"All the latest news?" Gastoni said wryly. Any news they received was hundreds, even thousands of years old, but it was still new to them. To them the Federation of Sovereign Systems had given way to the United System of Planets, and they thought of it that way, though they knew that undoubtedly one or more alliances of planets and races had risen and fallen. So the latest news was an ironic statement, but one they pragmatically lived with. Gastoni had once described it as, "You know the unihorn race has been run, the bets paid, and everyone has gone home . . . but you're still waiting to see who's been entered."

"Well . . ." Gastoni said, squinting at the ceiling. "There was a beauty of a revolution on Springtime about two, three years ago." He grinned, as they referred to events in that way, subjectively. "Heard Dexter bought it there, being a mercenary. Hydra started boycotting the Wolf clan for some idiot reason." He sipped at his wine. "They discovered fissionables on one of the moons around Xolotl and took it clean apart. What was left made a ring."

"They had an election on Terra," Konstantin said. "The government changed hands again and wanted to withdraw from the United System."

"Who won?" Rader asked, looking at the holograph of the original Tiger Guild founders that was fixed over the bar.

"Don't know. I didn't know which side won last time. It just doesn't seem to make much difference out here."

"Heard Savonarola voted in commercial slavery," Gastoni said.

"Well, that's what happens when you don't control your population. They breed themselves into disaster, and life gets pretty cheap," Korda rumbled. "Wasn't that started by some religious bunch?"

"Uh-huh," Gastoni said. "Can't get worked up, though, y'know? No matter what we think or do, it was solved . . . or terminated . . . a couple thousand years ago."

Wolf Briggs cleared his throat and looked at them. Gastoni signaled for him to go ahead, and the youth said, "They broke up Mercury?"

"*The* Mercury?" Konstantin asked. "Back in the Solar System?"

Briggs nodded. "Needed the material, they said, and it wasn't doing much, anyway."

"Yeah, but break up one of the original planets," Konstantin complained. "Jesus . . ."

"Only original to the Solar System," Rader said. "Very ordinary, beat-up, nothing world, really. Be better put to use as building material. What did they do with it, did you hear?"

Briggs looked embarrassed. "No. Just heard they took it apart. Maybe a Dyson sphere, or used it for the metals, I dunno."

"The Skrills hit Summer again," Konstantin said.

"They still doing that?" Korda asked, shaking his head. "Thought those rippers had blasted them good?"

"Oh, they did," Gastoni said cheerfully. "But the zongos are still poppin outta null-space, thinking they are hitting Summer for the first time. For them it's surprise, surprise—!"

"Those Moks," Konstantin said with a woeful shake of his head, referring to the vicious, war-bred race that fought as the Skrill shock troops. "Had a couple of skirmishes with them reptiles when I was a kid on Balanchine."

The conversation drifted into speculation on the mysterious Skrills and the generations-long war with humans, then into DNA regrowths, the near paradoxes of null-space travel that found sons and daughters older in subjective-years than fathers and great-grandmothers.

"New holofilm came in this winter," Konstantin said. "Sure did have a fanciful idea of livin' on frontier worlds."

"Most charged-up laser I ever saw!" cackled Gastoni.

"Heard Eric Wilde bought it on Ares," Konstantin said, throwing an immediate pall over the conversation, for the legendary hero at the beginning of the war with the Skrills had indeed touched them all. They looked at Rader, who was related genetically, his great-grandfather having been one of the tough rippers exported from Ares, where the original Wilde troop had settled.

Rader shrugged and raised his glass silently. The others joined him in the silent toast, and the conversation came to a stop.

Then came shouts and whistles from the lobby, growing louder and more boisterous by the moment.

"I think Liana is here," Korda said with a wide grin.

Several members of the Guild stood up, grinning in anticipation, eager to get a look. They were not disappointed. Liana came through the doors just ahead of several admiring trappers and hunters. She stopped, smiling, and they almost bumped into her. She stood boldly, all golden and scarlet, giving everyone a good look.

"Moya bogu!" Konstantin said in a grunt. "My god, my god . . ."

She wore sandals and a scarlet loincloth that fell to the floor in a silken sweep from a thin ribbon tied around her hips. Her smooth golden skin shone as if oiled, and between her full, bare breasts hung a delicate golden sunburst that was fashioned on Gilgamesh, a hundred light-years away. There were tiny, gleaming pi-pearls in her hair, which fell in a thick black cascade to below her shoulders.

"Gentlemen, the queen," Gastoni said, rising with the others.

Smiling, Liana came toward them, and the spell was broken. Others—trappers, miners, gem-hunters—shouted happy comments at Liana, and at Rader and Korda. Bare-breasted women were no novelty on most of the frontier planets, where personal freedom in dress and life style were private decisions, but a woman that was as attractive as Liana was rare anywhere. In their first year together Korda had killed two men who, at different times, had forced themselves upon her. And one time when Liana had been unable to persuade an ardent baron that his attentions were not wanted, she had been forced to kill him. Angry relatives wanted revenge, but she faced them down, a laser at her side. When they first arrived at Zikkala another man had died under Rader's gun when he thought to backshoot Korda and take Liana for his own. He had not been a guild member; no one had blamed Rader; no blood money was asked; everyone thought themselves well rid of an obvious troublemaker. No one blamed any of the men that had tried to get close to Liana, except that there was a common feeling that the dead—there were no wounded—had not been very bright.

A drunk made a playful, grinning grab for Liana, and without pausing, she bent back his finger felling him to the floor wincing but laughing. He climbed back into his chair, holding his hand, and was pummeled merrily by his companions.

Another man, someone Rader did not know, made a grab for Liana as she went by, taking a large handful of firm buttock. Liana didn't even look around as Korda broke his wrist with one blow. The man howled with pain, but Liana and Korda went on as if nothing had happened.

As Rader passed the wounded man, he said, quite cheerily, "Look, but don't touch." The man's face changed from drunken surprise and pained shock, to furious anger. Rader saw his good hand move.

The man froze, and Wolf Briggs gulped. Rader's Magnum laser was rock steady in his hand and poised just three centimeters from the man's nose. The room became very quiet.

"What's your name?" Rader asked in a soft voice.

"Uh ... Daniels ..."

"Citizen Daniels, I don't think Shorty would like to have anything extra to clean up. These bums are messy enough. I'm sorry, but I don't have one of the polite little stunguns that would only scramble your circuits."

"I . . . uh, I didn't mean anything . . ." There was sweat on his forehead, and he kept trying to look at the .2 millimeter hole of the muzzle, but it was too close and he kept going cross-eyed. "She's a . . . very nice looking . . . uh . . ."

"Lady is the word you want, citizen." Rader's gun went back into his holster with a slight sound. "Don't forget it." He smiled thinly, his eyes hard, then turned to join the others.

As Wolf Briggs edged past, the babble started again, self-consciously boisterous. Despite the chatter, he heard Daniels ask "Who *is* that zongo?"

"His name is Rader," Briggs said, confronting him, "and that's his friend's woman."

Daniels winced and held his wrist tightly. "You mean his lady, don't you?"

Briggs ignored Daniel's last remark and turned away to join his friends. Gastoni had the drinks poured and was grinning like a fool when he unobtrusively pulled up a chair. Rader squinted through the smoke. "Are you grinning like that because you like to see me in trouble, or because you're sitting next to Liana?"

"Hell, you weren't in trouble—he was."

"Maybe you were, after all," Konstantin said slowly. "That was one of Lockhart's men."

"All right, who is Lockhart?" Liana asked. "The name is new."

"He's the starbuck from Startrade."

"Isn't that the outfit that did the sub-rosa setup for that ghastly revolution on Steinberg?" Liana asked.

Gastoni scratched his beard. "They're a rough group. We hope they are just passing through. They came in on the *Cyrus Field* and say they are just vacationing before they go out on the *Astro Merchant,* which is scheduled in soon, or so they say."

"Oh—well, hell," Liana said, wiggling in her chair, "so Startraders sent some cleanboots. So there's another possible customer. Can't hurt to bid things up against Farplanet."

Rader saw Daniels leaving, cradling his wrist carefully in his other hand. He didn't look back, and no one left with him.

Another one to watch for, Rader thought.

Wolf Briggs saw the look on Rader's face and shivered.

Rader watched two old trappers checking and grading their catch of furs. A guild logo with the Rader-Chang-Korda mark was laser-tattooed on each hide. Between them the trappers had only two arms and two legs, but they had adjusted well enough.

I wonder if I could adjust to that kind of loss, Rader thought. *If I had to, I suppose. You can always do things when you must do them. Or almost always. Such as living without a woman.*

Rader thrust away the gloomy thoughts. The problem of sex had been solved, discreetly, long ago. Liana was Korda's woman, but she was friends to both. Sometimes she had come to him in the night, all honey and warmth and soft hands, to give her friend a gift only she could bestow. "Sometimes it gets lonely out here," she said once.

Liana was a welcome gift in the night, but not one he could keep, nor wish to keep. She was a special and good friend, but they were not lovers—not the way the word is usually meant. She bandaged their wounds, played chess with them, made them laugh and think, shared their life and was an equal partner. She was never boring, although at times she aroused all the other emotions, both base and noble. And sometimes she came in the night.

It's good, but not good enough, Rader thought. *I've been on twenty-three worlds and have known women of five races, some fine and superior women and people, but I have not found my woman.*

"Hey, Rader, is that true about the Kaleen havin' another gun?" one of the old trappers asked, breaking Rader's thought.

"I'm afraid so, Earl. They cut down Liana's Moonglow with a laser, but I took a needler away."

The one-armed, one-legged man whistled, shaking his head. "Son of a scabtree. Well, here's the tally ledger, Rader."

"Thanks, Earl. Stow it in the office, will you? I'm going over to the new dome, I think."

Earl looked at his partner, Keckner. "Damned fine stuff over there," he said to Rader. "Makes me wish I was fresh in with a winter's catch."

Rader waved and started away. Keckner called after him, "Hey, you gonna try for Alena?"

"Shut up, you zongo," snapped Earl.

Rader walked on past the loading dock, his smile fading. He saw Wolf Briggs trying out the sample saddle, with Bleek adjusting the pads for a good fit. *The boy's learning,* Rader thought, and wondered if *he* was. He walked on past the incubator dome, run by the United Guilds Co-op, where they stored and grew the mutated horse sperm and ova and created remudas as needed. He waved back at a few acquaintances lounging in the sun before Casey's Rainbow Bar and went on down the nameless street, toward the triad of pleasure domes.

Rader tried to remember what she looked like. It was funny how details dimmed and even changed, but you couldn't tell exactly where or how. He had thought about Alena Petrovna all winter and how he wasn't certain just

what shade her blonde hair was. He remembered the
honey-gold skin. He remembered the artfully concealed,
artfully revealed figure, one that rivaled if not surpassed
Liana's, except that no known guild member had ever found
out for sure—or at least no one ever talked about it. —

Alena Petrovna.

The last time he had seen her was the night before the
pack train left for Miracle Mountain and the home cave.
Her dome hadn't been erected yet, because someone had
dropped the catalyst at the wrong touchdown three planets
back and it hadn't caught up. So she had made a deal with
Lu and moved her contract girls in. Fresh girls on pioneer
planets were always good business, despite the attrition
as some girls found a place or a man they couldn't resist.
But they were mostly gypsies, like the supply ship's crew,
with seven-league boots spenning light-years and centuries, always a little anxious to see what the next star was like.

Alena Petrovna.

They had talked most of the night. He had wanted to
know about her, but she had been far more adept at prying
out the words from him. She now knew more about him
than anyone, except Liana and Korda. He had told her of
his childhood on Gilgamesh and how the natives there
called him Savage Flower. He told her stories of his great-
grandfather, one of Wilde's rippers, fighting the Moks and
their fearsome masters, the Skrills, the great enemies of
peoplekind. He had told her about the time on Mephisto
and about being in the mercenaries when he was no older
than Wolf Briggs. He told her of fighting on Robinhood
and Erin and Athena. He had spoken of Lorraine, the
woman on Athena, and about killing Dawson and getting
hit on Scee-icla-flair during the uprising there.

He had talked a long time about Zikkala, about the way
the sun came up over the Redpaws and about seeing the
vast canyons from their plateau, with the rainbow trees
filling the valleys and the tawny-brown look of the *rena*
grazing in the mountain meadows.

Rader shook his head as he walked through the dust. The
things he had told her! How he had met Korda on Horus
when he was thrown in jail by the priests, and how they
had busted loose and swiped the *Vasco Nunez de Balboa*

and the trouble they had giving it back to the owners on Aragon III.

I sounded like a goddamn holo-hero, he thought to himself ruefully. Thinking about it made him feel stupid and foolish. He almost turned into Curran's Saloon for a drink. When he came out, he could walk in the other direction.

But he didn't. *It had been just plain survival, not heroics,* he thought. *I just want a place not too full of people—but with just enough good ones to make it interesting. With some danger, so I don't get sloppy. With some beauty, so my soul doesn't shrivel. And with a woman. The right woman.*

That night he had thought it might be Alena Petrovna, but she had smiled and steered him away from becoming too intimate. Rader shrugged, feeling the heat of the Zikkala summer. *What the hell did I have in mind, anyway? Talking that soft flower into going out and living in a red-stone cave in the side of a cliff in Kaleen county? So the view was the Grand Canyon of Earth and the Spectrum Valley and Sorcerer Mesa all rolled into one. So what? So the air was clean and crisp and there wasn't an arological structure in sight. So what if you could get hypnotized watching the rainbow trees turning colors in the wind? Alena was a city girl. Barlwan, New Chicago, Diamondome, Tokio, Centauri Central, the big cities on Summer and Coronation—those were her kind of places. Fast, easy living, plenty to see and do, all clean and safe—safe air, safe ground. Holographics and health plans, and tomorrow's dresses today.*

Rader sighed. *Maybe if she could stand under a temple tree and listen to the tinkling flowers and smell the incense of the pollen. Or look up the hundred-meter interiors of the cathedral trees, with the clusters of blossoms like stained glass, and see the wind that had come across ten thousand kilometers of lush emptiness to stir the green leaves. Or see the white acolyte birds nesting and the sunlight coming down through the trees like rods of Zeus. . . .*

Rader stopped and looked up at Alena Petrovna's new pleasure dome. It was white, like all the others, to save on chemicals, and the entrance was pure, raw symbolism. The vulva-shaped entrance was lined with luxuriant carvings in

scarlet-stained *pungi* wood. The inner door was covered
with Grade II *monga* hide, beautiful and intricately pat-
terned. It opened silently at his touch.

There was a soft-lit chamber inside, with steps up to
another door beyond. It was carpeted, and sensuous music
filled the air. *Quite different,* Rader thought, from the
gaudy, loud, pulsating head-slam of Lu's, where you were
beaten about the head and mind with Alpha waves and
music, or the crotch-grab decor of Shamrock Sue's small
dome. *Something for everyone,* he thought wryly.

A lean, hawk-faced man in formal black approached
Rader with a polite expression masking his feelings. "Good
afternoon, sir. Welcome to Alena's. Would you care to
check your weapon, sir?"

Rader looked at him, then beyond to the checkroom
where an old trapper named Barnes, a Firster, sat with
an adventure story on a small reader. He looked back at the
man in black, pressing down the "hold" stud, just waiting,
without much expression on his crinkled face.

"No," Rader said, looking back at the maitre d'.

The slim man shrugged and smiled thinly, and made a
small, precise gesture with his hands, keeping them close
to his chest. "House rule," he said.

"Not my rule. Tell Alena that Rader is here."

There was a flicker in the eyes of the dark man, a
tightening in his face, and Rader's inner alarms went on
alert. The *maître d'hôtel* made another gesture, one of gracious resignation, and stepped to a hushphone. His eyes
never left Rader as he talked, looking at him flatly, without expression. Rader ignored him, or seemed to, and
studied the erotic paintings set into the carved *pungi* paneling.

"She'll be right down, sir," the *maître d'hôtel* said, a
cold envy in his voice. Rader grunted, not too graciously,
and continued his examination of the erotica. Inwardly, he
understood the restriction, and it was not an uncommon
one. Evidently Alena was playing it very cool and was
trying to keep the zongos fangless.

After a few moments the door opened, and the music
from within floated out, flowing with an almost visible
grace around the elegant figure of the beautiful woman
standing there, smiling at Rader.

"Hello, Rader," she said. She spoke to the maitre d' without removing her eyes from Rader, who was looking back, his heart beginning to pound. "I'll take care of this, Hayim." The dark-skinned man nodded politely and drifted toward the checkroom, picking up some papers, but keeping his eyes moving restlessly between Rader and his employer.

"You're looking well," Rader said as Alena closed the door behind her without looking at it and came down the steps to him. She was wearing a floor-length gown of dark shimmercloth that contrasted nicely with her blonde hair. There was a good starstone on her left hand, and small, matching jewels in her earrings.

She walked to him and took his hands. "I'm glad you are safe, Rader. I heard you had to fight your way in." He nodded, looking at her closely, with almost rude directness. She was aware of his scrutiny and stepped back with a soft laugh, spinning her body, letting the shimmercloth flow and run like a liquid rainbow over her lush figure.

My god, she's even more beautiful than I remembered! Rader felt an ache of frustration in his heart. Evidently Alena read the admiration—and lust—in his eyes, for she became flushed and suddenly awkward for a moment, before she regained her poise.

"Welcome to Alena's!" she said gaily. She seized his arm and pulled him happily toward the checkroom. "Come. Please." She smiled up at him as she added, "Without the gun, please."

Rader stopped, some of his happiness dissolving. "No," he said, a grimness shadowing his features.

The woman made a face at him and cocked her head. "No Kaleen inside, honest."

Rader had to smile at her manner, but he was stubborn. In a tone somewhat less harsh, he said, "I sleep with this, lady." At her smile, he smiled. "It's neither as beautiful nor as deadly as a woman, but it's comforting."

"Not even if I tell you it's a house rule and that everyone else in Shamrock checks their gun with Mister Barnes?"

Rader let his smile die away, and he glanced at Hayim. "He's wearing a flat stunpod under his left armpit in that nice store-bought, pretty suit. Probably a knife in his sock, too, or down the back of his neck."

Alena looked appraisingly at Rader, and without removing her eyes, she asked Hayim, "Is that true?"

"Yes, madame."

Alena pursed her lips, then spoke. "Hayim is the front. He's the one that has to go in if there is trouble. Slap a stunpod to a troublemaker's head, and there's no more trouble. No one is hurt. All he gets is a terrible headache the next day."

"I understand his function," Rader said. *What else does he do for you, lady?*

"I need him, Rader."

How often? Rader thought and hated himself. But he stood stubbornly, tall and dark, the smile fading into an uncompromising line.

Alena Petrovna shrugged winsomely. "Well, I cannot break my own rules, but I do want to talk to you. Come." When Rader did not move she tugged at his arm. "Come on, you stubborn bastard, gun and all. We'll go upstairs to my office instead."

Rader followed her up the steps, giving Hayim a parting glance and was surprised at the venom in his eyes. Barnes had returned to his Raven Blacksword adventure, his lips moving silently.

Just inside the double doors was a large sensatron cube, displaying the life-size image of a very beautiful oriental, lying like an ancient odalisque on a bed of gleaming silks and ornate cushions of shimmercloth. Beyond her, behind a pierced screen of wood, carved and jeweled, was an orgy of oiled bodies and sensual dancers, a writhing, murmuring vision of lust.

As Rader passed through the cones of projection from the Alpha-wave machines, he felt the heat rise in his loins and the old urge stirring his bood. The feeling disappeared, leaving only a lingering heat, as they passed by the endless loop of cycling hedonists, artfully captured by the sensatron's creator. They went into a passage, then up the curving inside of the dome to the living quarters and special rooms at the top of the big white pleasure palace.

"Wasn't that a Kendall cube from Kim Sung?" Rader asked.

Alena looked over her shoulder at him as they climbed.

"Yes. It's a duplicate, of course, but made under the artist's franchise. Kendall was very . . . sensuous."

Rader nodded, for Kendall cubes were in all the best erotica collections in that arm of the galaxy. *Just the thing as a showpiece in a whorehouse,* he thought. *She must think Shamrock is going to grow—the shipping costs for it must have been huge.*

They topped out and went along a curved passage past several brightly colored doors until Alena stopped before an inconspicuous white door. She put her hand on the ident-plate and the door hissed open. They went into a luxurious suite that was part office, part control room and, in an inner room, all bedroom.

Rader looked around him with appreciation. *Pungi* paneling, rich and lustrous, polished and well-fitted. *Torga*-hide chairs. Pools of warm light. Racks of tape blocks and a holographic well. A luxurious king *shoka* rug as big as a bed. A Moranian brass bowl filled with shelled sweetnuts. Wine and imported whiskey in a case of smoky thunderglass and polished rosewood. A flat oil by someone he did not recognize. A miniature sensatron of Borgman's famous *Venice Beneath the Sea.* One of McAllister's abstract carvings, which surprised him.

He must think a lot of her to give, or even sell, her one of his sculptures, Rader thought. *He keeps nearly everything he does.*

Alena crossed to a panel, pressed a stud, and music began playing. To the big hunter it sounded like Ravel, translated by the Xolotl Philharmonic. *Very appropriate for what I hope will be very appropriate.*

"Wine, whiskey, *pungi* juice—?"

"Whatever you're having," he said, looking at a small collection of vivid acolyte eggs in a glass case. A Kaleen headdress on the wall had some of the pi-pearls melted on one side. A shimmering emerald goblet held some polished warmstones from Yao-chang II. He glanced at the bedroom door, which was carved from dark, rainbow-tree wood and set with slices of fossilized shell.

Alena came to him with a goblet of primrose wine from Nuevo Monterey in each hand. He took one, and she gestured toward a chair. "Please."

He hitched his holster around and sat, suddenly feeling

awkward and raw. The gun *did* seem out of place in the lush and very civilized surroundings of a soft and beautiful woman's home. *Even if it is in a whorehouse,* Rader reminded himself.

"My informants tell me that you and Korda and Liana Chang brought in a fortune in prime *shoka*. Even a . . . what do the Kaleen call it?"

"A *tamir*. Korda got it. It was trying to eat me."

"Evidently none of you three digest very well."

Rader smiled faintly and took a sip of the chilled wine. "Why did you bring me up here?" he asked. "Gun and all."

Alena rotated the wine glass under her nose for a moment before she answered. The shimmercloth gleamed across her bosom, and Ravel plucked at Rader's mind from across the centuries and across the stars.

"Why do you think I brought you here?" she asked at last, not looking at him.

"I don't like games," he said. He put down the glass and started to get up.

Alena stopped him with a gesture, looking at him with raised eyebrows. "You don't give much, do you?" Rader just looked at her and continued to rise. She put down her own wine glass rather violently and got to her feet. "I need you," she said, looking right into his eyes.

"I'm not very good at opening front doors."

Alena smiled, her long hair swaying as she shook her head. "No, you see, I need . . . I need a champion. I've been stalling most of the winter, and now it is summer and my time is up."

Rader frowned in bewilderment. In the outback he knew the length of a *tamir*'s leap, how the *shoka* took bait, and most of the ways the Kaleen laid an ambush. But here, in this tiny bit of Inner World sophistication, he was lost.

"What the hell are you talking about?"

"Lockhart. Startrade Export-Import Ltd. They want to own me."

Rader felt a lurch in his gut and a sour taste come into his mouth. It was the second time Lockhart's name had come up, and neither time had been pleasant. "How?" he asked harshly.

"Startrade wants to own this," she said, gesturing around her. "And Lockhart—"

"And Lockhart wants to own you." Rader nodded. "I can understand Lockhart, presuming he's human or within enough decimal points to make it interesting. But Startrade—that's a big company. You have a nice place here, but next to the joints on Coronation or Centauri, well . . ." He shrugged. "Hell, even Steinberg and Y'bella, just to name some close ones, they have houses there that have been in steady operation for centuries! Why would they want this whiteball out on the edge of nowhere?"

"Have you been to Tura?"

"No, and I don't want to. That's the steam-bath planet next toward the sun, and *nobody* wants to go there. It's all marsh and grub land, with some very nasty flora and fauna.

"Well, Startrade wants it. Their search team just claimed it. They've been over there for four to five months. About ten days ago they came over here for some R and R." She shrugged delicately. "One of the men started bragging to one of the girls here. They've discovered a plant there that secretes pearl-like things. Big ones, as big as your fist or your head. Leaches the chemicals out of the soil, which is rich, then encapsulates the stuff into beautiful things. I saw one yesterday, Rader, and it was gorgeous!"

Rader spoke tonelessly. "So you want me to go to Tura and slice out these pearlloids, or whatever they are, and—" He stopped himself, inwardly furious and sad. His opinion of her sank swiftly.

"No, dammit! Listen to me!" Alena snapped at him. "The plants are big and carnivorous, and they have to tease the plant into disgorging the pearls. That takes time and equipment—and time means a lot of men. *Any* time on Tura is a lot of time, indeed."

Rader still didn't understand about the champion part, but the intensity of the woman's conversation convinced him of her concern.

"Even if the pearlloid is ruined," she said, "it's valuable enough to bother shipping back, just for the minerals. They are in almost pure form, chemically pure, if not atomically pure. One quick pass through the fusion torch and the mass accellerator, and it's done."

"So they found new baubles. So what?"

"Pound for pound they bring more than *shoka* furs, my friend. Plus, there's Jicron and the memoroids." At Rader's frown, she went on. "Jicron is the drug they get from the blossoms of this plant on Tura. It gives short-tem, low-intensity telepathic powers." Rader's eyebrows went up. "There's a kind of fleshy weed over there, too; grows in the swamps. From it they can make several types of memoroids—a total recall drug. You can bring back your earliest memories. Prenatal even."

"I don't think much happened to me then that I care to remember," Rader said. "But I still don't understand this champion business."

Alena leaned toward him, seeking to impress him with the importance of her words, but Rader was more impressed with her close-up beauty. "It will take a lot of people to harvest anything on Tura," she said. "There's a hundred men in the search team, and the follow-up ship will bring at least a thousand more." Suddenly she had Rader's attention. "And not one of them wants to stay on that steam-bath mudball fighting off the bugs and crawlies and risking some horrible disease not one minute more than they must. So the only way they'll work is knowing Startrade has some way of giving them some rest and relaxation. A pleasure dome or two, sports . . . a playground. Otherwise," she said with a weak shrug, "they'll exercise their options and jump for the next star on the route. That's the only way they can get men and women to go out blind, if they have big rewards and some say in their own destiny."

Jesus, Buddha, and Zeus, thought Rader. *Father of All.* A thousand workers descending on Zikkala to play. Not to love and cherish but to rut and drink and carouse. Hunting down the *shoka* and the others for sport, killing young and old alike, decimating the herds and prides. As powerful and as dangerous as the *shoka* were, they could not stand against a small army with any of the modern weapons.

And the Kaleen, killed for sport because they were different. An ancient story played out again, on yet another world.

"No!"

Alena drove her point home. "They're talking of headquartering here at Shamrock, with only a third of the men on Tura at a time. They are keeping this all quiet, of course, but a couple of their people love to impress Cleopatras."

Rader felt sick as she went on. "They are shipping in sport helos, plus ice-zoomers for the north country. They want to put in a dam at Harmony Canyon and make a lake out of the Marble River, backing it up through the Moon and Sunset gorges. Illusion Cave will be flooded, just to make a recreational lake. The cathedral canyons will be buried."

Something wrenched inside Rader, and he grew coldly, dangerously furious. "Go on," he said, with iced steel in his voice.

"They're buying up everything, starting now," she said. "They already have Lu's place and the Shamrock. Terry held out over in Blackbull, but . . . well . . . he fell down a canyon. Rita sold her little Nuevo layout and is moving on with the next ship heading toward Varuna. They have every house but mine. They're after several bars and even old man Benner's ship-chandler's yard. They make it look like tourists wanting to set up on a frontier planet, not a big company like Startrade taking over. If those bastards hadn't blabbed to my girls, I don't think we'd know what was coming off until it was too late. They want everything sewn up by the time the first crew gets here."

"They'll ruin this place—just as they did Indra and Ryan's Star," Rader said bitterly. Depression overcame him and he sank back into the couch. "It was that way on Gilgamesh, on Robinhood and Willis—and on a hundred other worlds where greedy men overpopulate their environment."

"Gilgamesh was your home, wasn't it?"

Rader nodded. "Poor distant, gutted Terra just never taught peoplekind anything, did it? There were always new worlds to screw up." He looked around the room sightlessly, his face stricken. Alena put her hand on his arm in concern.

"I . . . I thought I was safe here," he muttered. "It's a byworld, and here in the spur, I thought it would be out of the way of the main thrust of the empire of man." He shook his head angrily.

"I thought I could live out my life on this beautiful,

tough planet, growing old on a world I'd help explore . . . living in harmony with the nature of it . . . until . . ."

. . . until that day when I make a mistake or am too slow or stupid and die. If anyone is around, they might bury me in the side of a cliff overlooking a valley filled with rainbow trees and graceful wild rena drinking from clear streams.

"Now . . . now the Out Worlders will come, not to trade or live, but to ravage and change and soil and . . . and rape. And when they've totally gutted Tura, or when they think the fashions for pearlloids have changed, they'll move on, and everything will be left in shambles."

"Rader . . ."

He lapsed into a long silence, and Alena breathed softly, watching him. "This is a beautiful planet," he said at last, softly, sadly. *It lacks only one thing,* he thought. *A woman for me. One all my own.* He looked up at Alena and realized she was searching his face with an intent stare.

What about Alena Petrovna? he wondered, then asked her, "Why do you need me? There must be fifty guns that would stand by you. Hayim, for a start."

Alena smiled. "Yes, but there aren't fifty I want to stand beside."

They looked at each other for a moment that seemed to stretch and stretch. Rader felt the stirrings of a long-lost boyish hope. Then a persistent thought surfaced, destroying the mood.

"But why do they want to buy everything? Why not just move their girls and teams right in? They must have a hundred pleasure domes on their inventories."

Alena sighed and rubbed at one fist with her other hand. "If they can send out one search team and one Lockhart with credit vouchers, it's cheaper than shipping a pleasure team. They can move in faster, and if it starts paying off, they can bring down what they need from the follow-up ships. If not, the ships go on to the next stop, where the pickings might be better. We're just a convenience, a column in a ledger somewhere, a few milliseconds on a computer tape." She sighed again and looked up at the ceiling. "We'll be phased out as obsolete—just as soon as they determine it is necessary. Or convenient. Or commercially feasible.

They're a big outfit and look light-years and centuries ahead."

Alena paused, and her head dropped. The golden wings of her hair swung down to hide her face. "Free trips to the next planet, maybe even all the way back to the Inner Worlds on the circle flights. Heavy credit balances on Startrade's books, redeemable almost anywhere. The promise of leisure, the advantages of the technology and entertainment of the Inner Worlds. Not everyone likes it here, not forever, not for their old age." Her head came up, and she brushed back her hair. "Let me show you something," she said, rising.

Alena turned gracefully toward a large, concert screen and pressed a stud to start a tape block that was already in place.

The picture was from the original survey ship, the only airship that had ever flown over Zikkala, except for the landers coming down from the orbiting starships. The exploring flyer was sailing at its slowest air speed through the great unnamed complex of the cathedral canyons. Towering cliffs rose on either side, delicately tinted, intricately shaped and carved by millions of years of sluicing water and whispering winds. Spires and towers a thousand meters high, like citadels for gods. Arches and clefts and cups revealing hundreds of layers of stone in a score of colors.

The ship dipped and turned and flew through a massive arch and down past the three hundred-meter drop of Morning-glory Falls to the Green River below, leveling out over the lush, river islands crested with ancient, gnarled rainbow trees. The cameraship flew at the level of the water-worn gemstone strata, high in the sheer canyon walls. From each side, forests of *pungi* and *kurri* nested in steep valleys that cut down into the main canyons.

The edited tapes abruptly changed images.

The ship flew at maximum atmospheric speed over the Great Desert. The sea of sand. Tan, yellow, pale gold, rust, salt, white, flecks of black and umber. Here and there, jagged basalt monoliths thrust up through the blanket of drifting sand. The survey ship dipped low, racing just above the undulating dunes, accenting the speed, frightening a rare sandbird into flight.

Rader knew the tape well and looked for it. The distant black dot, quickly growing. Blackbull, the great black mountain, worn by time, carved by nature and by the labor of ancient Kaleen artisans into the hulking god-image.

The ship sped toward it until it loomed up faster and faster and the ship angled up and skimmed just over the horn spires.

The picture changed.

A Kaleen galley on the great deep blue expanse of the Great Sea. *Taba*-cloth sails dyed dull red, whitetops cresting the heaving waves, ribbon banners streaming in the wind. The frail ship was in pursuit of the green *skisporra*, the lethal whalelike mammal ten times the size of its pursuers. The tails of the Kaleen whipped up as they turned with astonishment to stare at the passing airship.

Then the screen changed: the Marble Mountains at sunset, all green- and gold- and pale-veined boulders. Through a steep pass, and the Shoka Valley lay before them, carpeting the basin with tall forests of temple and cathedral trees. A rushing river wound through intricate rock formations and under overhanging trees, through a lake alive with the delicious Umm fish, which had been named later, by the first explorers on foot.

Then Zikkala from space, blue and brown, with the fleecy white clouds of spring. The edges of the Great Desert were greening, and the sun sparked off the sea near the Wizard Islands, where the zesty *chorba* fruit was so plentiful.

Rader stared at the slowly turning globe, and his throat felt constricted. He had almost forgotten how beautiful it was, how unspoiled. Zikkala was a planet to fight for. To live for. To die on. The image faded, and he was back in Alena Petrovna's pleasure dome.

Rader's natural suspicions surfaced. "If what you've told me about Startraders is true, I'd fight anyway. But, why at *your* side?"

Alena laughed lightly and moved gracefully to the bar, where she poured herself a pale wine in a stemmed glass.

"You don't give away anything, do you? You are a very hard man, Citizen Rader."

"I survive."

"You survive by killing."

"If I must." She turned toward him and leaned against the bar. "If you mean men, then I do what I must, when I must." He gestured with his wine glass. "If you mean *shoka* or *tamir* . . . we kill only the old ones or those that attack us, which is often enough. We kill *rena* for food." He shrugged.

"But you kill."

"Everyone kills. If you don't kill your meat yourself, you hire someone to do it, or he hires someone."

"Not everyone is a carnivore." She was baiting Rader, and he knew it.

"Not everyone survives. I survive."

"Yes, that's why I want you on my side."

Rader narrowed his eyes at her, studying her carefully. Then he set down his goblet and stood up, looming over her, a lean, hard man in black. "If I fight, it will be for what I believe in, not to save your whorehouse."

Alena looked at him, her violet eyes wide. "You could make a case that they were the same thing. Unless the beautiful Liana has changed greatly, you might be interested in what we supply here."

Rader laughed in her face. It was a short, loud, rude blast. "Women certainly know how to utilize their scarcity," he said and swept Alena into his arms and kissed her. She stood passively until he had finished, but there was fire in her eyes. "If I am going to fight big bad Startraders, I might as well have the fringe benefits."

Alena's smile faded. "I am not a fringe benefit for you or anyone. I wish to hire you to defend me, nothing more."

Rader's eyes gleamed. "Do you want me to gun down Lockhart and the Startrade Board of Directors in the street?" His face grew even harder. "I am not a hired gun like some adventure-tape holo. I fight when I must—and run when I must."

"That is why I want you to fight for me. For Zikkala. For yourself."

The tall dark man looked at her a long time before answering, searching her face carefully. "Quite a speech," he said at last. "You left out Mother, God, the First Principle, the Blackbull spirits, and apple pie."

Alena stepped away from the bar and strode across the *shoka* rug away from him. Rader watched her bottom and couldn't help grinning. She was obviously trying to keep it from swaying excessively, but nature had outpointed her. She turned and looked at him from across the room, her face serious and thoughtful. He hid his smile and waited.

"I want you to fight for me because I want to survive. I want you to fight for me because men whom I trust say you are the best. I want you to fight for me because I am afraid. I will pay you well, as much as I can afford, and back you up with everything I have. But I am not part of the spoils, Citizen Rader, not for you, not for anyone."

Rader said nothing. This was a new side of the beautiful flower from Civilization. He felt a grin twitching madly at his lips before he suppressed it.

His gun flashed into his hand, swept across the room away from her in a deadly arc, and slid back into his holster unfired. "You think that is all I can do, all I've done, all I can ever do?"

Alena shook her golden head. "And you do not know me," she replied. She crossed to the couch and curled gracefully into one end, her back against a fur pillow. "I was born on Canaan," she said, and Rader's heart sank.

Two billion people on two small continents, bulging at the seams with all birth-control devices and methods forbidden by the ruling religious hierarchy. The quality of life had been disgustingly low for more than two centuries, and sinking lower. It was a stinkhole that forbade migration to other planets for religious reasons. A stern, austere religion controlled everything, demanding sacrifice, with an avenging god for a policeman.

"I was born a slave," Alena said, her eyes on Rader. "All very legal, of course. My parents were indentured servants, sold into servitude by their parents to keep them from starving. But I was one of the lucky ones. I was born in the House of Themis, and to the household of a kindly old man. He said I reminded him of his dead mother, and I suspect I might have even been his genetic daughter, although my mother would never confirm or deny."

Alena picked up her wine glass, swirled it, and looked

into the bowl for a long moment. Rader stood awkwardly, waiting. "He alone kept me from being sold when the Themis fortunes changed with a change of First Bishops." She shrugged slightly. "I was young, I was beautiful, and I used him because I had to. There was no other way out." She looked up into Rader's eyes, seeking understanding and finding it.

"Oh, I could have pleased a new master and found special favors for a few years, but in the end I would be sent to the kitchens or the fields, and I would still have been a slave on god-fearing, goddamned Canaan. So I played upon the old man. I learned songs his mother had sung, I dressed as much like her as I could, I studied old tapes and learned to walk and move like her. He *had* to save me."

Alena looked at the starstone on her finger and turned it to catch the light. "He had hidden a small bag of starstones and emeralds that the family and the creditors did not know about. He sent me away secretly, first to Coronation with a forged passport, then to school on Flowerworld. He gave me a new name and a chance."

And you wind up an outplanet madam, Rader thought bitterly. His feelings toward the woman were mixed and mostly confused. He was attracted and repelled. Alena angered and excited him.

Her eyes searched his face again, then she took refuge in a swallow of wine. "One of the family . . . wanted me. He was sent to school on Flowerworld, saw me, and . . ." She paused and took a deep breath. "I was free, but they seized the money and made trouble for me. I escaped. I ran to Athena, to Malenkor, to Steinberg, to Ryan's Star. I used men. I used their desire for me."

She straightened, bringing her head up proudly. "No man took me by force . . . or bought me. No man took me who I did not want. My shame is that I manipulated their desires. I used my beauty as a weapon. I have been loved, but . . . I have not loved. I . . . I was afraid to love . . ." Her voice faded, and her eyes dropped for a moment, then rose again to look defiantly at Rader.

He took a deep breath and stepped away from the fire of her gaze to pick up a flagon and fill his goblet again. Then he looked back at her with a faint smile. "Everyone uses what he or she has," he said.

"I came here because it was where the supply ship was going, and I thought I'd be safer out here, with a better chance for making it big. It was just a way station to somewhere when I came here with my girls. A location for a quick killing, then move on with the Guild ships, to even newer worlds, where they'd be even hungrier for what I have to offer." She shrugged. "I fell in love with a planet."

They were silent a moment, and Rader tasted his wine, leaning his hip against the bar. She spoke again, softly, more hesitant in manner. "I'm twenty-four, Rader. I've been running a pleasure dome for over three subjective standard-years. I'm good at it. The drinks are not watered, the psychedelics are pure, and the prices—for everything—are fair." She gestured toward the floor. "There is beauty here, and rest. If a man just wants to rut in a warm hole, he can go elsewhere." She smiled suddenly. "And there's fun here, too, Rader. You grim man, you—you can laugh here."

"Startraders runs a good house, too."

"I'm certain you would know," she said and lowered her gaze, her smile melting away. Just as quickly, she lifted her head and put out a hand toward him. "I'm sorry, I thought —I'd hoped you would be—different."

"I'm a man, Alena. I'm the way I am, the way men are."

She looked at him for a long moment, and slowly her face cleared and her smile returned, almost shyly. "Do you realize that is the first time you've used my first name." She stopped and tilted her head at him. "What *is* your first name, anyway?"

"Rader will do."

Alena rolled her eyes skyward and made a gesture with her hands. "I forgot. Never ask *that* kind of question in the Out Worlds." She paused and looked at him shrewdly, smiling. "Friends?"

Rader grinned in spite of himself. He nodded and saluted her with his glass. She sat up, kneeling on the couch, and reached for his hand, pulling him down to her. She took his glass and put it on the polished fossil-leaf table. With a tigerish noise, she threw herself at him, her arms around his neck, bearing him back into the pillows, her body pressing tightly against him.

"You may kiss me now," she said and made her mouth ready.

But Rader didn't react. He just looked at her, a small smile on his lips, until her eyes popped open, large and violet and somewhat surprised.

"Are you asking or telling?" he said.

She tipped her head to one side, raised her eyebrows, and tugged him with her as she fell back to the other end of the couch. Her voice, soft and husky now, made it a question. "Kiss me now?"

They kissed.

They kept on kissing, and Rader kept changing his mind about her. By the time they stopped, Rader thought he was either being a full zongo, top-button fool, or that just maybe he was in love. Or both.

Alena smiled a delicate secret smile and pushed him back, rising to her feet and taking his hand. She lead him through the carved rainbow-wood door into her bedroom.

They kissed again by the bed with its deep, golden-brown covering of *tangri* furs, then she stepped back with a smile. With a gesture almost theatrical, she touched the neck-fastening of her shimmercloth dress and gave her body a wiggle —the garment dropped to the floor like a falling of stars.

Rader almost gasped aloud, for she was the most beautiful woman he had ever seen, blonde and golden, taut and tawny, without a blemish, at the peak of her physical beauty. He had seen women all over the Perseus arm, from the virginal test-tube miracles of Diamondome to the skilled courtesans of Athena, The Teacher, and Anubis. He had seen the genetically sculptured women of Coronation's Erosphere and had looked upon the Black Queen and Chota Malor. He had seen the mistresses of kings and popes, ministers and lords. But Alena had a oneness, a proportion and color and sculptured texture that pleased Rader with a deepness he had not suspected.

Dressed, she had been disturbingly beautiful, but nude and expectant, she seemed to be in her natural state, a loving woman, a complete woman. Rader felt very hairy and bony—and very male.

He was aware of her smiling as she stepped toward him, her full breasts swaying gently, their tips crested with hardening pink. Her mouth was warm and moist as it rose toward his. Her skin under his fingers was on loan from a pagan love-goddess. Her violet eyes closed as their lips touched.

Zzzzzzzttt!

Alena froze, and her eyes flew open. The dreamy expression died. She spoke a single short word in a language unknown to Rader and looked into his eyes. "I'm sorry, that's the emergency signal." She turned quickly away to the bed-head and hit the audio toggle on the console there, unselfconscious in her nudity.

"Yes?" There was enough ice in her voice, Rader thought, to frost Tura.

"Sorry, Miss Alena. Mister Lockhart is here. With some friends." It was Hayim's voice, controlled and hard. Without thinking, Rader's hand touched the stud on his holster, releasing the magnetic lockdown. Hayim's voice had that kind of quality.

"I'll be right down." She clicked off and scooped up her dress and started to step into it, then stopped. She shot Rader a grin and tossed the garment aside. It fell to the floor like a fluttering rainbow bird. She went to a wide closet and slid one of the doors aside. Her fingers ran down the line of luxurious dresses, until she pulled a deep red one from the hanger.

"I think it's time, Mister One-Name Rader. Are you my champion . . . or not?"

Rader felt the tensing of his muscles as his body made itself ready for combat. He merely nodded at her, for he was already running through the disciplines he had learned on Mephisto. He forced his body into calmness, then ran it again until it was not forced. In this state, his mind and body were combat-ready and not preprogrammed into any conditioned response. He could not act instinctively, relying upon his mental computer to choose a course of action that was suitable.

As Alena slipped into the red dress, Rader unfocused his eyes and ran through an even deeper discipline. He remembered his teacher on Mephisto, an old man who could be incredibly deadly. "You must learn to short-circuit your mind so that you react subconsciously—but with exactly the right move. Someone, some thing, comes at you, and you absorb a score of things about their attitude and condition—speed, distance, weaponry, balance, intent, posture, their commitment, and so on. Everything changing every second, every split second. It is much too quick for conscious thought. You must develop a kind of instantaneous computer, so that you can feed in the data and come up with the proper counter. When you are doing it right, the counter just flows. It is inevitable—so inevitable that it can often look as though the opponent cooperated in defeating himself."

When Rader looked out of his eyes again, Alena was sliding open another closet door to reveal a rack of good, expensive outback clothing. A Marlin jacket better than his own. A thermal suit, a camouflage tunic, and one of the latest Aquagills. She reached up to a shelf and drew down a slim one millimeter Starr Target needler. She smiled wanly at Rader as she slipped the small weapon into her dress. Evidently the dress was made to hold it, because it seemed to disappear into the ruffles and frills somewhere under her bosom toward her left armpit.

Rader looked admiringly at her. "I believe that no one has taken you by force."

Alena grinned briefly at him and checked herself in the mirror as she passed. She stepped to his side and put her palm against his chest. "There will be time for us."

"I know," he said wryly, "but survival comes first."

Alena gave him a fleeting grin and went into the office part of her quarters. "Come on, champion, I think it is time for the jousts."

She ran a house check, camera by camera, checking first the inner rooms, then the lobby where Hayim was. She zoomed in on a man in his middle thirties, backed by two others. He had dark wavy hair, worn full, and a beautifully cut Ambere suit in bottle green. His gun-belt was well fitted, ornamented and black, and the gun was a GE-500 needler. He was extraordinarily handsome and exuded confidence and poise.

Rader reached past her and zoomed the picture back to full. Alena touched a fingertip to a man who had his right wrist in a cast and wore his gun belt in an ill-fitting, left-hand holster. "He's one of Lockhart's men," she said.

"His name is Daniels," Rader said. "We met today." Alena shot him a look but said nothing. She ran back through the cameras until Rader stopped her on one of the main-room screens. "There, that one near the edge of the stage—is he yours?"

"No, but I think I saw him with Lockhart once." She moved the cameras around the room. A well-built brunette was doing a fair imitation of a Shanga belly dance for an enthusiastic afternoon crowd. She pointed again. "Four and five. Osbourne and Novak. They were with Lockhart, too."

Rader flicked back to the lobby camera and studied Lockhart with a grim smile. "He can't be a bad guy. Any vidtape, casting director would make him the holo-hero in a second. Look at those shoulders. Look at the way he wears that confident, I don't-care-who-owns-it smile. Got to be the good guy."

Alena hit him with her elbow. "I hope you don't fight like you think. He's the point man for Startrader. He's the one that engineered the takeovers on Xarris and Michelangelo. He fixed the Omigron scandal, according to the blabbermouths on the *De Forest*. They say he rigged the *Christiaan Huygens* disaster. He was a kingmaker on Sundark and Imexicrom. No one knows how many people he's killed—or had killed."

"My, my," Rader said softly, studying the man who stood smiling and confident, probably realizing he was under surveillance. "A real bad person." He straightened and put his hand on Alena's bare back. "Will Hayim back me? I know he'll back you—I can see it in his gizzard—but will he back *me?*"

"Yes. I'll let him know."

"What about your other people? Barnes in the checkroom? Anyone on the main floor?"

"There's Henri. He runs the shows and . . ." She turned to the scene in the main room and gasped. Rader's eyes snapped to the screen where a body had just slammed back into the stage, spraying blood all over the naked dancer. The body folded and fell to the floor, brutally carved into barely attached chunks of meat. The dancer ran off screaming, and the audience was on its feet, impotent for lack of weapons, and staring at the body—and at the killer.

"Henri!"

Rader reached across and turned up the audio. "You all saw that!" a burly Startrader said to the crowd. A small three-bolt laser was smothered in his meaty fist. "He insulted me and then started to draw!" The killer pointed at the stunpod that had fallen from Henri's jacket. No one contradicted him; he had two bolts left and Startrader behind him. At least no one on that floor contradicted him.

"Poor Henri," Alena said. "He loved me. He came from Steinberg just to . . . They . . . they must have said something about me."

"Love can make you vulnerable," Rader muttered, watching the killer stow the weapon in a left forearm holster and swagger out. He switched to the lobby camera and saw the man nod along with Lockhart, with smug satisfaction. Alena stared sightlessly, her eyes brimming.

Rader stood up. "You're staying here," he said harshly. "They'll cut you down, trying to get me, or Hayim, and say it was a terrible accident."

"I'm going down," she said with sudden determination, wiping at her eyes angrily and starting to rise.

Rader grabbed her by both arms and pressed her back into the chair. "You are staying *here*. You hired me to fight for you, and you'll do as I say when it comes to fighting. Now, you just get on the tube and find Korda, Liana, Gastoni—anyone in the Tiger Guild. I need someone to watch for backshooters." He started for the door, but she stopped him as he touched it.

"Wait." She was busy with the control deck. "Hold it, I'm routing a call . . . through . . . the Pink Shoka . . . ah! Charlie? Call Hayim for me. . . . Yes, route me through. . . . No, don't ask . . . then find Korda and Gastoni, and Liana. Tell them Rader needs them, here, *now!* All right." Alena looked up at Rader and grinned briefly. "Hey, sir champion, shouldn't you be wearing my colors?" Then she sobered. "Hayim? Act as though it was a reservation coming in from outside." On the screen, Rader could see Hayim with the hushphone to his head. "Rader is coming down. I want you to back him all the way. Barnes, too, if he will." She paused, listening. "And thank you."

Alena clicked off and looked at Rader. "Good luck," she said, her voice and gaze level. Then her hands were busy on the console. As he was going down the corridor, he heard her call to him. "Come back. I hate unfinished business."

He grinned and went bounding down the curving stairs. *She just might do,* he thought happily.

Rader slowed at the sensatron and came through the doors into the lobby slowly, casually, letting a number of men swarm past him to pick up their weapons from Barnes and leave. Many of them gave Lockhart, then Rader, wary looks. None of them were Tiger Guilders, and in a few moments the sound died and there were only nine left: Lockhart and his five, Hayim, Barnes and Rader. While the customers were leaving, Rader stood at one side of the steps, looking at Lockhart, their eyes locked as they exchanged silent information.

Then, as the last customer left, Rader broke his gaze with Lockhart, who had lost the edge to his smile, and raked across the other Startraders casually. "Hayim," he said, "Miss Petrovna will not be down. She's busy with the books." He moved down the steps, unchallenged, and into the room, ignoring the tough young men with Lockhart, who remained silent. Rader pretended to see Barnes for the first time and moved closer to the checkroom door.

"Barnes! I haven't seen you since the spring meet at Blackbull three years back!" He looked over the counter as he exchanged rough insults with the old man. He smiled thinly at the laser the legless man held in his one good hand, low and ready behind the counter, resting it on his uneven stumps.

"Well, keep your tanks filled," Rader drawled, turning back toward the men in the room and moving a little away from Barnes.

Lockhart and his men were spread out across the opposite wall. Lockhart's smile was back to full intensity, his teeth white and perfect. Rader grinned himself as he spoke.

"Startrader Lockhart, I presume. My name is Rader."

"Citizen Rader," he replied with warmth. "Are you . . ." He hesitated for a moment, his eyes shrewd upon Rader without his smile dimming a lumen. "Are you speaking for Citizen Petrovna?"

"I am." Rader's gaze swept across the others. Hayim was deceptively casual, almost as if he were afraid and did not want to become involved and was trying to find a discreet way out. *"I just work here,"* his manner seemed to say, his dark Arab countenance bland with forced unconcern. *If he ever comes after me,* Rader thought, *I must be very alert.*

"Do you speak well?" Lockhart asked, his voice amused. Six to one amused. "Are you accustomed to public speaking?"

Rader looked around the lobby casually. "This does seem awfully public, doesn't it? Well, it matters not." *Take the initiative.* "Miss Petrovna has told me of the marvelous plans Startrader has for our little backward mudball. Going to make it a garden spot, I hear."

Lockhart's eyes lost most of their amusement, but he continued to smile until Daniels made a sudden move; Lockhart shot him a venomous look—and the man stopped, looking uncomfortable.

"Thank you," Rader said. "I imagine Miss Petrovna values the carvings behind him."

Lockhart recharged his smile. "Yes, regrettably some of today's weapons are almost too good at their job." His left hand rose casually to tug at his ear, as if perplexed. His smile became a little rueful. The man on Rader's far left started drifting to the side. Rader pinned him with a look and he stopped, but the next man moved as well.

"Hayim," Rader said softly.

The Startrader toughs were suddenly looking into the mouth of a Magnum in the Arab's steady hand. The two hired guns looked and saw death sliced thin.

"Citizen Lockhart," Rader said pleasantly, "I'm afraid you and your guests will have to leave. Your party has disturbed the serenity of this place of rest and joy."

Lockhart nodded, all toothy urbanity gone. He sighed dramatically and shrugged. "I can see that you are not a businessman. I came here to talk business."

"You're right. I am a very poor businessman," Rader said. "I'm a hermit, really. I like to be left alone. I like my friends to be left alone." He started to add, "I like my planet to be left alone," when Lockhart interrupted with a sneer.

"You have whores for friends, then?"

Rader pressed back the immediate impulses and put a faint smile across his face. "Yes, I have women friends who sell their bodies for pleasure. Of course, if I thought you meant to include Miss Petrovna in that category, I would have to kill you, and frankly, I don't know if I can afford it.

"You see, this is Zikkala," he continued through Lockhart's frown, "and we have bound ourselves by the Common Rules of the United Guilds. Any man who kills in a duel must pay blood money to the family of the killee." He shrugged slightly. "I'm just a poor outback hunter, Startrader Lockhart. I'm sure that since you are such an important man with that famous organization, they would ask a great deal for you—all your travel expenses out here, executive replacement training, burial plot, and I don't know what all."

There was a silence, and Rader smiled innocently. "I'm certain you did not wish to give the impression, however inadvertent, that Miss Petrovna was included in that earlier remark. No, of course you didn't, but just to keep the record clear I'm certain you would wish to inform your friends here of that fact."

Rader looked serenely into Lockhart's eyes, the hard, trained muscles at rest, the sensors alert, the brain ready to respond in whatever manner seemed appropriate. Lockhart stared at him, his eyes narrowing, his body tense beneath his negligent pose of confidence. For a long moment, the two men faced each other—the air was electric with tension. Rader knew Lockhart was more afraid of dying than he was; the knowledge was sadly exhilarating.

The man from Startrade's main office calmed his face, then spoke in a bland, businesslike voice. "Yes, you are correct. It was a carelessly worded remark. No one would care to slur Citizen Petrovna in any way." Without waiting for the order he was certain Rader would give, Lockhart started toward the outer door. "Come on," he said gruffly, "she can't see us now. We'll conduct our business another day."

"Oh, there is just one more thing," Rader said, turning after them. They all stopped, looking back. Rader's eyes pinned Henri's killer. "Have you made arrangements for the blood money to be paid to Henri's family?"

Left alone and singled out, the burly killer glared belligerently back at Rader, turning slowly to face him. Confident of his gunspeed and the backing reputation of Startrade toughs, he started his pressure.

"Screw blood money. Where I come from, if you die, you die; if you kill, you kill."

"I see," Rader said quietly. "Well, the law can extract the credits from your estate."

The man tensed, his hand twitching upwards involuntarily. "You mudball skinswapper, you ain't takin' nuthing from Paulie Smith!"

And he drew.

Rader released his mind, and it chose the appropriate response. The ruby-beam from his laser struck Smith just below the sternum, cut up through his heart in millisecond pulses, splitting him open in a gaudy, bloody wound. The Startrade tough jerked as the red beam scarred the *pungi* panels behind him. Smith's corpse fell back with his death cry fading. He hit the wall, then bounced wetly forward, hitting the polished floor with a clatter, his unfired laser spinning through the splatters of blood.

Lockhart's nearest man stared, then went for his weapon as Paulie Smith was still collapsing. Barnes drilled a huge, five millimeter hole through the counter and through the one called Novak. The man spun, then crashed down into the lurid, spreading mosaic of blood and gore, his gun thumping into a gobbet of Smith's back and sliding off.

Lockhart was frozen, as were Osbourne and Daniels, who looked very pale. Only Lockhart's eyes moved, from the bloody corpses to Hayim. The Arab was grinning an ancient murderer's grimace, and the Startrader realized that he was only two ounces of trigger pressure from death. His lips twisted in a sick smile, his handsome face sallow as he looked at Rader. "You must be rich around here to afford so much blood money."

Old Barnes cackled loudly. "You don't understand our laws, Citizen Lockhart, *sir*. Your kind never does, 'causa ya think other folks're unimportant, lessen ya can use them."

He licked his lips. The old cripple was enjoying himself hugely. "Y'see, we pay what we think it was worth. It's a matter of honor—course ya might not unnerstan that. If the family or maybe friends don't think it's enough, they can take it ta Guild arbitration, and if the court ups it, they take it outta his guild stash." The multiple amputee cackled again. "I think Clem Peterson will agree two credits a head would cover it."

Lockhart stiffened. "Perhaps." He looked at Hayim, then back to Rader. "Except that your Marshal Peterson will be replaced soon. The Federation of Sovereign Systems is sending in a new marshal. He's scheduled on the next ship." His color was returning, and his smile was vulpine. "Blood money might get to be very expensive around here."

Lockhart turned and left, with Daniels scurrying behind and Osbourne making an unhappy tail. Rader gestured at the bodies. "Let's get these bagged and the place cleaned up. Signal the Guild for a coffin for Henri."

Hayim turned to the hushphone without a word, and Rader grinned at Barnes. "You are much neater than I am."

"I didn't have to draw. I had a bead on him already." He laughed in a croaking rasp. "They'll kill me for it, but what the hell, huh? That *tamir* should have done the job winter 'fore last." He chuckled again, a bubbling laugh that ended in a wheeze. "They'll be paying so much blood money, they'll wish they never heard a Everett Barnes!"

Rader laughed and spoke to Hayim as he hung up. "Better get Clem in here and get the blood money registered. I have a hunch Citizen Buttermouth Lockhart is thinking of sending us into bankruptcy legally. I saw how quickly he picked up on the law." He dug into his pocket and pulled out a five-stellar tab and tossed it to Barnes. "Take it out of that—and thanks!"

The old trapper's one hand snagged the coin out of the air, and he laughed again. "No, sir! No, *sir!* I'll pay for my own kill, thank ya, and you'll have the change." He flipped the coin and caught it. "Damn, I thought them days was a gone forever."

Rader aimed a thumb at the *pungi* wall where there were two smouldering marks. "I think we need some new decor around here, though."

"Aw," Barnes said, "they'll love it. Ya know how it is, they'll come ta look at the spot." He cackled happily to himself again as Hayim restored his weapon to the secret crevice below the hushphone.

"And thank you," Rader said to the Arab.

Hayim bowed slightly, his face unreadable. "It is as Miss Petrovna wished."

Alena Petrovna burst through the double doors and threw herself at Rader, who caught her, laughing. The tension was draining out of him, and he felt good.

"Rader, you damned fool bastard!" She kissed him, full and hard, and old Barnes snickered loudly. As she pulled back, Rader caught a glimpse of Hayim, his hawklike face tight, shifting his intent gaze away. *He won't try to kill me until this is over,* Rader thought. *Then I must watch for him.*

Alena shivered as she looked at the bloody remains of two human beings. Then she brought back the gladness. "Rader," she said breathlessly, her face young and bright. "We won!"

The big man's face hardened. *Is she really that naive?*

"Round one for Citizen Petrovna's Pleasure Palace," he said. "Round one only. Do you understand?"

Her face clouded, and she pressed herself to him, her fists against his chest. She sighed, deeply and with resignation. "Oh, I was hoping . . . ah, well." Her head came up, and she spoke quietly. "I thought you were crazy, doing what you did." Her eyes flickered as two crippled extrappers came from the rear of the dome and started to slide the bloody pieces of Smith and Novak into plastic bags. "Ugh. You certainly are a messy champion to have around. Look what you did to my wall."

Rader smiled thinly and pulled free. *She's tough,* he thought happily, *but not hard.* "I'll pay for new panels," he said.

"Oh, no! No, you don't! The blood goes and those bits and pieces of red stuff hanging there . . ." She paused slightly, paling for the moment before continuing. "But the panels stay that way. I'd be dumb to remove them. People will love seeing them and telling each other the story. Lockhart won't be quite so frightening around here from now on." She grinned at Rader like a little girl with a delightful secret. "I have it all on tape, you know. How you made him crawl and everything."

"Alena, I—"

Korda came through the door in a rush, a big Excalibur laser in his hands, a great black tiger with very big teeth. Liana was right behind him, leaping sideways in the opposite direction, her own needler traversing the lobby swiftly. Their faces were severe masks of fierce readiness. Wolf Briggs came in after them, breathing hard, wide-eyed, but holding a weapon at the ready.

Hayim did not move a muscle, and even old Barnes stopped his cackling. Rader, who had heard the pounding feet coming, simply grinned. "Late as usual. Someday they're going to get me, and you'll feel guilty as hell for . . . oh . . . maybe all afternoon." Although his words were light, he was glad to see them.

"Huh," rumbled Korda, his eyes moving in slits from Hayim, to Barnes, sweeping across Alena to the bloody carcasses being bagged. Wolf gulped and looked away. "Both?" Korda said, indicating the bags.

"No, I got one, ya tanglefoot!" Barnes snapped from the checkroom. Then he grinned widely and slapped the countertop with his one good hand. "Just like the ol' days in the Starvault!"

Liana lowered her needler and relaxed. Evidently she had borrowed the gun, because she had no holster and was still wearing her loincloth. She looked at Rader, then at Alena. "Have we started a war?"

"There's no need for you to get involved," Alena said quickly, and Liana frowned at her.

"What do you mean? He's involved, isn't he?" Liana indicated Rader, then tossed her long black hair back.

"Yes, but you—"

They were interrupted as people from the main room began to crowd out, looking at the mess. Barnes began to tell the story to whoever would listen, so Alena tipped her head toward the private rooms, and they went up.

"You're going to need someone to watch your back," Korda muttered to Rader as they passed into Alena's quarters.

"Nothing new about that," he replied.

They dropped onto couches, and Alena poured some

wine. Rader held his glass to the light and had dark thoughts.

Had they started a war? One way or another, Lockhart would get even—maybe more than even.

Are there any in the guilds who might have friends in Startrade?" Briggs asked.

"Not likely," Korda said. "Not real friends. But there are a few locals who are unaffiliated."

Liana put down her glass. "May I ask just why you were down there blazing away in the first place?"

Rader explained to Korda's unreadable face and Liana's knowing one how he had come to be Alena's "champion," although he did not use the word. It felt silly to him, somehow, to thus label himself.

Liana stood up as Rader finished, her breasts bobbing and the pi-pearls gleaming. "All right, so we have a war to fight. You better order replacements for the medikit and get plenty of vitamin-complex sets from the Guild stores." To her it was settled, and now it was time for logistics.

"Uh, a war?" Wolf asked.

"No, this isn't quite yet a Guild thing," Rader said. "If they mess with the guilds . . . well, then maybe you could call it a war. Until then, it's just a fight betwen the good guys—us, naturally—and the bad guys—them."

"Wolf," Rader added, "why don't you get a rig together and head out for the hills. You can draw on my account for what you need."

The boy blinked and swallowed. "What do you want me to do?"

"Do? Oh, no, just go hunting, trapping, gemstone looking. Whatever you had planned before."

"You're trying to get rid of me," Wolf said sullenly.

"This isn't your fight, boy," Rader said. "We've had experience, we have a stake here."

"I can fight."

"I'm sure you can, if you need to. But you don't need to."

" 'Cause I'm not in your guild?"

"Aw, hell," Korda said. He looked at Rader. "This isn't going to be just a Guild thing, y'know." Rader nodded. Korda looked at Briggs. "We'll find something for you to do, Wolf."

"Liana," Alena said, "would you care to decide on the fashions for this war?" Liana got up gracefully, and they left the room. Wolf looked after them with some confusion, but he said nothing.

There was a long pause, broken only by a gurgle of wine into Korda's goblet. Barber's *The Fortress Keeper* gave way to Reymundo's *The Planets of Aragon* on the music player. Korda sighed at last and set down his goblet.

"It's not going to be easy," Korda muttered. Rader nodded.

"I'm a little annoyed with myself for assuming you and Liana would join our little war," Rader said.

Korda waved away his doubts, then flipped a thumb toward the closed bedroom door. "You want her?"

Rader nodded his head again, but slowly. "She's . . . interesting."

Korda's mouth smiled on one side. "The trouble with frontier planets is that you don't have the widest selection possible."

"It only takes one," Rader said. "You have Liana, and I'm . . . I'm looking." He turned toward Wolf and smiled. "What's your preference?"

"Me? Oh. I'm looking, too. I'm still, uh . . ." He looked uncomfortable, and Korda spoke up to cover his embarrassment.

"Lockhart will have more men here soon. They always follow a search team with a good number of general workers, rough boys, accountants and a whole damned takeover force. If we pressured him into a fight, they'd probably use it to bring the Patrol down on us. They always have a few blackcoats on the supply ships. Or do you think he's bluffing about a marshal coming in?"

"No. But we better call a Guild meeting, a full meeting, as big as we can get it, and tape it for Blackbull and Nuevo. Even if they don't listen to Alena, they'll come to look."

Korda snorted and wiped at his face with a big hand. "This can't be handled just by a bunch of wild hunters shooting every Startrader or blackcoat that sets down. There will always be more of them coming along. It's the policy, and if Startrade is seeking to develop this area, then you can be damned sure they'll have more coming, as support troops."

Wolf made a sound, then looked embarrassed, but Korda gestured for him to speak. "Go on, boy, you were on the *De Forest*. Say what you think."

"But the law . . . I mean, a Patrol marshal . . ."

Korda interrupted him with a laugh. "If the law is coming out on a Startrader's ship, then you can be fairly certain Startrade owns him. They'd be sure of that before they started." He shrugged. "They cover their bets. They like things legal, or close to it. It's the way they work. All legal, at least on the surface. So whatever law comes in will be their law."

"Is the Patrol that easily bribed?" Wolf asked nervously.

Korda nodded. "Some people are, and Startrade is an expert at sniffing out those that are possibles. Then they'd seal 'em up and arrange for their transfer to the frontier worlds."

Rader smiled without mirth. "You can be sure Startrade gets the bribable ones assigned to them and the incorruptible ones to Farplanet's sectors."

"But Farplanet comes here, too," Wolf said. "This is a free zone, isn't it?"

"Yes," Rader said. "But a long, long time ago, back on some Inner World, there was a touch of discreet pressure . . . a bribe or dab of patronage. Then some judge gave discretionary powers to a tame marshal coming out here. He can declare us outlaws, deed our land to someone's pet dog or a tame court-trustee, and . . ." He shrugged again. "They'll run right over us."

"But Startrade won't have an armored division behind them," Wolf said earnestly. "Just what they have here and what comes in on the next ship."

"But that could be a thousand men," Korda said. "Three thousand, maybe. And machines. Technologies we know nothing about. Hypnosis drugs, telepathic controllers, continental energy suppressors . . ." He gestured with both hands.

Rader said, "A lot of those things are designed for total extermination, alien hostiles, or civilizations more highly mechanized than what we have here. Inner World people always seem to think in terms of mechanistic technologies or mudhut nothings. They won't want to eliminate us, not without some pretty good reasons, lots of strong evidence of what baddies we were—things that will hold up in court against our Guild lawyers. Their suppressors won't stop our flyers, because we don't have any. Their radios won't work any better than ours, in all probability—not in this sixty-year sunspot cycle."

"So it's a guerilla war," Korda sighed.

Rader's face brightened somewhat. "Now that's something I can understand. Hit 'em and run. We did that on Robinhood, when I was in the Merks. But that alone can't win a war."

Wolf's eyes got round. "You were in the Mercenaries?"

Rader looked at him with a sour expression and snorted. "Yeah, and we ate children and lasered pregnant mothers." He snorted again and turned to his wine.

"I didn't mean—I only know what I heard—"

"Don't believe all you hear, boy," Korda said. He tipped his head at the youth and asked a question. "Which side are you on?"

"Yours. Of course. I'll fight if I have to."

Rader chuckled and looked at him with a smile. "If I have to," he repeated. "Good answer. Don't get to thinking of yourself as one of those Inner World holo-heros, boy. They have a very short life expectancy."

"Yeah, right," Wolf said, looking serious. "Never meant that." He looked pleased.

The door opened behind Rader, and he saw Korda's eyes. He looked quickly over his shoulder, saw Liana and Alena enter, and for a long moment he held his breath.

Liana had discarded her loincloth for a black *silkon* one with silver highlights, formal length, and strung with pi-pearls found in the depths of the Wizard Islands lagoons. The ebony panels swirled around her flaring, golden hips down to the tips of her high-heel sandals. Her long thick black hair had been braided and rolled and arranged into a high, fancy headdress with a filigree centerpiece of Khortan silver, set with ancient Anubis emeralds. Another emerald hung on a fine silver chain between her firm bare breasts. Her tawny skin glowed, and her hair was as dark as a Rimworld night. She came smiling to Rader, slanted eyes dancing, and with a turn sent her *silkon* loincloth swirling as she plopped herself down in his lap and kissed him soundly on the mouth.

Rader was almost as surprised as Korda, who also found a golden queen approaching him, smiling warmly. Three drinks back, he barely knew her, and now she was coming to him, wearing a savage costume never worn by any primitive on any planet.

She had sandals with things that crisscrossed up her calf, their tips wound with copper wire. On her left wrist was a primitive wooden bracelet, carved with hydras devouring each other in a circle. Low on her hips was a supple *monga* hide strap, set with small metal knobs, from which hung a chocolate brown *tangri* pelt, striped with bands of rich gold. A thin metallic chain hung loosely around her waist, to which were attached small gold, silver, copper, and iron coins from Caliban and Hammurabi. Her breasts were bare and her nipples hard. Her thick mane of golden hair swung long and free. Earrings of small golden firefalls, fashioned by the slave jewelers of Varuna, hung on either side of her head.

Korda stared at the vision of the golden savage that was pulling at him, forcing him to heave his one hundred five kilograms of hard muscle to his feet. Alena pulled him toward the tape-block player. "Help me select something appropriate," she said, standing close to him as she fingered the blocks.

Liana breathed in Rader's ear. "How's that for a feminine wile?"

"Is that supposed to be subtle, or am I dense?"

"She's making friends with Korda, dum-dum. Nothing makes a man feel better than to have a beautiful woman make a fuss over him. Well, almost nothing else." She rose from his lap and brushed a breast across his face.

"Stop that," Rader said. "You two are about as subtle as a *tamir* in rut."

"And for the same reason, lover."

"Huh?" Rader looked from close-up Liana to far-distant Alena.

"She wants you. We got that all settled in the bedroom."

"A lot of things get settled in bedrooms, lover," snapped Rader, "but my future is not one of them."

"Sorry. We divided you two up. You have nothing to say about it. You are in our power. Our feminine wiles are duralloy *shoka* fangs, powered by the darlingest little fusion plant you ever saw."

Rader pulled his head to one side and put his hands on Liana's slim waist and looked at her sternly. "What are you *on?*"

"Uh," Wolf said, but they ignored him.

Liana danced away, laughing with a silvery delight that brought a smile to Rader's lips but confusion to his mind. *I'm not sure I like what's happening,* he thought, *but I think I'd be a fool to start complaining. What is there to complain about, dum-dum?* he asked himself. *Is it because you don't feel in control, lover?*

Somewhere there was a diabolic Rader, laughing in the echoing nothingness. Rader felt as if the Fates had tangled a stitch.

Alena seemed very interested in him, and Rader felt the strong chemistry between them—but he wondered if she was just a skillful actress, binding her champion to her in ways money would never do?

Once, Rader had been rich, briefly, a long time ago when he had been mustered out of the Mercenaries on Athena with the loot from three worlds. He had spent it on wine, women, and a battered Explorer-class starship named *Catherine of Aragon.* There had been scented Athenian women, beautiful and experienced, who seemed to find the young warrior irresistible. They writhed their sleek, pampered bodies over his, with stunning smiles and whispered hot words, proposing bizarre, exotic fantasy fulfillments.

As the novelty waned, Rader had come to realize that as far as they were concerned, any physical attractiveness he had for them was a plus, a dessert to the main course of monetary transfer. He had bought Caren a graceful crimson flyer, because she said she liked to make love while dipping and swooping through the great thunderheads. He had taken Aucturon to Falcon's Lair, the dome at the top of the world, for a week's high living. He had drunkenly let Bridget con him out of the Odin ruby, for which Ladislaus and Hrushevsky had died. In exchange, she and her three sisters had performed in ways he thought impossible. One of the cleopatras in the etroticon had stolen the perfect little crown-gold figurine, while two of her kind slavishly acted out one of Rader's minor fantasies.

In the end, he was left with enough credit for port duties and not enough for landing fees on Horus, which had started the trouble with the priests. Rader had been burned, and not even the relationship with Lorraine, when he was still a mercenary captain, had helped.

Liana came back, her *silkon* panels streaming and the pi-pearls glittering, to stand before him, a golden animal with a fine civilized polish and dancing dark eyes. "It's time for dinner, *tjinta*."

"I think I'll have to go," Wolf blurted quickly.

"Oh," Liana said with a pout, "stay."

"Let him go," Rader said. He got to his feet and stuck out his hand in the ancient gesture of friendship. "Thank you, Wolf, for coming to help."

"Yeah, sure." The boy looked pleased, and then Liana came to hug him. He blushed and stumbled back towards the door. "I'll see you later, huh?"

Alena left Korda and smiled at the boy, who didn't know where to look. "Listen, Wolfgang, when you finish what you must do, you come back. Tell Hayim I said you were to have Table Ten. You see the show and enjoy yourself. It's on the house."

"Yes, ma'am, thank you." He stumbled as he went out, and Alena closed the door behind him and put her back to it.

"Oh, dear," she said. "I had forgotten how young they can be."

"He's not bad," Korda said. "Good instincts. I had to shove him out of the way coming in, earlier."

Liana took Korda's arm, hugging it against her breasts and kissing his shoulder. She made low animal noises and called him *upendo* and *amour* and *nor tuk* and made him smile.

Alena put her arms around both of them and looked across at Rader. "Citizen Champion Rader, I congratulate you on your friends." The expression in her eyes changed, and her smile became less sure. She broke away and came to him as he rose, tall and lean and sundark.

"What's the matter?" she asked.

"Nothing."

"Nothing?" With that face? I'd hate to see you really concerned." She put her hands on his chest, breasts thrusting out in perfect firm splendor, and smiled. "Having second thoughts, Rader? Wondering if I'm worth it?"

"Zikkala is worth it. That's enough."

Alena pursed her lips and drew herself in close, her fingers digging into the fabric of his tunic. For a long moment she stood there, head down—the scent of trumpet flowers and the fresh clean aroma of a woman assaulting Rader's senses. Then her head came up, the fine blonde hair swinging back, and she put her arms around his neck.

"Too fast for you?" she asked softly. "Not for me. I've been looking for you for a long time, Rader, a very long time. You, Rader. I didn't know your name, and I'm not even certain now what it is." Her brows darkened. "Yes, I want you to fight for me . . . and for a planet I think is worth fighting for. I'm not the spoils of war, Rader, but if you want me, you have me. For as long as you want."

Alena pulled back her head and looked at him with a small, crooked smile. "I've never said that to anyone before. I ask nothing of you that I do not know you will give anyway." She hesitated. "If I please you, we can be together until . . . until we part."

Rader looked into the violet depths of her eyes. *You're supposed to be able to read the soul in the eyes,* he thought, *but you look and find, then look and lose . . . and make up your own ideas about what you have found or lost.* "What if I do not please *you?*" He was immediately angry with himself, wondering why this woman so often made him feel like a fool, saying foolish things, talking instead of acting?

"You please me," she said, smiling and rising on tiptoe to brush her lips against his. She started to move away, then stopped, and her face sobered as she looked back at him. "I am not in love with you, Rader . . . not yet. I do not love you . . . yet. I promise nothing. I like you, *amo,* for you are *malmola,* hard and intelligent, and I like your friends. I think I will fall in love with you, but I will not say what I will do or think or feel until I know."

"Fair enough," Rader said, a glow starting in his heart. If it was a game she was playing, she was setting dangerous rules. Then the mad satyr deep in Rader said, *"But later she can say, 'I told you so! I promised nothing!'"* He forced his thoughts away, buried them deeply, and smiled as he took her arm.

They went together to Liana and Korda, who had been watching them. They all smiled broadly and happily at each other, even Rader, who was the last to smile. Korda lifted a thunderglass goblet and rolled the camarrafano brandy in it.

"We who are about to dine salute you."

When dinner was over, Liana and Korda exchanged knowing looks. They traded farewells and went off to their own bed chamber.

Alena smiled and shut the door behind them and set the alarm. She touched the light control and dimmed the panels even further, leaving only a few small pools of light in the shadowy room.

Rader watched her walk by, a half-naked golden savage with hundred-credit perfume, to program the music cubes. Then from a cabinet she took a slim handblown bottle of pale-blue *ploom* wine and two small wine cups.

She walked to Rader with her eyes downcast and very much aware of his gaze on her. She knelt beside him on the *shoka* rug, poured the two glasses full, and handed one to Rader as he lounged back against the embroidered cushions.

They sipped the delicately scented wine and did not speak, listening to the music. Alena shifted and lay against a cushion, her body relaxed and lovely in the soft light. Leisurely Rader ran his eyes over the beautiful woman as she kept her eyes on the wine in her glass. She was breathing slowly and deeply, her big breasts rising and falling steadily, the firefalls at her ears shivering. She knew she was being inspected and was obviously nervous, although Rader could not imagine why, as she was the most beautiful woman he had ever seen.

Her hair was fine, long and thick, and the lean hunter reached out to smooth his hand down her shoulder and arm, feeling the sandlike texture of her spilling hair, rolling on her skin. When he touched her, she shivered like an excited mare but did not speak.

The delicately smooth texture of her flesh, the fine golden hair, the fullness and firmness of her breasts, the pink-brown nipples that were puckering and hardening in a sign of her inner feelings—all these things intrigued and excited Rader.

But more than the physical beauty was the radiant inner beauty of the woman that excited Rader. She was tough-minded and intelligent but was neither hard nor insular. *How did you last this long, on your own, and stay this way?* he thought. That tiny alarm rang again in his mind, perversely discordant. *Or are you acting? The sweet, warm beauty in trouble, playing out some complex game of deceit and greed?*

Rader's mind was blurred by the beauty and desirability of the very available Alena. He put down his glass, took hers and put in on the table. *Actor or survivor, he thought, who cares?*

He put his hand on her arm, and she came to him suddenly, in a rush, breathing hard and clinging to him, burying her face in the hollow of his throat. Rader held her, stroking her back, running the gold hair across her shoulders, inhaling her, letting the reality of her soak into him.

Alena Petrovna.

Alena Petrovna and that old beat-up Rader, the fighter who hated to fight, the lover who was hesitant to love.

"Rader," she said into his throat.

"Yes?"

"What a strange, harsh name—Rader. You sound like a pirate."

"And Alena Petrovna does not sound like someone running a dome full of cleopatras."

Alena pulled away from him and searched his face. Rader thought she was going to cry.

"Do you hate me for being a madam?" He started to speak, but she put her fingers quickly against his lips, then dropped them to his tunic, where she plucked at the fabric with nervous concentration. "No, of course you do. No man really wants a woman in my business."

Rader tilted up her chin and looked into her wet violet eyes. "Do you sell yourself?"

She shook her head vigorously. "I tried once, but I

couldn't go through with it." She looked up at him once again. "My god, you know I'm not a virgin . . ."

"Virgins are a great responsibility," Rader said and smiled. "Besides, they're always wondering about what they're missing and probably fantasize about it so much, the reality couldn't possibly match up." Again, he smiled at her—and slowly her own smile returned.

"Hell, if you're wondering about your social status or something, I was a mercenary for three years, and the only thing lower than that is a six-year merk—"

She was kissing him. . . . he was kissing her.

Then they were kissing—and it was the kind of touching that only lovers know—the devouring, sensuous experience of flesh upon flesh. His hands told her of desire and lust and gentleness. Her tongue spoke of surrender and giving and sharing.

They rose at last, breathing hard and almost groggy. Alena said, "Time to play the unfinished symphony."

In her bedroom Alena once again stripped away the carefully primitive costume until she stood naked and more savage, more basic than ever before.

Rader's black tunic joined the rest of his clothes, and Alena devoured him with her eyes as he came to her. They kissed again, bodies pressed together, with a kind of wildness loosened in the room. Alena was focused upon his maleness, hard against her stomach, and she writhed against him with a moan.

The beautiful young blonde looked up at him at last, staring into his eyes with a peculiar intentness. "I'm afraid I won't please you," she said, then quickly ducked her head into his throat. She started kissing him down his chest. "But let me try . . ."

The sphere of light cast pulsating shadows over the surviving Kaleen as they knelt in a line on the smoothed stone floor.

We mourn the unfulfilled, the voice said in their minds. *We mourn what shall not be for those who shall not continue. But rejoice in the testing. The time of the nest awaits you. Shir-ka-kaloon, my father, my son, mother of us all, will be with you.*

The Kaleen warriors waited, sensing more to come. The

voice came again, solemn and neuter in their expectant minds.

We are at the time of our greatest testing. The scaly beasts of claw and fang were not so formidable. Not even our brothers, our sisters, were so honorable a foe. Your nesting will achieve great heights, perhaps the greatest purification ever.

There was a pause.

The cycle will be completed. We shall all be elevated. The cycle was before and shall be again.

Again a pause.

I am Kaleen-ka, Mother of broods, Father of the nest. I mourn with you, and I shall rejoice with you.

The pulsating sphere of light expanded, charging their minds with wordless fire, then shrank, sinking into the rock and disappearing. The chamber was dimly lit as the Kaleen warriors rose to file out, a renewed determination in their double hearts.

Rader stood looking at the still body of Barnes so carefully arranged for the funeral. The old trapper lay with his one hand upon his chest, wearing his best and only suit of formal city clothes. He looked distant and thoughtful—and somewhat younger.

"Heart attack, huh?" Rader grunted, looking across at Russ Holtan and Konstantin.

"That's what Levesque said, but . . . well, I dunno," Holtan said, his hand stroking his thick, dark beard. "I always thought he was pretty healthy."

Konstantin and Rader exchanged looks. "Lockhart?"

"That would be hard to prove," Rader said. "People *do* die of natural causes even here in Zikkala, and if Lockhart slipped him something, it probably wouldn't show up in an autopsy."

"Calkins says a Farplanet ship will be coming into orbit this morning and that the shuttle will be down by this afternoon. Maybe they'll have a diagnosticon, and we can find out."

"And maybe not." Rader turned away from the bed and

walked into the hall, followed by Holtan and Konstantin. "Lockhart said a Union marshal was supposed to come in. It would be just like them to bring a tame badge in on a Farplanet ship instead of a Startrader. No—hah-hah—evidence of collusion."

"He may not be a bought gun, y'know," Holtan said.

"Yeah, sure—only how did Lockhart know a marshal was coming? He doesn't look like the precognizant type to me."

"Well, maybe he won't be on this ship," Konstantin said hopefully, limping along on his crutch.

"That'll give us a bit more time," Holtan muttered.

"I'm not sure which side time is working on yet," Rader said.

The shuttle came down that afternoon, landing on the plain outside the western gate. It loomed up over the rock-melt barriers, indicative of the monstrous size of the interstellar globes that sailed the galactic seas. The bulbous lander opened its large cargo hatch, the crane slithered out of its hole over the opening, and the crews appeared, rolling crates out and hooking them on. The passenger hatch popped, and the extender slid out. A black-clad man appeared on the platform almost at once and stood looking down.

Someone in the ground crew waved, for Farplanet was a good outfit, shrewd but fair, and the only complaints lodged with the guilds had been over accidental mistakes and a few unimportant misunderstandings. They were commonly considered a far cry from the world-gulping reputation of Startrade Export-Import Ltd., headquartered on Centauri Central, Beta Centaurus XIX. But still, Farplanet *was* a huge corporation and suspect on the face of it.

The crates of tapes, with coded information on everything from *ji-ja* music and the Transmute games of Berry III to the latest reference books on molecular constructs, gravitational studies, and social dynamics, came down on the cables. The blue-striped vitamin boxes, cerise hormone containers, and white-banded medical supplies came down next. Guild buyers and skilled psycho-technicians regularly sent samplings of various cultural entertainment to outlying planets and these came down in Guild-sealed crates.

Rader watched the man up on the extended passenger platform watch those working below and wondered about him. He was too high to get much of an impression, except for the usual Patrol black uniform.

More Guild stock began coming down: artificial hands and legs, tanning solutions, exotic herbs and frozen foods, some Quar elixir, game tapes, Guild advisories on upcoming cargoes and policy updates, Sakimoto holos, tape blocks, Moltari *drebna*.

And a Union marshal for Rader.

He came down, lean and arrogant, booted and grim, wearing a gun that Rader did not recognize. He swung aboard the platform, lowering a small, Zeus fusion-power plant and rode the cable expertly to a landing.

Lockhart, flanked by Daniels and Osbourne, walked out to meet him, and Clem Petersen was with them. The Zikkala-elected marshal looked uncomfortable but game, and Rader jumped down from the rock where he had been watching and walked out to hear better.

"Ah, Marshal Gossett!" Lockhart said smoothly to the grim-faced lawman. "I'm Lockhart, Startrade commander here." He gestured toward the others. "Daniels, Osbourne . . . and Clem Petersen. He was elected peace officer by a citizens committee here—oh, four or five years ago."

Lockhart made the election sound like children playing, and Rader grew grimly cool. He hoped Clem would keep his head as the Union marshal looked him over contemptuously.

Rader inspected the new force from civilization, with clinical exactness. The United System lawman was big and looked tough, but then they had to be or they didn't last. Rader instinctively disliked the man, and it wasn't just the uniform, it was the man himself. Rader had met many Union badge-toters that were good men, and fair. The vibrations from this blackshirt were bad.

Gossett's voice was contemptuous and challenging as he sneered at Clem. "So you're the far-end constable that drilled Coughlin, huh?" He looked Clem up and down, with disgust on his face plain to see. "Maybe you'd like to try some of your outworld backshooting on *me?*"

The deliberate provocation startled Rader. He had to be Lockhart's tool since few marshals would press matters on such a crude level, so quickly and so obviously illegally. There had to be great pressure building, he thought. Also, someone had to have briefed the marshal on the local situation between the time the starship left null-space and came on planetary drive to Zikkala orbit. Rader looked narrowly at Lockhart and saw there a careful attempt to cover up great concern.

"Ah, Marshal Gossett," Lockhart said, "you have not met the pride of Shamrock, the owner of our finest pleasure dome . . ."

Rader saw Alena coming through the gathering crowd of hunters and townspeople. She wore a severely cut jump suit of clinging brown, and her hair had been pulled back and tied in a luxuriant ponytail. Around her hips was a gun-belt, and Rader's heart leaped. In his world, in any outworld, if you wore a gun you were considered capable of using it—and people acted accordingly.

Alena's hand rested gracefully on the marwood butt of her Starr Target needler. Her eyes were frosty as she swept her gaze over Lockhart's group, but she did not flinch under the frown of the new marshal.

"Marshal Jake Gossett, this is—"

"Alena Petrovna," she said, interrupting Lockhart's smooth speech. Rader drifted closer. Lockhart saw him, and Rader felt cold pleasure as he saw the momentary widening of the Startrader's eyes.

"This is all very pleasant," Gossett began abruptly, "but I'm here to bring law and order to this god-forsaken ball of crud, and I haven't time for whorehouse cleos."

There was a silence so sudden that Gossett stiffened, his eyes moving around warily. He followed the track of several pairs of eyes and discovered Rader. He half-turned to keep the lean hunter in view.

Rader spoke into the silence, his voice deceptively mild. "Mister Lockhart, it seems to me you have indiscreet friends."

"Rader," Alena said, "it's all right."

He ignored her and moved to the left, bringing Lockhart

and his disciples into line behind the marshal, forcing the blackshirt to turn and making Lockhart nervous. The handsome Startrade leader looked at Clem, who had stepped to the side, his face bland and calm.

"Marshal Gossett," Rader said quietly, "I believe *our* marshal informed your organization that Zikkala was not a signator to any System pact: therefore, we don't really need a big scary Union marshal here at all, legally or otherwise."

Gossett sneered. "If we waited for the paper work, we wouldn't have gotten out of the Perseus arm. The Patrol goes where it is needed."

Rader smiled thinly. "Exactly. Where it is needed. It is not needed here. The *Winthrop Aldrich* won't be leaving orbit for a day or so. Why don't you borrow a horse from Mister Lockhart here and look around at our god-forsaken ball of crud . . . then go home."

Gossett's eyes flicked beyond Rader, then around at the faces, stopping for a second on Lockhart's. The Startrader slid his eyes toward Rader, and the marshal turned fully to face him, a cruel smile twisting his lips and disappearing into the bleak dark spaces of his eyes.

"Are you trying to run me off, sonny?"

"Oh, no," Rader answered. "I'm just informing you that since you have no legal status here, we welcome you as a transient tourist . . . and that's all."

"As far as we're concerned, Zikkala is part of the United System, and I'm here to bring justice."

"Justice is a very big word, Marshal. Like love and freedom and death. It would be an injustice to myself . . . just as an example of our thinking here on this god-forsaken ball of crud . . . if I permitted any further insults to Miss Petrovna, either by word or tone."

"Rader, please," Alena said. She stepped toward Gossett. "Marshal, I've come to discuss your legal status here. I spent an hour this morning looking through the Tiger and Dragon Guild files, and nowhere do I find that either guild or any individual member or company under any commision has filed—or even petitioned—for System status." She spread her hands and looked at Clem. "Therefore, as much as we enjoy talking to visitors from the Inner Worlds, we simply cannot allow you to be under the impression that we are—or ever have been a System planet." She smiled and glanced at Rader as if to say, *"There, that's the way, you gun-man you!"*

Gossett looked at Lockhart over his shoulder, and the handsome Startrader's expression was frigid. *Don't look at me for every turn,* he seemed to say.

On the periphery of his vision, Rader saw Wolf Briggs in the crowd and hoped the boy would remain cool. *Where is Korda? Will he finish checking the bales at the warehouse and get here?*

Clem Petersen stepped forward, a mild-appearing man who possessed both tact and a fierce tenacity that had caused many a rough hunter to watch that he didn't offend. "Why don't we go up to the Guild Hall and discuss this? The boys up top would like to set up for trading, and we have a couple of warehouses full of *shoka* and other goods we'd like to trade." He started forward and men moved behind Rader.

"No, goddammit," Gossett snapped, and everyone stopped. He looked hard at Clem. "I am officially informing you, before witnesses, that I am assuming lawful command of the armed forces and constabulary of Zikkala, Loki IV, RS catalog number 39-733-906. You will disarm and place yourself under my orders or suffer the penalty."

Everyone stopped breathing. Clem sighed in the silence. "Miss Petrovna was quite correct, and I'm certain that a computer check will verify our status as a free planet. It is true that we have not yet petitioned for an official ruling under the Free Planet Act, but—"

Gossett drew.

Clem tried. He was fast, and he tried hard, but he really hadn't expected such a violent, final solution so soon, and he died. The gun Rader couldn't identify burned a large messy hole through Clem's chest, and his guts were starting to spill out in oily gray coils splashed with red, as Clem fell backward.

Rader's hand streaked to his gun butt, but even as he moved, he sensed a movement behind him. He threw himself sideways, his gun swinging up to bear on the black-clad Union marshal, hoping to hit him even as he fell. But a nova exploded on the side of his head—he was falling in slow motion, everything blurred and confused.

He still fired, but the wavering laser-beam missed by a few millimeters and sprayed Daniels' brains all over the Zeus fusion-power plant still on the pallet.

He was crumpling into the red dust and deeper into blackness, where he heard someone call his name . . . and deeper . . . into the blackest part of all . . . into oblivion.

Even in oblivion they called his name, only softer, quieter. It was a word, sometimes his name and sometimes just a sound, a thing without meaning. Gradually, faintly, he realized it was his name. There were other words, then his name again.

Rader . . . Rader . . . it's me . . . Rader, darling . . . oh, Rader . . .

"Rader, wake up!"

The pain came before anything. A great throbbing, conquering pain. Rader groaned from the sheer enormity of a pain that throbbing, that demanding of all his life force.

"Rader, darling!"

A voice. A woman's voice. She knew him. She liked him.

With an effort like lifting a boulder with his tongue, Rader forced open his eyes. Rock-melt. Gray rock-melt streaked with dull red. Then a face, framed in blondeness, came into the narrow slit of his viewscreens.

"Rader? Are you all right?" It was Alena.

He closed his eyes. He was alive, and Alena was with him. He moved his lips, and somehow the words didn't form. He felt Alena as she touched his lips with a damp cloth. He felt her press her face next to his, her hair falling across him, to whisper into his left ear, the one opposite the spot where a rabid *shoka* was tearing off his head.

"You're in jail. *We're* in jail. One of Lockhart's men hit you from behind with an iron bar. You have a concussion, but Levesque says you'll live. The medikit says you'll live. *I say* you will live, so stop shamming and *live,* damn you!"

She moved back, a smile trembling on her lips as Rader forced open his eyelids again. He felt very tired. He tried to smile but was startled to see the tears suddenly gush forth as Alena's face crumpled. She buried her face against his chest, and he felt her shake.

"Oh, god, Rader, it's been two days, and you haven't stirred! I was so scared!"

His voice croaked, then the words came. "You . . . in here . . . with me? Korda? Liana? Others?"

Her blonde head came up, and she wiped ineffectually at the tears. "Korda disappeared. Clem is dead. Russ Holtan lost a chunk of side in that shootout. Liana . . ." She pressed herself to him again and whispered in his ear. "I think Liana is still here in Shamrock, hiding. But I don't know for certain. They threw us both in here, and I had only seconds when Levesque was here with the medikit. I tried, honestly I tried, Rader, but that bastard Gossett was wearing a permovest under his tunic. My needler knocked him down, but it didn't kill him and they grabbed me before I got another shot in! I should have aimed for his head!"

She clung to him in impotent rage, and Rader's head throbbed even harder as his growing anger raised his blood pressure. "You . . . with . . . me . . . here . . ." Every whispered word was an effort.

"They said I could nurse you, instead of keeping me in another cell. They don't want you to die as a martyr, they want to discredit and humiliate you. But I know they'll kill us both when it's the right time for them!"

"Lockhart—?"

"He's hunting Korda and the others. A lot of men just headed out, back into the hills. But they didn't know the marshal brought in a flyer. They're hunting them from the air! Oh, Rader, the marshal didn't come alone! He had deputies—they were probably Startraders he deputized. One of them is the zongo ace that crushed your head. And lots of Lockhart's men already here have been deputized. Now the marshal can hunt us down with a legal force and get that goddamned Startrade outfit what it wants!"

"What . . . did . . . Korda . . . do?"

"Someone told him, I guess. I think they expected him to try to rescue you, but he just disappeared." She looked worried. "He . . . he didn't run out, did he?"

Rader forced a faint smile to his lips. "No. He . . . knew . . . I was . . . hurt?" Alena nodded. "Then . . .

he . . . will . . . wait . . . outside . . . and . . . Liana . . . inside." He closed his eyes as a wave of pain hit him. When it had passed, he asked in a weak voice, "How bad am I?"

"Levesque was worried about the motor responses on your left side. Can you move?" Rader tried, but his arms felt like lead and trembled. He went limp, gasping for breath. Like an animal he drew into himself, summoning up sleep, using the disciplines to drive back the pain. "Rest," he said in a whisper.

Alena held his hand and looked around the rock cell wearily. She laid her head against his side and closed her eyes, curling as well as she could against his pallet, which rested on a rock-melt ledge.

At last she slept, twitching in her dreams.

Rader awoke groggily as he heard the cell door rattling. He opened his pain-clamped eyes to see Lockhart entering. Behind him were a couple of men. All were armed, arrogant and tough looking. Only Lockhart was smiling; but his smile was without humor, merely a facial gesture to emphasize his superiority.

Rader lay without moving, just watching them, but he was silently using the disciplines to force back the pain and the weakness. His body seemed sluggish and unresponsive. He knew he was in no condition to do anything at all, but rather than reveal his weakness, he stayed quiet.

The two guards stepped out from behind Lockhart, theirs eyes on Rader, their hands not far from their lasers, which gave him some satisfaction.

Lockhart finished his silent superior examination of Rader, then looked at Alena. He permitted a carefully controlled expression of sadness to cross his handsome face.

"Too bad, too bad," he sighed. "You could have provided me with considerable amusement, out here on the edge of nothing."

"And what would you have provided me?" Alena answered, her voice remarkably calm, even faintly mocking.

Lockhart shrugged delicately. "You are beautiful. I admit that freely. I have never minded extending my protection and generosity to a beautiful woman. You could have been the queen of this mudball world."

Alena was silent a moment before Rader felt her move on the bench behind him. She stood gracefully, stepped forward and, with excellent aim, spit right in Lockhart's face. He looked startled, and the men behind him half-drew their weapons. With an angry gesture Lockhart wiped the spittle from his face, and his lips curved in a vicious smile.

"A theatrical gesture, Citizen Petrovna." He looked at his hand, half-turned to the guard on his left and without a word wiped his hand on the man's tunic. There was a flicker in the guard's dark eyes, but he said nothing as Lockhart turned back. "Very well," he said rather briskly, as if informing them the interview was over and that they might leave his imperial presence.

To Rader, Lockhart said, "Too bad about you. From the moment I arrived here all I heard was stories about the great Rader, the world-hopping thug, the fast gun and great warrior." He snorted contemptuously. Their eyes locked for a moment, and Rader saw tension appear in the Startrader's eyes. "Yes," the handsome off-worlder said softly, "we might have made an interesting pair . . ." His voice trailed off, and he seemed to shake himself, a surprisingly frank smile coming to his mouth. "Childish, isn't it? Who is the better warrior? The challenge of the jousts, the dusty, street duels before space travel, perhaps even back in the days of primitive man." He made a small gesture with his carefully manicured hands, as if regretful. "But this shall not be, this possibly legendary meeting of Lockhart and Rader. You will die; I shall live. You will be forgotten; I shall rule a dozen worlds."

"You couldn't rule a space pebble," snapped Alena.

He smiled at her in a sad, wise way. "Oh, but I shall. The Empire of Mudballs, perhaps, but an empire, Citizen Petrovna. By the time Startrade hears about it all, I shall be rich and powerful—and in control of a respectable collection of space." He shrugged again, almost a comical shrug. "By the time they try to *do* something about it, it will be too late. The worst that can happen is that I shall be Startrade's conquering hero, the one who stuffed their coffers with treasure."

Alena sniffed. It was all she did, but Lockhart flushed and his smile disappeared. There was a volume of rebuke in that sniff, and Rader almost smiled. He saw Lockhart's eyes swing from one to the other, before he spoke. "People like you have such little dreams. A piece of land, a dome, a full belly." He snorted contemptuously through his nostrils. "There is no power more mighty than the power of a great dream—and I have that dream, and I have that power." His clenched fist rose before him. "You shall not stop me, your shabby little mudballer shall not, your guilds shall not—! Not even Startrade Export shall stop me!"

Alena sniffed again. "Power ennobles, is that it? And absolute power ennobles absolutely?"

Lockhart's face grew pale and pinched, and for the first time, Rader saw beneath the mask of his handsomeness, saw the tension and fear, the madness and cruelty. And for Alena, Rader felt fear. For himself he felt little. He had faced death many times, and in some ways he was already accepting his own death in this conflict. For the beautiful Alena he felt a chill, damp fear. But in a strange way it made him feel good; it had been a very long time since he had worried that much about anyone.

Lockhart forced the dark expression from his face, and then a bright, toothy smile appeared, almost as if by magic. "Why do I waste my time with you? You are yesterday's business. It was petty of me even to come here to gloat." He smiled on a moment, looking from one to another. "Yes, gloat. A theatrical gesture on my part," he said, bowing slightly to Alena.

Lockhart turned away and the guards backed out. The man from Startrade paused in the doorway and looked sadly at Rader, but the sadness was mock pity. "Too bad," he said softly. "Goodbye, Rader. Killing you in a fair fight might have helped me greatly in the future. A little advance publicity never hurts. 'The man that killed Rader on Zikkala.' They would have been afraid of me, and that might give me an edge somewhere, some time . . ." He shrugged again and left without another word.

The cell door clanged shut, and there were only the muffled sounds of them leaving. Alena stroked Rader's face as he let himself sink back into healing sleep.

Rader winced at the loud clanging, and he struggled up from a deep sleep into blinding pain. Booming iron-on-iron sounds echoed in his hall of blackness, and a sneering voice demanded something, someone.

The lean hunter lifted his lids like rusty hatch-covers and saw the huge dark figure of a man pulling at Alena, dragging her toward the cell door. She was fighting him, but her words were lost in the sea of pain that flooded over Rader as he tried to rise. He fell back, weak and dizzy, as the sneering man dragged her out. He twisted on the ledge, pressing himself up as Alena struck the man in the stomach, then raked her nails across his face. She broke loose and backed into the cell, her jumper ripped, her eyes jumping from the burly guard to Rader, who now was almost sitting up.

"Don't, Rader!" she yelled. The guard stepped toward her, cursing, and unclipped a nervelash from his belt and struck out at her.

Alena staggered as if gaffed by a giant hook, her nervous system going into shock at the incredible pain. She swayed and fell to her hands and knees. Rader staggered to his feet, his head swimming, the room blurring. He croaked her name, took a step and fell to one hand and one knee. He almost passed out as his head seemed to slice open and fall apart, but he reached out for the guard.

The man easily avoided his slow and awkward attack and negligently backhanded him across the face. Rader's head snapped, and blackness was instant, but brief. He opened his eyes to a slit and tried to rise against the swords of pain, but the guard was already dragging Alena's unconscious body out through the cell door, the collar of her jumpsuit gathered in his meaty hand. The suit had ripped, and one naked beast jutted out through the tear.

The thick door thudded shut, and the exterior bar

banged closed. Rader's face hit the cold rock-melt floor, bringing oblivion, if not peace.

Time stretched out, then contracted, then stopped. There were jagged shards of time and images falling through Rader's mind. Alena's face, intense and open-mouthed in orgasm. Paulie Smith's entrails exploding against the wall. The *tamir* looming over him, fangs opening with a snap, his laser in the red dust beyond his reach. The Kaleen blade rising up from the *scrit,* his arm going back, the feathered spear lifting, and Rader's hand moving in slow motion toward his holster. Korda smashing through the priests to his side. Buckling up in the drop shells, armored and tense, as the ship came into the atmosphere, ready to spew mercenaries like seeds. Alena, waking him in the night, her mouth on fire, her perfumed, glowing flesh, her screaming voice ripping open the black dome, letting in the crimson sky . . .

Alena's screams brought Rader back. He lifted his head and cried out a curse, for the dripping blood had soaked through the bandage and had stuck his face to the stone floor.

Another scream came, this one longer than a breath, dying at the end, but longer than anyone should scream without passing out. Rage gave Rader strength, and he levered himself to his hands and knees, his head hanging, dizzy, dripping new blood, as he fought back the blackness of vertigo.

He crawled to the thick wooden door and clawed his way up, breaking fingernails against the rough, hard surface. At last Rader stood on his feet, swaying, fighting blackout, until he could stand without grasping at the boltheads on the door. His fingers poked at the metal-covered observation slit, but it was securely fastened.

There were no more screams, and that frightened Rader more than anything. He leaned back against the wall next to the door and fought at calmness. *If she is dead I will kill them all, all the way back to the home planet head office,* he thought with a snarl. *I'll burn them down, I'll slice them through and let the guts spill out and watch their faces as they see themselves. I'll burn and bomb and kill and kill . . .*

There was a noise in the corridor, and Rader pressed himself back, summoning up the hidden resources, running the disciplines against pain as fast as he could.

The slit opened, and for a moment there was silence. Then a rough laugh came from beyond the door. "Okay, hero, get out where I can see you." Rader didn't move. "Move, scum, or your lady friend gets hurt."

Rader heard Alena give a sudden moan, and he moved as quickly as he could to the center of the cell. *Live,* he told himself, *survive, Then kill. Take what you must, then kill. Survive and kill.* The cell door opened, and the big grinning guard stood there, a nervelash ready in one hand and supporting a naked Alena with the other.

With a hoarse curse Rader took a step forward, but the leering guard prodded Alena in the side with the nervelash and she jerked awake with a cry, rigid and wide-eyed. Then she fell forward to her knees and rolled over to lay sprawled on the cold floor, moaning faintly.

Rader took another step, a low animal growl in his throat, his fingers curling. The guard's piggy eyes changed as he raised the nervelash threateningly. "Don't make me do it! I hit you with this and it might kill you! It's my ass if you die before they want you to!"

"Get out!" snarled Rader, and the burly guard moved back a step. Then his bravado returned, and he laughed obscenely at the injured hunter.

"You can have her for a while, grubber! She's no good to use that way!" His laugh brought a surge of manic strength to Rader and he lunged toward the guard, his hands reaching out. The guard moved quickly through the door and slammed it shut as Rader hit it futilely. The man's laugh came through the open slit into Rader's face. "Now it's your turn, big man. Nurse her back quickly. She's the kind of prime cleopatra we love to interrogate."

Rader spit through the slit, and the guard cursed. "Damn you, I'll be glad when they give us the word on you!" His cruel voice shifted and he sneered through the slit. "Get her up and around, dirtgrubber. The second time is the time they'll talk. They'll do anything . . . *anything* . . . to keep us from using it again." His lewd laugh was stopped by the slam of the observation slit's tiny door.

Rader turned with great pain and looked at the naked, sprawling girl. Except for the raw red marks at her wrists and ankles, there was hardly a mark on her. His stomach turned, and he staggered. *They brought a shockquizzer with them!*

He half-fell to his knees and looked close at her body, seeing the small burns and bruised flesh at her nipples and crotch, where they had attached the electrodes. The vomit of rage rose within him, but he fought it back, feeling impotent and helpless. He had seen the priests on Horus use the electrodes on the heretics. He and Korda had stared out through the bars in helpless anger as the victims writhed and jerked in sweaty nakedness on the racks, their voices hoarse from screaming, then screaming silently as the electricity tore at their muscles. Hearts failed, minds broke, people became vegetables, bodies wrecked by the spasms, genitals forever intimidated—all in the name of some god. Rader remembered one girl—young, pretty, olive skin gleaming—screaming herself into death as the greedy-eyed priests watched her naked, humiliating end.

Rader found his fists curled into hard hammers, bruised by the rock-melt floor, and he forced quiet upon himself. Slowly, painfully, he moved her from floor to ledge pallet. She jerked when he touched her and made a fearful moan.

They'll die screaming, gobbets of flesh still alive, their blood turned to acid. Rader swore a silent and terrible oath of revenge.

He crept to the bucket of water and tore a piece from his tunic to make a washcloth and sponged her face and body. Every movement was precarious, and the daggers still plunged into his head. He whispered soothing words into her ear and wished with all his heart he could do more.

The hours passed. A greasy bowl of dubious stew was served them through the rusty feeder lock. Rader held up Alena's head and forced a few drops into her mouth. She stirred and did not cringe when he touched her, but she did not awaken.

Please let her mind come back, Rader thought. *Don't let*

*it hide away from the hurt and pain and humiliation. Come
back, Alena.*

Slowly Rader regained some of his strength, and the
greater part of the head pain eased, as long as he did not
move too much or too often. He was regaining some of
the control of his left side. Alena still did not waken, and
he kept the single thin blanket tucked in around her nude
body and watched.

Night came when the last candle stub flickered out.
Shamrock hadn't had much use for a jail before, just a
quartet of sturdy cells for drunks to sleep it off and keep
from hurting anyone. The cell was not overblessed with
conveniences.

In the darkness Rader listened for whatever sounds he
could hear. Once, he thought he heard the fluttering de-
scent of a flyer, and several times the sound of coarse
laughter came to him. Once, someone slid open the observation slit and shined a light in, playing across Alena's
blanketed form and Rader's scowl.

Some time in the darkest part of Rader's personal night,
Alena stirred and he slipped his arms under the blanket
to clasp her to him. He whispered her name fiercely again
and again until at last she spoke.

"Rader?"

"Yes. Don't speak." He let out a long sigh. He could not
remember when such a feeling of gratitude had enveloped
him. *She was whole!*

"Rader . . . I . . . couldn't help it . . . I'm sorry . . ."

"Never mind. I know, I know. Sleep."

"No . . . must talk . . . must tell you . . . they hurt
me . . . I couldn't help screaming—!"

Rader spoke through stiff lips. "I know what they did.
Now, go to sleep. You need sleep. Everything will be all
right."

"Rader . . . they tore off my clothes . . . I was so groggy from the whip . . . I couldn't . . . they laughed . . .
they're Lockhart's men . . . deputies . . ."

"We'll take care of them. They have no right to be
here. Now go to sleep, Alena, rest . . ."

"No, must tell." Her lips were dry, and she licked her
tongue across them, her blue eyes staring at Rader. "They

hurt me . . . that machine . . . I couldn't help myself. They touched me, Rader. Everywhere. I feel so . . . dirty. I was helpless. Spread out. Tied. They've done . . . that . . . to women before. They . . . told stories."

"Never mind, Alena . . ."

"They told me how I'd beg, how others had begged to be allowed to . . . to do terrible things. I spit on them. They gagged me and then . . . later . . . they took it off because they liked to hear me scream. Oh, Rader!"

"You couldn't help it." His hands stroked her hair, and he felt her tremble. In his mind the guard was being fried with the edge of a laser beam. "No one can help it. Your body betrays you." He took her in his arms, holding her tight, feeling so sadly frustrated that his mouth tasted metallic.

She whispered on, as if compelled to rid herself of the words. "I think they were under orders from . . . Lockhart . . . not to . . . take me. They wanted to break me, to make me grovel . . . they said so. Maybe that's what . . . Lockhart wanted. Break us all, one way or another. Once . . . once they thought I was still unconscious, and they were talking. One of them . . . was . . . touching me. I could barely keep from shivering at his touch . . . but they were talking. They haven't found Korda or Liana. That boy, Wolf—he tried, but they beat him up. There was trouble with Gastoni. He shot one of the deputies. They've declared martial law."

"Just what they wanted," grated Rader. "Now they can declare anyone they want to be an outlaw."

"They . . . oh, darling! They want to send you to that hell-hole planet, Tura! You and the others they've caught. A work gang. They know you'll die there, but then it won't be their fault." His entire body shivered, and Rader wrapped himself around her, sliding onto the ledge and gathering her tightly in his arms. She had a spasm, jerking in his arms and gasping.

"Oh, Rader, I couldn't help it! The first pain—it was like an orgasm and they . . . they laughed at me as I . . . oh, god." Rader made soothing sounds and stroked her hair, and images of the deputies with their genitals ripped out by metal pinchers flickered through his head. She was sweating again, but he didn't want to release her to get the wet cloth.

"I couldn't help it. I was helpless! It was like . . . like my body wasn't my body. It just responded and . . . they knew! The orgasm seemed to go on forever—for hours! I couldn't stop it!"

Rader made quiet murmurs into her ear while his heart raged against the cage of his helplessness. "Then it got worse. I didn't know pain could . . . I cried. I screamed. Oh, god, I feel so filthy!" She turned her face into Rader's throat "Rader . . . will I . . . will I ever be able to please you again? After what they've . . . I'm afraid, Rader . . . maybe I won't be able to . . . feel anything again."

Rader patted her gently. "Go to sleep, Alena. You need rest. Don't worry. We have friends. You'll be all right. Go to sleep, now."

She pressed herself against him, and after a time he thought she was asleep. His mind was a black swirl of hate and anger, and his thoughts were of escape and revenge and death.

Then she spoke with a whisper. "Rader?"

"Yes, I'm here."

"I love you."

He seemed to swell, like a blossoming explosion of light, a roaring, soundless nova. He knew she *was* the woman. *The* woman. The pain was nothing, the fear and helplessness nothing, only bugs scampering in the mind. *She loved him!*

His lips moved, but no words came. He had never said it. Not ever. Not once. Not even when it would have been easy and pleasure-giving. The words were simple and basic and beautiful.

"And I love you."

Rader held her and the nova within him softened to a warm glow, a solid, steady fusion of the mind and heart.

I have found the other half of me, he thought.

"I commit to you," he said in a whisper, but she was asleep. It did not matter. He had said it, and he would say it again.

Rader's jaws clenched, and he held her protectively. *God help Startrade,* he thought grimly, *because I won't.*

In the place of those-who-learn, nine young females and six young males sat before Ka-morro-ma, who was old and had been old in the time of the parents of the young. Like their teacher, they sat in the position of the flower, rising and falling with every slow breath.

Let us consider the unfulfilled spirits of those who are not with us. Ka-morro-ma's thoughts were in their minds. He began with a centering, focusing chant, both with his mind and in his thin voice, and the learners followed.

They had much to learn, and the tests of the enemy were difficult and deadly.

In the morning the guards came. There were two of them, and they held the nervelashes menacingly as they gestured from the cell door for Alena. She cowered back against the wall, mouth open, halfway to madness. Her eyes flickered from the contemptuous smiles to Rader and back.

Rader rose slowly, carefully, looking for openings and weaknesses, his injured body testing itself. They watched him, and one laughed. He flipped out the nervelash carelessly, and Rader just barely dodged it. The man laughed again, but his eyes kept jerking away from Rader to look at Alena, whose body was only partially covered by the thin blanket she clutched to her breast.

One guard backed Rader against the wall by threatening Alena. The other suddenly grabbed for her, ripping away the filthy blanket and flinging it into a corner. His coarse face tightened as he looked her over.

"Hey, she's better stuff than you crudders said! She's real fine, even for a cleo!"

Rader growled and took a step forward, but the guard extended the nervewhip toward Alena's bare flesh. "No," she whimpered, "please . . ."

"Come on, beauty, be nice to us and there won't be any more buzz-buzz."

"Hey, take it easy, Sayles," the guard watching Rader said. "You know what Gossett said about her. Later, you know . . ."

"Oh, for Hydra's sake, will you shut your port? He said we couldn't actually, you know, do it. But he didn't say we couldn't have a little fun with her, did he? There are a lot of things a girl can do for a man—if she's willing. Look at the Virgins of the Venus Temple. You just keep an eye on the hero there." He grinned down at Alena, who had sunk to her knees. "Come on, beauty, or the bad men will hang you up again."

Alena whimpered again, hunching her shoulders. Rader tensed, forcing the disciplines on himself. *Be ready.*

Alena clutched at the guard's boots, then at his trousers. "Please . . . please," she said. "Not that again. I couldn't stand it."

The guard watching Rader grinned over his shoulder at Sayles. "Hey, what did I tell you? Give a night to think about it . . ."

Alena came up on her knees, nude, looking up at him with a fearful expression. She clung to the man, pressing her big round breasts against his legs. Sayles and the other guard exchanged looks of smug lechery.

"I'll be good," she said shakily. She got onto one knee, and her hands fumbled at his belt. "Let me show you. I'll make you feel something special." She was looking up at him, and when he looked again at the other guard, his thick lips curling in lewd anticipation, she drove herself upward, her thigh muscles powering her rise. The top of her head struck him under the chin, and his head snapped back with a loud crunching snap. Then she threw herself back, holding his belt, her feet arching him over, throwing him headlong into the rock-melt wall. He fell and did not move.

Rader had been moving from the moment of Alena's contact with Sayles's jaw. He threw himself in a body block, getting under the beginning of the nervelash whipstroke and hitting the remaining guard in the midsection. Rader dropped to the floor, the shock to his injured head making the cell fade and eddy in waves of pain.

His head cleared before the guard got back his breath.

Rader seized the butt of the nervelash and crashed it into the guard's temple. Then he whirled to see Sayles slump to the floor, his head a bloodied pulp. The turning gave him vertigo and he fell, catching himself with one hand and cursing his weakness. He struggled erect as Alena came to him.

Her face was white and she laughed nervously. Her body trembled, and her eyes were large and wet. "Is he dead?" she asked in a hoarse whisper, looking away from the body.

"Yes." He broke away from Alena, who swayed. He bent over the figure of the guard he had hit and began pulling off his clothes.

"I . . . I've never killed a man before," she said shakily. "I don't think I like it."

"No one but zongos likes it. Remember what they had in store for you—then get into these." He tossed her the tunic and struggled to get the man's trousers off. He looked up at Alena and saw that the gray tunic covered her almost to the bottom of her buttocks and he let the limp leg drop.

Neither guard had a gun on him, so Rader picked up a nervelash and stepped to the cell door, looking out warily, leaning against the side of the opening.

"Are you all right?" Alena asked with concern.

"No, but I'll manage." He turned back into the room and picked up the second nervelash, held it butt up and twisted the setting. Then he motioned Alena out of the cell. As she left, he leaned over the unconscious guard and jammed the whip into his slack mouth. At once, the entire body went rigid.

Rader felt no regret as he went out the cell door and toward the heavy door at the end of the short, dim corridor. By the time anyone found the guard, his mind would be burned out—or he'd be dead. That he was brutally cruel in his action did not concern Rader. He had sworn an oath of revenge.

Rader looked through the open viewslit and saw the guardroom beyond. Two burly men Rader did not recognize and a sullen free-lance miner named Morton were sitting around a battered table, drinking *pungi* beer. One of the girls from Alena's was curled up in the corner with bruises on her shoulders and face.

Rader pulled Alena back down the corridor and whispered in her ear. "They didn't hear anything, but they'll expect those bastards to come through there with you any minute now. Now listen. Take off that tunic. I know I'm asking a lot, but it's the only thing I can come up with."

Alena dropped the tunic to the floor. She was still white, but there was determination on her face. "Whatever you say."

"I'll open the door, then you go through fast, yelling like hell, scared to death. Hit them at the table, knock them around as much as you can without looking suspicious, then get over to where Mara is."

"Mara?" Alena's head jerked toward the guardroom.

"Never mind. This will help her, too. The table is straight ahead, and Mara is in the corner to the right. They'll be watching you, so . . . so show off that pretty flesh. I'll go for the gun-rack on the left."

Alena shivered and crossed her arms over her naked breasts as Rader pulled on the uniform tunic over his own blood-stained clothes. "All right . . . I'm ready," she said in a small voice.

Rader took her arms and looked into her eyes. "You were just fine in the cell. You'll be fine this time, too. I'm sorry we've had to use you like this, but we need an edge, a diversion."

She nodded. "I understand."

Rader said, Don't think about it. Just *do it!*" He turned her toward the door, and they moved quietly. Alena still hugged herself as Rader checked the guardroom through the viewslit. Then he jerked his head at her, and she put down her arms stiffly and inhaled deeply, thrusting out her bosom. Rader gave her a fast, hard grin and put his hand on the door, the nervelash coiled in his other hand.

He slammed open the door and shouted, "Get in there!" in a loud, rough voice. Alena staggered in, long blonde hair streaming, arms out, breasts bobbing. Heads turned, but she was already falling across two of the men. She was wide-eyed with fear but made no attempt to cover up her nakedness as she struggled out of the clutches of the laughing men. She pushed herself away and fell to the floor by Mara, covering the cowering girl with her body, emitting little cries of terror.

The men rose, grunting, and started for her, crude phrases of animal-like endearment on their lips.

"Freeze."

They stopped. The tone in the voice was enough. Very slowly they turned their heads and saw Rader with a laser in his shaky fist. One of them twitched as he suppressed a move toward his own weapon. Rader smiled thinly, and all three of the men knew they were looking at their own death if they attempted anything.

"Drop 'em . . ." Gingerly they lifted out their lasers and lowered them to the ground with extreme gentleness. At a gesture from Rader they edged toward the rough rock-melt wall, then halted on command and faced the stone.

"Get her up," Rader said to Alena. To the guards he said, "Anyone else in here?"

The guards exchanged quick looks, then one said, "Cell Four. The magkey is over there." Rader did not take his eyes from his prisoners as he told Alena to go open up the cell. "Put that on," he said, pointing at a coat hanging over a chairback. Alena picked it up as she went out.

"Mara," Rader said. The girl brought up her head, her eyes blurred and unfocused. Rader's grip on the gun tightened. He saw the faint bruises on her wrists and ankles.

Russ Holtan came through the door, his face battered and a bloody bandage on his side. He winced as he smiled at Rader, then he picked a laser from the rack.

"Thanks," he said. "They were planning to ship us to Tura right after the trial."

"But you're the Guild starbuck here," Rader said. "Surely the law wouldn't—"

"Don't fool yourself. They're taking no chances and wasting no time. Tura's a treasure house for Startrader. I'm only beginning to realize how big. Survivors write history, remember? You saw the so-called law here. There's no help coming—we have to do it ourselves."

Rader nodded in reluctant agreement. "Mara . . . we'll have to take her, too. She needs attention. We can hide her out with—" He stopped and looked at the three guards. "Morton," he said softly, "won't they be worrying about you over at Gorchakov Two?"

"Aw, Rader, I quit there last week . . ."

"And hired out, huh?"

"Jesus, man, I was flat. I'm not in any guild, y'know. No free handouts to Morton. But listen, I had nothing to do with what they did to the woman, honest! I wasn't here, I was just—"

The nervelash struck out and laid a ribbon of fire across the backs and nervous systems of all three men. They yelled and arched their backs. Rader hit them again, twice, as fast as his arm could swing, a vision of Alena, tied down and naked, searing his mind.

"Rader!" Holtan gasped, clutching at his arm. "You'll kill them!" Rader thrust him aside, his brain on fire, and the whip struck again. The men screamed. Two of them caught it across the neck and passed out, their screams dying in their throats.

Alena grabbed at Rader, shouting into his face. "Stop! Please stop! Rader! *Stop!*" The tall hunter stared wildly at her for a long moment, his face twitching and his hands trembling with a terrible anger. Abruptly he threw aside the nervelash as the third man slipped into unconsciousness and fell. Rader glared around him, then pointed at Mara. "Pick her up! Let's go!"

Rader stepped to the rack and pulled down his own gun and holster and put the belt around his hips as they went out. He checked the laser as they hurried down the narrow street between the domes, with the extra gun in his armpit.

The two men and two women stole through the night to Levesque's quarters. Without a word he slipped out into the night with them and guided them next door to the Guild dome. He took them quickly down in a secret cellar, where they put the dazed Mara on a bunk.

"She'll be safe here," Levesque said. "Only a few council members know of this bolt-hole." He looked at Rader critically. "You are better, but you're in terrible shape. You better hole up here, too. You won't be doing much fighting, not for a while, unless you want to kill yourself."

Rader ignored him. To them all he growled, "I'll not hole up here like a hurt *tangri*. I'm goint to cut those bastards up!"

"One good hit, one good fall, Rader, and you've had it," Levesque said. "Do you want to spend the rest of your life as a vegetable, with people feeding you, cleaning up your bed?" This stopped Rader, and he glared at Levesque for a long moment.

"All right, but not here. I'm going home. I'll get well and come back."

"Better know what else has been happening," Holtan said grimly. "The *Aldrich* lifted yesterday, but they left a big Patrol communicator that can cut through the sunspot noise. That means they have communications, and we don't. And they have a lot of 'deputies' guarding it." He sank down into a chair and breathed deeply but in pain, holding his injured side. "They've got us sealed up, split up. I even heard some talk about sealing the system, quarantining it, forbidding any ship to land . . .'

"By the time they get through there won't be any evidence against them. If they haven't gotten rid of *these* wart-makers, they'll have sent them on, keeping them two or three jumps ahead of any honest law that might come this way. And when the Guild starts to wonder why they haven't heard from us, they'll have a documented story all put together—a bunch of zongo hunters and grubbers, out of their pods on Eroticene and *pungi* juice, who took on the Patrol and lost. Who will say different?" He sat down heavily on a crate and glowered at the floor.

"I'll stay here and nurse him," Levesque said. "I'll be the information center. When she's well, I'll send her out with someone, maybe Xavier or Zaiman, or someone."

"What condition is the town?" Rader asked. "And what do you know about Nuevo Monterey and Blackbull?"

"The people or the town? The town is all right, except for a few laser slices in Curran's. The warehouses are untouched. Everything's okay there. Almost everyone has ridden out—or walked out. Anyone coming in with their loads after yesterday has been turned back. They haven't touched the Guild domes, yet, but they control everything else."

Levesque wiped his face with his hand. "They brought in at least thirty men on the *Aldrich*. They landed first over at Neuvo and dropped some, then hopped the lander over here and set down the rest. Gossett deputized them all, plus a few renegades like Morton and Hansen. They really stacked the deck."

Rader nodded sadly. "Yeah." He thought a moment, then asked, "What about those Moltari over at Blackbull?"

Levesque shrugged. "Don't know. There's only that bunch at the south end and four or five scattered around. We haven't had much to do with them. Too busy, or . . . y'know, xenophobia." He repeated his shrug. "They're just here to suck pods and be anthropologists, or whatever it is they do. Study the Zikkalans . . ." His voice, weary and bitter, trailed off. "And I heard they aren't due for pickup for ten, maybe twelve local-years. They're suppose to live about five hundred standard, so I guess fifteen or twenty years on some research station isn't much to them."

"Didn't someone tell me there was some kind of cyborg over at Nuevo?" Rader asked.

Holtan nodded. "Yup. But she went out on the last ship last summer. Something to do with nutrient flow or hormone regulation or something. No, Rader," he sighed, "there's just us. Those Moltari aren't fighters . . . at least this bunch aren't, as far as we can tell."

"They're a pretty advanced race though," Rader countered. "One of the first to sign up with the old Federation. Fought the Skrills right along side us. They gotta have some kind of power. You don't fight the Skrills and the Moks and stay off the extinct list without some kind of . . . of something . . ."

Holtan shrugged. Rader sighed, his eyes looking at Alena fussing with Mara, then swinging to Levesque. "You're right, you unlicensed gut-cutter. I better hole up." He looked at Holtan. "I'll head west, toward Destiny Mesa, then north to the cave. Why don't you cross the Marble and go over into Shoka Valley? I bet Gastoni is holed up there. Only don't look around his dome. He'll have a hidey-hole someplace. Go around April Mountain and up the Marble to Neuvo. Tell everyone. Dammit, this is one time I think having some communicators would help!"

Holtan nodded. "Thinking the same thing myself. Well, you watch out for the Kaleen."

Rader scratched at his unshaven cheek. "I wonder. Look, they have even more to lose than we do. Worse comes to worse, maybe we can get a ship in here and get out. But

Startrade is certain to kill off every one of the Zikkalans. One look and you know they'd make a lousy slave race, so Startrade will kill them off. Maybe some kind of bug, sprayed from a flyer or dropped upstream in the water. So why don't we get them on our side?"

Holtan raised his eyebrows. "How? Think they'll see a difference between us and Startrade? Both human, both invaders."

"Maybe . . ." Rader chewed at the inside of his mouth. "Think on it. I've sat by their fires, and they knew I had killed their brothers. They even seemed to have respect, in their way. I'm not the only one who's sat with them. Korda, Greg, McAllister, you. Maybe we can start there."

Alena spoke. "Where are Liana and Korda?"

Holtan made a face. "Korda took off I heard, god only knows where. But Liana is here, and that new kid, Wolf Briggs." He pointed above ground.

"Here?" Rader asked, his eyebrows lifting.

"Sure, why not? Look, not everyone has gone on the warpath. There's a few who think it will blow over or that it's a thing between you and Lockhart and they should keep out."

"But don't they *know?*" Alena asked angrily.

"Yes, some of it, but they don't all believe it yet. When I spread the word that they were sending Rader and me off to Tura, the entire membership of both guilds will start aligning their focusing deflectors and heading in." Holtan made a face. "Startrade is playing it very cool. No use getting anything more stirred up than necessary, is their line. Having *no* survivors would look pretty suspicious . . . not that they wouldn't be willing to brazen it out if they had to. But the way I see it, they're willing to take the chance, just for appearances." He glanced at Rader. "I think they picked on the wrong man. No one in either guild is going to think Rader here went zongo."

Alena smiled weakly at Rader. "See, I was right in picking you, champion."

"It could be a slaughter," Levesque said. "All those hunters and trappers heading in, thinking it's some kind of punch-out, and running up against a Union marshal, a fortified town, and a lot of high-powered weaponry—plus, a flyer with a big Prometheus laser. There's another one at the gate."

There was a long silence, finally broken by Rader. "Tell everyone to get ready, to raise a little hell around their home base if they get the chance, but to sit tight until you give the word. We'll have to work out a plan first."

"They'll slice up every trapper's dome with that big flying Pro," Levesque said. "Just sit up there, out of reach, and carve things into garbage."

"Maybe," Rader said. "It'll keep them busy at least. We can always pop up new domes, we can always build again —but we can't raise the dead."

Holtan rubbed his hand on the butt of his stolen Patrol laser. "Rader, look. I'm a good starbuck for the Guild—and so is Manning, at Dragon, but neither of us is goddamn general."

"Neither am I," Rader said.

"No, but they all respect you, and you were a captain in the Merks. You know that kind of action."

"Hell, Gastoni was a major in the Rangers out of Malenkor," Rader said. "Charlotte Calkins was a sergeant-major in the Imperial Marines in the Barbarossa system. McAllister was a *murra* in the Sunstar Brigade."

"Yes, but they'll all listen to you," Holtan said.

"Don't give me an indispensable man speech. No one is that."

"No, but you have the respect. You also have the best nerve." Holtan grinned. "And the meanest s.o.b. when you get started." He grew serious. "Will you command?"

Rader took a deep breath, exhaling noisily as he looked at Levesque, who nodded. "All right, but I don't like it much. If you get a chance to fire off something to the Guild Council—or *anyone* out there—you better make it official and designate me as Tiger Guild warlord." Holtan nodded.

"Come on," Levesque said, "I'll take you to Liana."

Liana bounced up from the bed with a laser in her hand when the door to her dome-top room opened. She threw it into the pile of papers and equipment littering the bed when she saw Rader, flinging herself on him with a harsh cry. She made a fuss over him as Alena came in, but the blonde

woman went straight to the bed, where half-buried was
Wolf Briggs.

Liana tugged Rader toward the bed as Alena gave him a
quick examination. He groaned as she probed his bruises,
but Liana said, "He's stiff and sore, but not terminal." Alena
looked at the battered youth with empathic sadness, and he
smiled back weakly at her.

"What's this all about?" Rader asked, gesturing at the
mess.

"It . . . was a plan to bust you out of jail. I was going to
have some of the girls protest Alena's arrest out front—as
a cover for me while I cut into the jail from the back. Oh,
don't laugh. It was a great plan, even if those goddamn
walls would take me an hour to slice through with this
damned little laser!"

Rader hugged her tight, then indicated the clothes Alena
had on. "Get her dresed in something for the trail, and let's
get out of here. Do you know where Korda is?"

"No. He told me to hole up here, and then he just went
pop!" She sighed. "You know him. Gotta do things his way.
He probably went out to get an army together."

Rader pawed through a big plastex trunk, jerking out
various items of clothing and equipment. He tossed Russ
Holtan several items and told him to change and get going.

Wolf Briggs raised himself up, his face puffy and
blotched. "No, you don't," snapped Rader. "You lie down
and take it easy."

"I wanna go," Wolf said, his voice muffled and choked.

"You're in terrible condition," Liana said.

"Look at him," protested Wolf, pointing at Rader.

"Him, oh, he's used to it," Liana said lightly, but when
she turned away, her face was troubled. She gave Rader's
head a critical look, but she knew better than to try to
dissuade him. To Wolf she said, "You get well, and be our
fifth column here in Shamrock."

"They might not bother you, if you don't try anything
more," Rader said. "You're not a guild member, and can
say you are just a tourist."

"But—"

"Shut up," Alena said firmly. "We're asking you to do
something very dangerous, I know. Staying here and being

a spy is maybe too tough a job for a young man like you, but—"

"I can do it," Wolf said, his eyes blinking as he fought back the headache pain. They had beaten him quite badly.

Rader looked at him solemnly. "You can pass, you know. Being the inside man is . . ." He hesitated. "It's a tough job."

"Never mind me. I'll do it." He fell back on the bed, exhausted, his voice weak. "I won't let you down." In a few moments he was asleep, and Rader exchanged looks with the women, and they smiled, faintly.

Twenty minutes later, Rader was leading his horse behind him as they slipped through the dark streets toward the main gate. Following were Alena and Liana, weapons in hand and leading their animals with the other. Ahead of them was the well-lit main gate guarded by armed men and a Prometheus laser. With Russ Holtan going out through the small eastern gate with Levesque's help, Rader thought to provide a little distraction at the main gate.

He signalled the women to wait and handed Liana his reins. Rader's gun was at the ready as he slipped forward, silent as a cat in his soft boots. A tiny, combat cover was over the blinking ready-light, and his body was relaxed by the disciplines that so often served him. His head wound was reduced to a throbbing, dull ache, and he felt every step. The tall hunter pulled down night goggles to peer through them at the guards he could see, then searched the darkness for any that might be hidden.

Four. Plus one at the Prometheus.

They'd never be able to just gallop through with any chance of survival, no matter how swiftly they went. The Pro would sweep across the night plain in a rain of millisecond pulses, and they'd be dead meat.

Take out the Pro. Divert the guards. They were too spread out for even his fast gun to get them all before someone would fire back—*and maybe get Alena or Liana.*

Rader leaned back against the chill rock-melt and thought furiously. *Should we try for the back gate, too? No, too difficult to get the horses through. Only way out is through here. Divert the guards. I could go through Denny's hut and up onto the wall, then creep up on the Pro. But I'd need a diversion.* Radar grinned. *A good guerrilla would make the diversion count, too.*

The flyer.

Where was it? Rader went back along the wall and asked Liana a softly whispered question. "By the Dragon supply dome" was her answer.

Rader thought a moment. "Look, I don't have time to think of something fancy. If it worked once, maybe it'll work again." He smiled reassuringly at Alena, who was still white-faced. He started to say something, but she put up a hand. "Whatever you say," she whispered.

They hitched the animals in a triangular space between three domes, and the two women disappeared into the darkness. Rader went around the domes and slipped into Denny's deserted hut and up through the roof hatch.

The hut was built against the exterior wall, and the roof was an extension of the parapet walk. The wall itself was barely visible as a darker mass against the night sky. The nebula of The Sorcerer was overhead, and Tura was a bright spot on the eastern horizon. Lao-tzu and Sargon were bright diamonds in the constellation of The Jeweled Sword. Just edging up from the horizon was the galaxy known as The Wall of Stars. Neither of Zikkala's moons were visible. Jörd, the moon the Zikkalans called Pulamo, was occulted and unseen. But Skidbladnir, the second and smaller moon, would be up soon, and the satellite the Zikkalans called Theka would flood the plain with brilliant moonlight.

Rader took his time, moving slowly across the roof and onto the parapet walk, keeping close to the darkest shadows. He crawled as close as he dared to the Prometheus gunner sitting atop the gate arch, then lay unmoving, studying him.

The big laser was mounted on a tripod at the top of the gate, where there were no walls. It could fire easily in any direction, but its advantage was also a disadvantage because there was little protection. Furthermore, it was pointed out across the plain toward the hills, which meant Rader would have to turn it, taking precious time. The gunner was quiet, but the constant turning of his head indicated his alertness.

Bit by bit the light grew as Rader waited. Skidbladnir was rising. Rader edged slowly, silently into the pale moonlight to look down at the four guards. He could hear them talking quietly. They were alert but not at peak. As he watched, one of them said something and a light suddenly flashed on, flooding the gate area. Rader froze, his eyes sliding to the Pro gunner. The light was from below and the top of the wall was still dark, but Rader was afraid he might present a silhouette, so he carefully slid back into the dark shadows near the parapet and waited.

There was a whoof and a burst of light beyond the nearest domes as Alena and Liana set fire to something near the flyer's landing disc. The guards below came alive, and the Pro gunner wheeled his weapon around. Rader grinned, gathering himself, knife in hand, his gaze going from the gunner to the street and back again.

The two women came running down the street, wide-eyed, their clothing torn, and as they came around Dome One, Liana threw away a burning piece of clothing. *Nice touch,* Rader thought.

Wildly disheveled, and obviously frightened, the two half-nude females ran toward the gate as if for help. Rader had counted on none of Lockhart's fresh new guns having seen either girl, or if they had, it was too dark to make proper identification. He saw a black smear of soot across Alena's face, and realized she had thought the same thing.

"Help us!" Liana cried. "They're all dead!"

"Look out!" Alena sobbed. "It's burning—Lockhart—oh, my god!" She sobbed out something incoherent, falling to the dust in a tumble and rolling toward the shelter of some crates. Liana staggered a few steps further, stumbled to a halt, holding her side as if hurt, and slumped sideways.

The guards were milling in consternation, and two of them moved out toward the women. Rader acted. He ran out onto the gate top, and before the gunner could react, he had one hand around his face, jerking his head up. He jabbed his knife into the side of the man's neck and ripped the blade out. The gunner died with no more than a gurgling squawk. Blood splashed over the Prometheus laser. Rader threw the dead man backward and swiveled the Pro downward, aiming over the edge as he snapped off the safety and the gun blinked its ready-light.

"Don't move!" he said in a voice loud enough for only the guards below to hear. They all turned and looked up, but Rader decided that instinctive move didn't count, as none raised their weapons.

Liana came erect, her laser coming out of the wad of torn and burned clothing around her arm. Alena rolled out, her weapon straight-armed at the guards, her face intent.

One of the guards uttered a short, definitive curse that Rader hadn't heard since Athena. But no one moved. Liana ordered them to toss aside their weapons, then went quickly and efficiently along, gathering them up and not getting between them and the Pro. Alena got to her feet, her gun held with both hands.

"The flyer wasn't there," Alena called up to Rader.

"Too bad. It must be out hunting with infrared. Well, get the horses." She backed into the darkness, then turned and ran. Rader spoke to the guards, quietly. "Put your hands down and get there by the guard-room door. Watch 'em, Liana."

Rader ran back to Denny's roof, then took careful aim with his hand weapon at the dark bulk of the Prometheus. A one-second burst cut through the gun as if it were butter, and it fell in a clatter. The bits were rolling about on the archtop as Rader dropped down and ran out through Denny's door. He saw Alena leading the three mounts up the dark street toward the lighted gate.

Rader ran past Liana and lifted the gate bar. He shoved one side of the heavy gate open, and when it moved an alarm went off. Rader cursed his stupidity for not checking for additional security, then gestured toward Alena to pull the horses through. She mounted as Rader, his gun on the guards, motioned Liana through. He gestured down the street toward the center of Shamrock. He could hear the city coming alive as the alarm rang incessantly. "Run," he said.

Three of the guards started slowly, then were running hard within a few meters. The fourth man backed along the wall, fearfully. "Don't kill us," he said. "Don't kill me, I—"

Rader looked at him in disgust. He turned and gave a two-second burst over the pile of weapons they had captured, then slipped through the gate. He pulled it shut behind him, ignoring Liana's urgings to mount up. He thumbed the laser to a different setting, then fired at the metal edging of the heavy gate. There was a flash and a dull, melting red glow as he fused together the steel lips. The wood caught fire and burned with a thick oily smoke. It would slow down pursuit for only a few moments, but now was when they needed moments.

Rader ran to his mount, took the reins from Alena and vaulted into the saddle. They galloped into the night and were quickly lost in the darkness beyond the gate light. Rader looked back and saw there was a spreading glow reflected on the white hemispheres of several of the central domes.

The tall hunter heard the unusual sound of a flyer's vanes and looked up and back to see a spear of red light strike down from the sky. The animals shied and screamed. The fire-lance struck again, closer, then again, closer still. Rader saw the winking muzzle of a big laser firing at them as the copter overtook them.

Infrared spotters! "Spread out!" he shouted over the pounding of hooves and the rising flutter of the flyer. His own weapon leaped into his hand and he fired, but he had forgotten to reset from the torch position he had used on the gate. The flyer veered from the beam of heat, and a shot from the Prometheus went wild.

Then the ship was coming around in a tight circle, the Pro burning a dotted line of melted glass in the sand, straight toward Rader, who had pulled his frightened mount to a halt.

The gun reset, Rader forced calmness upon himself and took careful aim, holding the laser with both hands. He fired, and the ship quivered, briefly lit up by the fiery beam. The Pro's beam veered away, then sharply back as the gunner corrected, just missing the tail of Rader's mount. Rader tried to sight again on the ship, but it was past him and beyond, angling away at a slant. He twisted in the saddle and fired again, then again, but he was not certain he had scored hits.

Rader drew his reins tightly, calming the horse, and listened. He could hear the women galloping and the diminishing whirr of the copter's blades. Then there was a thump and a sliding, ripping sound. Then silence.

Wounded, but not killed, was his decision. He wheeled his mount and raced into the night toward the fleeing women.

Rader lifted his head wearily, fighting the throbbing pain, and turned in the saddle to scan the land and the sky behind them. Nothing moved under the furnace of the summer sun. No distant dust clouds, no growing specks in the sky, nothing. He turned back, automatically checking the terrain ahead, squinting through reddened eyes and the blurring mist of pain. He felt the blood-dampened bandage on his head and fought the blurriness away.

The women plodded ahead, slumped in their saddles, dusty and bone tired, their mounts walking steadily but slowly, with lowered heads and drooping tails. Rader fought the weakness and the desire for healing sleep, knowing that if Startrade's thugs came now, he would need every bit of energy and as much time as possible.

They had ridden west along well-traveled trails, not north as their pursuers might have expected. When they hit the Marengo River, they would swing right, hopefully beyond the first search patterns if they rode hard enough. Rader thought their improvised escape route would work, providing the blackcoats were rattled enough by the incapacitated flyer. With their new radios, capable of cutting through Loki's intense sunspot interference, they might be able to box them in. The standard, Guild saddle-radios had not even been made operational, and the only radio powerful enough to cut through was the jointly operated planet-to-satellite one, used to contact ships, and that was in enemy hands. *The communications net gives the Union marshals an advantage that might be crucial,* he thought grimly.

Rader shaded his eyes and saw the characteristic humps of a volcanic formation, worn smooth by time, jutting up from the tawny-gold and red of the desert. He called ahead, "Bear left— we'll rest in those rocks." His voice seemed cracked and dry, and the low call made his head throb.

The got off stiffly and stretched. They loosened the cinches and tied the animals near tufts of sugar grass. Rader said, "Keep up the sky-search. We may not have knocked their flyer out for long, and with heatscopes they can find us easily, even in this desert—if they get close."

Alena sat down with her back to a worn red boulder the size of a supply dome and closed her eyes, huddling deep within herself, wrapped in the torn fragments of her clothes.

Rader distributed some of the dried *torga* meat, and Liana found a fistful of half-ripened appleberries, which she shared. They ate in silence, sipping from the canteens, too drained by the desert and the long ride to talk. Rader passed around some stim-tabs he had found in the saddle's medikit and said to keep them for the right time.

He squatted down by Alena as she sipped some water. When she finished, she stared out over the hot plain sightlessly, looking dully over her forearms at the sand and rocks.

"You all right?" he asked. She nodded. "Reaction to all this finally setting in?"

She gave another weak nod, and her gaze slid down. She closed her eyes and rested her forehead on her forearms. "Yes." She took a breath and opened her eyes. A hand dropped, and she began drawing scrawls in the sand by her side, away from Rader. "I've been thinking. I tried not to think, just to let time pass . . . to endure . . . but I couldn't stop."

Rader waited patiently. She ran her tongue over her teeth and closed her eyes again. "It's the killing. You being hurt. The jail. The things they . . . did. Oh, Rader, I didn't know it was going to be like this!"

"Want to give up?"

Alena turned her head toward him, looking at him through red-rimmed, half-closed eyes. "You know better than that. We can't stop now . . . but I didn't know it was going to get you hurt. And Barnes killed, Clem . . . Russ and Wolf hurt . . . even those . . . those guards . . ."

Rader lifted an eyebrow. "You wanted a champion, but you didn't think he'd get hurt? Or hurt anyone else? This isn't a hologram play, Alena. They don't get up when the cameras stop."

Her face was anguished. "I feel . . . so responsible. All those men. Ours, theirs . . . dead . . . hurt."

"You're not responsible, Startrade is. No man is fighting

because of you . . . not even me, really," he said. "I got involved because I had to. Maybe now, I'm fighting harder —because of what they . . . because of things that happened. But you just told me something I didn't know, Alena —that's all."

She started to protest, but he stopped her. "Listen to me. When man went out into the stars, he discovered more planets than he ever thought could exist. We spread out for a thousand years, like yeast boiling over. We filled up prime worlds and ruined them, one after another, just as we did on Terra."

Rader touched her arm. "Not everyone wants to live out on the edge of the map. There are plenty who like their comforts. They like their arcologs filled with a half-million people, their wallscreens, sensatrons, places where it never rains, neat little constructed mountains where they never get dusty or muddy. They live vicariously with sensory recorders and holographic shows. They breath safe, filtered air and live neat, safe lives in domes and arks, with the rain falling only when they're asleep and just onto the farmlands. They pretend to admire the brave pioneer, but secretly they think he's a zongo sucker—and they're very suspicious of anyone who goes out beyond a connection to computer entertainment."

The tall hunter's head wound pounded, and he closed his eyes for a moment, running the practiced disciplines to set aside the pain, making it a thing apart, something observed and not a real part of him.

He opened his eyes and stared at Alena. "But not everyone wants to live like that. Civilization has many advantages. I miss the *chula* dancers, the art galleries, the sensory tapes about places I've never been. But the Guild sends us the book molecules and lots of holo-stories and sensory tapes. I'd miss them if they didn't come, but I would never trade Zikkala for them."

He leaned closer to her. "The dream of every man is to find some place to live in peace . . . but not in boredom. Death by boredom is the unkindest cut of all."

Rader straightened and looked out over the hot red-gold plain and up into the clear deep-blue sky. "I've been many places, but here is where I have chosen. The Elaan Gardens are prettier, the *xarol* islands more flamboyant, and almost anywhere is bigger than Shamrock." He looked down at Alena again. "If it wasn't worth fighting for, I'd ship out and go hunting one that was." He grinned at her. "I always avoid a fight, but I never run from one."

He touched her arm, and she shivered, drawing the rags of her clothing about her, retreating into her own closed world again. Rader sat back with a sigh. "Do you think we are savages here? Killers? Just killing for fun, for adventure, for ego, just killing for the sake of killing? You wouldn't be the first cleanboot that thought so."

Rader took a deep breath and let the air out explosively. He sat quietly for a minute. "I know we are rather primitive here compared to where you've been. I know it looks like a holo of ancient Terran cowboys and redskins, or merks and mudballers, or whatever. With Startraders here it's like the simple landgrubbers against the big powerful land-grabbers." Rader picked up a pebble and threw it out into the desert. "But this is the way it is here. We're out at the edge of so-called human civilization. Even with the null-drive ships, we are a long way out. We have horses instead of ground cars or flyers, lasers instead of pocket television communicators. We kill our own meat, not dial it or choke down compressed and flavored algae."

The big hunter looked at her for a long moment. "Do you know how I feel when I kill a man? I feel terrible. Even when the entity is not even remotely human, I feel terrible." He leaned forward and spoke intently. "And it feels *good*, too, all at the same time, because it means I lived, that I am alive and he, she or it isn't—because he tried to kill me and didn't."

"And the guard on the wall?" she asked softly.

"He would have, if he could. That was his job. Was there any question of that? I feel no regrets. He knew the chances when he hired out. He let his ego think he could handle it against the Tiger and Dragon Guilds." His voice changed. "The things I regret are the things I could have prevented or changed—and didn't. Once, on Erin, in the mercenaries, I thought I was one hell of a starbuck sergeant and I took a shot at a *clorg* cyborg—right past one of my own men. And I missed. I took that boy's left leg off. They grew it back, of course, and he had a two-year vacation with pay and a slug of fancy psychotherapy, but I *hurt* him and I didn't mean to. He may never be the same again. It took something out of him. I've heard re-grows tell me they never really believe that new limb is really theirs. That I regret. Killing one of Startrade's toughs won't keep me awake, but I remember that kid and the look on his face as he lay there, looking at the stub spurting blood."

Alena was silent a long time before she spoke. "I—I love it here, but it has become so—so terrible."

"It will be good again. Maybe this will teach us something. That the price of liberty is eternal vigilance, as the man said. We all thought we were 'safe' out here on the far edge of nothing, that the rest of mankind was too busy breeding and trading and fighting to give us much bother. We thought they were building toward Andromeda and out from Centauri Central, away from the Skrill empire. We were wrong. The spoilers have come." Rader spat into the sand.

"We thought only a few trader ships would come all the way out here because we were in a backwater, because there isn't an earth-type planet within three star systems of here, that we could live out our lives and not be plugged into the great human galactic civilization any more than we wanted."

Rader put a hand to his head for a moment, feeling the pulse of blood. "But this is out home and those greedy bastards have busted down the door and gotten their feet on the carpet. If we lose, Zikkala loses—and the Zikkalans, too. So forget your guilts, forget the pain, forget it all, save it for the day after victory. Now get on your mount and let's ride."

Rader stood, fighting the wave of dizziness. Alena looked up at him strangely from within her wadded nest of rags. "You enjoy it, don't you? The fighting, the running, the chance at bravery, the need for courage, the odds?"

Rader brought a grin to his dusty face. "Yup, I suppose I do. That's always a hard thing for a woman to understand. Maybe it goes all the way back to the cave. I know I feel more at home in our cave, before a real fire, than in *any* palace I've been billeted in. Maybe because it's *our* cave. We discovered it, fixed it up. In a way, it's the first real home Korda, Liana and I have ever had."

The tanned hunter took a moment to scan the desert.

"Yeah, maybe it's in our chromosomes to be like we are. All of us who really live here on Zikkala. The ones that aren't just tourists. We recognize it in each other. The will to survive, to be more than just survivors, but *free* survivors, doing what we want."

Rader made a little laugh. "Maybe it's all ego—the fighting, the winning. But living on the edge of death is—*living*. Back in civilization you still see it. Not every survivor lifts ship for the far planets. They climb mountains, scale arcologs, race flyers, take the subs down, train *tigras*. No one makes them do it. They *want* to do it, because doing it makes living sweeter."

He shrugged. "Some have different ideas of living on the edge. They try drugs or high finance or having two mates. That instinct breaks out even if you try to keep it down. It breaks out little, or it breaks out big."

Rader smiled and extended his hand to her. "Speaking for myself, I don't like to be pushed. You can talk me into anything, but you have one hell of a time *making* me do anything."

Alena took his hand, and he raised her up. "You're right," she said. "I don't think I do understand. Maybe I grew up on too many worlds where everyone *had* to learn to live together, to keep the rough edges hidden, to take the little annoyances, to avoid the involvement and confrontations."

"Social oil," he said. "Every time one of us hits a planet where they ask you to check your weapons at the spaceport, we want to turn right around and lift off."

As they walked to their mounts, Rader added, "People always think everything can be settled by talking it out. And often it can be, if people are willing to try and understand each other. But when the irresistible force meets the immovable object, the fighting starts. The zongo who said war solved nothing was no student of history. Entire races have been obliterated, whole philosophies gone, worlds blasted, cultures diverted into entirely different lines of development. Maybe the result isn't the best or the nicest or the most logical or anything but simply the *result,* but it does solve things. Now mount up. I want to be at the Rhega Rocks by nightfall."

She climbed into her saddle, and Liana joined them.

Alena looked down at Rader as he gathered in his reins. "There's a side of you I'm not certain I like. It—makes me uncomfortable. I've never known a man quite like you."

"Be uncomfortable as you ride. Liana, take the point."

The sun moved down the sky, and their shadows lengthened behind them, bringing the landscape into sculptured relief. A few kilometers to the northeast Rader saw a brief flurry of dust, but it did not persist. The land grew less barren as they dropped down the gentle fluvial plain from the Shamrock highlands to the Marengo River in the west.

They rode until just before dusk, making camp within a semicircular cluster of age-old volcanic bubbles, hollow and exposed to the weather by millions of years of erosion. The redstone cliffs rose above them, erupting from the sandy plains in great frozen bubblings of stone.

Liana insisted Rader rest while she gathered dried firewood from the scrub *pungi* thickets around the caves. Rader had to agree. If he passed out, he would become much more of a burden on them than he was.

He watched the women building a fire as deep inside the bubble complex as possible, right on the site of a number of ancient fires. Liana went out again to gather some greens she had noticed.

Rader leaned back against a rock and wondered where Korda might be. *Did he head straight home? Probably not. He was certain to come back when he thought I'd be well enough to travel. But how to contact him? Was he alerting trappers? Almost certainly,* Rader thought. He cursed the sunspots that effectively isolated them from each other. Communications was a necessity in a war. Their lack of communications might prove fatal, he thought gloomily. *I'll just have to try and read the minds of my friends.* Not telepathy but long familiarity with them and with their type. But it was far too late for regrets. The next important decision was agreement on tactics and strategy. But even after that was made, how would he communicate with the outlawed hunters?

The fire before him grew, and the flames illuminated bands of carvings and paintings across the top and sides of the ancient bubble. Quite realistic and recognizable *shokas* and larger-than-life *tamirs* battled puny Kaleen natives. Several figures were lying under talons in twisted positions of pain and death, yet the Kaleen warriors stood fast before the charge of a massive king *shoka*.

From some of the dead pale blurred shapes were rising —the spirits of the dead. On the ceiling there were other, more defined, blobs of pale color. They seemed to float over the scenes below, dancing among carved stars and a sunburst.

"Look," Rader said to Alena, pointing at the paintings. "Are the stories painted there much different from those in the grotto at Trois-Frères on Terra, or the Emerald Caves on Coronation? Even the *xerons* have nine-million-year-old versions of the same thing. Primitive intelligence surviving. Man against beast, man against man, man against nature."

"And man against God?" Alena asked.

"Sometimes," Rader shrugged. "But those battles are somewhat less tangible than these." He gestured at the murals. "The man-God battles or explorations or meshings are all things each man must fight alone. They are seldom truly shared experiences."

Alena looked at him across the crackling fire. "Are you trying to justify something?"

Rader grinned weakly and leaned back against the rock, gently feeling the side of his head, amazed that it hadn't ruptured, and spilled his brain with a soggy plop to his shoulder.

"No, not unless explaining counts as justifying. I may be putting it too simply, but survivors are survivors because they survive." He closed his eyes, his chest rising and falling slowly. "There are many reasons men kill. Survival. Food, which is survival. Passion. Hatred. Some code or honor or some religion. Killing so that your god or credo is no longer threatened. Killing because you feel small, to tear down others. Killing for material gain, or power. Killing for warped pleasures. But it's usually fear, which translates into survival in some form."

Rader opened his eyes and looked at Alena. Even in her rags and coating of dust, tense and bewildered, she was beautiful. "The fact is that a number of powerful people are quite unemotionally trying to kill me, kill my friends, and in time, my planet." He waggled a hand. "Kill, neutralize, eliminate, *falan*, remove, pick the polite word. We must adjust to that fact. They are not going to just go away because someone points out they are acting illegally or immorally. If we adjust to that state of mind, to those facts, and *do* something about it, we might just stay alive. If we do not, we will be dead, or as good as dead."

Alena said nothing, and after a moment Rader said, "Patrol corruption is nothing new. But we are a long way from arcolog monitors, from courts and writs and cease-and-desist orders." The throbbing in his head made him seek the darkness of closed eyes once again. "If you think there is an alternative to survival, you are already dead."

Alena licked her lips and sighed. "But why must things be so harsh?"

"Because we have passed the point of polite conversation. That point was reached in some boardroom or at some company starbuck's desk when the order was given to go ahead. 'If you meet with resistance beyond a certain limit, then do thus-and-so.' Lockhart is just the hard point, but greed threw the spear."

Alena took a long deep breath, then let it out slowly. She looked up at the murals, lit by the flickering fire. One cluster of figures showed primitive Zikkalans stalking a graceful *rena,* and a celebration around a fire. "What you are saying is that those who live by the sword stay alive."

"Only if they understand that a sword is not a man's only survival tool. In fact, it's not even the best." He tapped his head, wincing because he had tapped the wrong side. "This tool in here is the best."

Alena nodded morosely, and Rader opened his eyes to grin weakly at her. "Once, on Athena, a friend of mine named Weber said, 'What's the use of surviving if something worse is always going to happen?' What's your answer to that?"

Alena stirred the fire with a stick. "Because we must, I suppose. It's instinctive. If you don't survive, then nothing you believe in survives, unless your death ensures that survival."

"Nothing lasts forever," Rader said. "Everything changes, even the race of man. Only the changes are slow, and no one generation really sees it. Perhaps some day men like me will be extinct. But until then I'm living right up to the last minute of the last hour. If I go hard, I won't go alone."

Alena looked at him a long time, searching his battered

face. "You—frighten me sometimes. You seem so—cold, sometimes, so—calculating—yet—I feel safe with you."

"But," grinned Rader.

"But nothing," Liana said as she entered. She dropped a double handful of a nameless lettucelike plant on a smooth rock. "Let's eat." She took up a flat pan and began dropping in shreds of *torg,* some *chandthrut* eggs she had found on the trail, and a few herbs she had gathered. Her slanted eyes squinted through the smoke at Rader. "You know, *nur tuk,* I love you, but sometimes you do talk on and on. Why don't you eat and make love to her and everything will look different, no?"

"The universal panacea, Liana? Love therapy?" Rader caught Alena's expression, and he stopped, his heart sinking. The miniature lightning bolts ripping into the most delicate, intimate parts of her lovely body had done more to her than he guessed. The suggestion of lovemaking had made her draw in on herself. She sat within her swaddling of rags and was staring blindly into the fire, her mind a thousand parsecs away.

Rader glanced at Liana and the conversation moved on to her preparation of the *chandthrut* omelette and whether she should slice in some wild buttoneye, then comparing this cave to their own, then on to what to expect of the morrow.

"We should be at Greentree Valley by noon tomorrow," Rader said. "We'll bathe and hunt, then we'll go on up the Marengo and along by Destiny Mesa."

"Yeah, you could use a good shot of *ploom,*" Liana said. She scooped portions of the omelette into the metal plates from the saddlebags and settled back to eat. She was chewing on a tough shred of *torg* but held up her end of the conversation that they wordlessly hoped would draw Alena back into life. The blonde woman was silently, mechanically munching the meal and staring into the fire.

"Why do men give places such lurid names?" Liana asked. She intoned a series of names. "Destiny Mesa, the Wizard Islands, Spectrum Valley, Gilgamesh, the Starvault."

"Sometimes because they are descriptive," Rader said. "Or he does it scientifically, with Greek or *xeron* roots, which we usually shorten. This ribopolynucleotide molecules become *messenger* RNA or just RNA. Man names places in honor of, or because of. The early explorers of Terra often named places for the saint's day they found it, or for a king or patron, or for someone whose favor they were courting. Or because a single strong or unusual element attracted notice. Spectrum Valley *looks* that way. The Wizards loomed up out of the coastal fog like hooded priests. Destiny Mesa's name came from the first man who hit there in the spring and found himself downwind from a thousand hectares of blossoming *ploom*." Rader smiled. "Old Schulz just went up and was a long time coming down."

He stopped and put down his empty plate. "Things and places are named by usage or unusual events or whim. The Windsong Caves could be called nothing else. The *Pink Shoka* is whim." He gestured around him, giving Alena a quick glance. "The Zikkalans call this *Rhega-ploor-kar-mala,* which means Stopping Place of the Old Ones, but we shortened it to Rhega Rocks. Everywhere that we've shipped ova there is a Dead Horse Creek and every dangerous chunk of dirt has its Dead Man's Flats or Dead Man's something.

"Sometimes people are names for reasons of sympathetic magic, hopeful that they will take on the characteristics of that object or power or person. Young Briggs, for example. Maybe his parents named him as they did, hopeful that he might prove a musical genius. Primitive tribes often name children after powerful beasts or forces of nature."

"You know the name in all of Zikkala that I like best?" Liana asked. Without waiting she said the word, savoring it with her omelette. "Pungi. *Pungi.* Punnnngi. Pun-gee! I just love it!"

"That's because you like the juice," Rader laughed. "Alena, what's your favorite name on good old Zikkala?"

There was a silence as the dying fire crackled. Alena seemed to pull herself back from somewhere. She raised her head and looked at Rader for a long moment. "Yours," she said.

They looked at each other, firelight flickering in their eyes. Liana scraped the last morsels of food into her mouth and gathered up the metal plates. "I'll just go scrub these with sand," she said. At the curving edge of the nearest wall she looked back briefly to say, "Warm tonight. I think I'll sleep out by the horses."

Neither Rader nor Alena replied. She lay back on her blanket and slowly peeled open her tattered cocoon of rags. The firelight gleamed on her flesh as she held out her arms to Rader.

"Hold me," she said. "Make it all right again."

They plodded through the summer heat, the heads of the animals drooping, and the three figures on their backs bent and weary. Rader forced his head up from time to time to look around at the carved-bare badlands, seeing through a mist of pain. Greentree Valley was just beyond the rough country. Twice he saw dust, to the north and southeast.

Kaleen scouting parties? he wondered. *They use captured horses now. Or Startrade searchers? Korda? Some trappers running a warning trail?*

He kept his hand near his laser and kept the trio moving. There was nothing else he could do. They rode through the badlands that edged the desert, then crested the ridge and looked down into Greentree Valley, a wide delta of lush foliage through which the Marengo River flowed. Rader's head was pounding painfully, and he called a halt once they had gained the shelter of the thick forest of huge cathedral trees. He was afraid of passing out, falling, and becoming even more of a burden. He was ashamed of his wound and weakness, though he knew he was being illogical.

They made camp under a fifty-meter high cathedral tree. The wind sighed through the leaves; the white acolyte birds were going through their mating flights; and high up, the warmer air was making the leaves change color. The cathedral trees were related to the small rainbow trees, though not as colorful, and their leaves changed color through the greens and blues in temperature differences.

The tree was old, and the center trunk long ago rotted away, leaving only a scrubby mound in the center of the network of interlacing branches and vines that had re-attached themselves to the soil. The result was a churchlike interior, with colorful blossoms serving as stained glass windows, and the bright leaves and flowers of parasitic plants adding to the intricate, moving designs. All around them was the majestic forest, but only the tops of the trees received the sun and there, backlit by Loki, were nature's abstract paintings of flower petals.

Rader lay on a blanket over a bed of blue moss and listened to the sounds, each blending with the other in nature's arboreal concert. The valley was a beautiful one —and even more startling to find after the long, dusty desert journey.

This planet is beautiful, Rader thought. *But is it really beautiful enough to die for? Is anything that beautiful?* He looked at Alena, bent over a small fire, cooking some wild butterbuds and chopped nuts from the tree. *Was she?*

Alena turned her head to check on him, concern in her eyes, and it was a moment before they both realized they were staring at each other. She smiled, her long blonde hair falling forward. She brushed it back, her smile becoming shy until it forced her to laugh. They had looked at each other and smiled and laughed, and Rader felt good. Her shock at the bloody killing seemed gone—or at least under control.

Yes, maybe there is something beautiful enough to die for. Rader laughed to himself. *But the last thing a man should do, is die. The very last thing.* His brief doubts about the pain, destruction and death that was being caused left him. *Let them decide if their greed is enough to die for.*

The afternoon became evening, and Alena sat next to him, insisting upon feeding him bits of butterbud and slivers of redroot and juicy sections of the fruit Liana had harvested by climbing high up into the cathedral tree's interlocking maze of limbs.

Liana was now stalking the surrounding forest like a lithe phantom, her laser ready, and her ears open to the night. Far away they heard a *kurri* give a hunting howl and closer, the trill of a dancerbird. Alena lay down on the blanket and slowly peeled open her tattered cocoon of rags.

The firelight gleamed on her flesh as she held out her arms to Rader.

"Hold me," she said. "Make it all right again."

As they buried the dead, physically and spiritually, Shir-ka-kaloon appeared, a fiery ball of cold light floating over their heads.

Those who survive the testing will be among our greatest, were the words heard in their minds. *You must draw upon the resources of the nest and vanquish all before you. You must succeed on this level of experience before you can rise.*

The Zikkalans continued to cement the mortal remains into the crypts of living rock. Then they prayed, but not for the dead.

Next morning, Rader and the two women rode north along the river, through mottled glens of light between the groves of great trees. They startled *rena* feeding, and once they saw a family of bluefox with their tiny, fluffy babies. They crossed the wide Marengo at midday, then went along through the yellowtail and the shrine bushes growing in the meadows as the big trees thinned out. Then they saw the distant hump of Destiny Mesa just before sunset.

They camped back from the river in a cluster of rocks that could be easily defended and made a fireless camp. "There's a lot of activity around Destiny this time of year," Liana told Alena. "The Zikkalans come from everywhere to be there when the *ploom* blossoms."

"Then why are *we* going near there?" Alena asked.

"It's sacred ground. If they don't get us before, they won't touch us up on top?"

"But coming down?"

"We'll worry about that later," Liana said. "Without a medikit, the *ploom* is the best thing for Rader. Hell, I think it'll be even better than a starship robohealer."

"I thought *ploom* was some kind of psychedelic pollen?

"It's more than that—it's a balm. It's a high, all right, but it's more. It's a healer in the quantities we'll be getting."

"The wind is blowing the other way right now," Rader said, "or you'd be feeling so good you couldn't stand it." He grinned at her. "Wait until tomorrow."

"Why don't we just bypass it?" Alena asked. "You're looking better, and if there are that many Kaleen coming there . . ."

"Not just Kaleen," Liana said. "Every tribe sends parties, to make sacrifices and gather pollen."

"And to bypass it would take us out of our way," Rader said sleepily. "We're going a long way, and we might have to fight a lot. I may seem like one of those indestructible frontiersmen of space to *you,* but I feel as though my head's about to fall off and embarrass me a lot.

Alena came over to him and lay in his arms. Liana took a blanket and snuggled up on the opposite side, turning her back to them and putting her laser right where she could grab it.

Alena kissed Rader's cheek and wiggled in close. The delicate aroma of the bluemoss was in their senses as they drifted off to sleep. Liana stirred only once, when a *kurri* snatched a dancerbird in midflight.

The sky was lightening in the east by the time they were approaching the foot of the narrow trail up the mesa's steep side. Once they were on top they were safe, but until then Rader went first, his laser out and ready, with Liana watching the backtrail.

He was feeling good, and already the day was dawning beautifully, with the cool grays and blues rising slowly through the spectrum toward the rose-reds and golden tans of the midday rocks. Far below, the thick green-blue band of forest lining the Marengo was quivering with changing colors as the air warmed.

Rader smiled. The Kaleen would never stop him. He swung his weapon toward every rock and cleft as he looked, a fiercely joyous feeling growing in him. The headache was gone by the time they topped out on the mesa. To the east the golden rays of Loki were breaking through the remains of the clouds that had passed over in the night.

"It's beautiful!" Alena exclaimed, the morning breeze lifting her hair and streaming it behind her. She jumped down from her animal and started to run; Liana followed, bright-eyed and smiling. Rader gave the steep trail one last swift search with his dark eyes before he, too, dismounted, tied up the horses and raced after Alena and Liana.

The *ploom* thickened and grew taller toward the center of the vast purple field that covered the thousand-hectare top of the flat mesa. Seven million square-meters of psychedelic plants waving in the sun. Their blossoms wafting the nearly invisible pollen into the wind until it became like dust, a purple cloud blowing westward in roiling dark columns.

Liana began to tear off her clothes, dropping them behind her in careless abandon until she was nude. She even discarded her weapons belt. Long black hair flying behind her, as she raced into the tall purple plants, plowing through the outer fringes of the tall purple plants, laughing joyously, her skin quickly mottled with lavender pollen.

Alena stopped, and Rader caught up to her—then they laughed and ran together. She stopped and, with frantic eagerness, stripped away her tattered rags, flinging them into the plants gaily, smiling up at Rader while he, too, undressed.

The last thing Rader discarded was his laser. He put it down carefully. *This is sacred ground,* he reminded himself. But he memorized where it was, just off the trail that lead toward the heart of the purple field.

Naked and together, Rader and Alena ran down the narrow path, between the progressively taller *ploom* plants. The trail curved, and suddenly they were running toward a small pool fed by a spring. The surrounding plants were three meters high, the ground blackish purple with pollen. Dancerbirds zoomed and banked through the sprays of pollen carried up by the breezes. The surface of the pool was blotched with floating islands of pollen. Liana was already in the water, sleek as an otter, her hair like a blackwing's feathers, flowing behind her as she rolled in the dark waters, golden brown and glistening.

"*Aiiiya!*" she cried as they came through the swaying

purple blossoms. She jackknifed through the surface of the water, breaking up the purple islands, kicking her way down. Alena and Rader dived into the water from a shaped rectangle of rock that jutted into the pool.

The coolness embraced them, stroked their naked flesh. It was murky beneath the surface, the water saturated with the fallen pollen. Alena and Rader surfaced together, and she threw herself into his arms, half-drowning them both, kissing him hard, spitting out a thin paste of pollen, then kissing him again, pressing her body against his in bold demand, locking her legs around him.

Liana came sputtering to the surface, spraying water in every direction. "Look!" she said. She held up an intricately fashioned headdress, made of beaten gold and uncut polished jewels, with trailing chains of finely woven seathorns and pi-pearls. The netlike headdress had a polished red-stone at each golden crossing, and in the center of each stone was a tiny starburst of light.

"It's incredible!" Alena said, reaching impulsively for it. Liana surrendered it with a smile and dove underwater again. Alena swam to the edge and walked up until the water came only to her knees. She stopped and untangled a string of the pi-pearls before putting the headdress on. She then turned to the only mirror around: Rader's eyes.

She laughed brightly, spreading the streamers of pearls, and asked, "Where did it come from? Who left it here?"

"It's a Kaleen headdress. The whole bottom of the pool is covered with things like that."

"It's gorgeous! It would be a star attraction in any museum in the galaxy!"

Rader nodded. "But it will never see a museum. This place is sacred to the Zikkalans, and none of us are going to take any of it away." His face darkened for a moment. "At least no guild member would. But if some of those Startrade muckers find this . . ."

He took a deep breath, and the frown left his face. "That piece took some Kaleen artist several years to make, then the tribal queen wore it here. She threw it in along with all the other jewelry and objects they wanted to sacrifice. Then she made love with the king, right there on the stone pier, and any child born of that particular union is destined a chieftain with certain advantages and responsibilities."

Alena fingered the delicate trailing ribbons of pearls and curling seathorns and asked softly, "Would they mind if I wore it awhile?"

"No." Rader smiled, then ducked as Liana splashed to the surface again, with another headdress plus a gathering of muddy bands and necklaces in her arms. Her white teeth flashing, Liana waded ashore and washed the treasure off in the pollen-saturated water. She dumped the discovery on the flat, worn stones of the pier, and there was a sudden flurry of choices and decisions that left Rader ignored. He floated lazily in the water, paddling only to keep them in view as they dressed, and watching the intricate weavings of the dancerbirds as they gorged themselves on pollen.

"There!" Liana said, and they both turned toward him, pagan goddesses from the dawn of imagination, golden and jeweled. Each had quickly and cleverly adapted the alien artifacts to heighten her own beauty, and each turned expectantly to the mirror of Rader's eyes.

"We are the sacrificial virgins," Alena said proudly.

"Yes, you high priest fella you!" Liana called. "Come and get us!"

Rader flipped over and swam to the edge of the pool. As he came striding up out of the scented, lavender water, they laughed with delight at his erect manhood, then swiveled and ran into the forest of *ploom*. Dripping, Rader plunged in after them.

The purple, velvety leaves brushed against their wet naked bodies until they were painted bizarrely with the pollen. The women cried out and broke apart as Rader closed in, and he ran after Alena. She curved back toward the pool, sweeping the tall plants aside, causing showers of lavender dust to fall behind her. Rader cut across the curves and shortened the distance.

Alena broke from the thick brush and threw herself into the still rippling pool, and Rader plunged in after her, catching her in the water. They laughed and wrestled, but she had no intention of stopping him. He pulled her out onto the mossy bank . . . and they made love for a very long time.

It was like nothing that had ever happened to either of them. The psychedelic powers of the pollen heightened their awareness, bringing them closer. Rader was ultra-aware of every inch of Alena's lush body, of the texture and minute coloring of her skin, of the gracefulness of her muscles, of her heartbeat and breathing. He imagined he could feel the cool cushiony moss beneath her back and his own weight upon her, and when he cupped her full breasts, he sensed the touch from both sides of her skin.

They spoke, but not in words. Their bodies joined and fused and became one, and *they* became one, and there was nothing else. Unseen were the nodding purple blossoms and the deep-blue sky and the ripples in the lavender-coated water. Unheard were the gurglings of the spring, the bird cries, the hiss and rustle and rasp of the plants in the wind. There was only flesh and movement and an atom bomb of pleasure going off in slow motion.

There was no knowing when the ending came. It seemed to go on and on, and then they knew they were less high and then less and less until they lay panting side by side, a cloven oneness, Alena-Rader and Rader-Alena . . . and then Alena and Rader.

They knew the tie was never to be broken again. Time and distance and circumstance might stretch that line thin, but it would not be broken, never severed, never frayed through.

Alena rose at last and solemnly removed her jewelry, standing on the stone platform, and dropped it back into the pool, piece by piece. "I think we did this in reverse," she said, smiling, as she lay back down next to him.

They huddled together, not cold, not too warm, looking up at the sky, watching the dancerbirds swoop and bank, listening to the rustle of the *ploom* and feeling very good indeed. There was no place they wanted to be but right there.

After a long time, the two lovers heard movement. Rader raised his head to see Liana coming slowly back through the *ploom* along the single narrow trail. She was trailing a large headdress of golden wire, strung with carved jewels. She walked silently out onto the stone pier and dropped everything in, piece by piece, as Alena had done. Then she looked at them, a serene smile on her face.

"I had a mystical experience," she said. "I sat on the western edge of the mesa with the pollen blowing out past me. After all those orgasms I began to see that clear light . . ." She stopped, and a smile tugged at the corner of her mouth. "Let's go home, Rader. I want Korda."

Without a word Alena and Rader rose, and they went back through the *ploom,* picking up clothes. Alena kept only her sandals and used a tattered ribbon of fabric to fashion a skimpy loincloth with her weapons belt. The tattered cocoon was gone forever.

Liana said, "There's a group of Kaleen gathering pollen on the west end." At Rader's sharp look, she shrugged. "I saw them, they saw me. Nothing happened. They just looked at me tripping and went back to bagging the stuff."

"Not all of them," Alena said softly.

Two dark, shaggy heads were looking through the tall stalks of *ploom.* "Don't move," Rader said quietly.

"I didn't plan on it," Liana said.

The two figures stepped into sight, warily watching the half-dressed humans. Another pair of Kaleen warriors were behind them, eyes dark and cautious. "Go on dressing," Rader said. More Kaleen appeared, then more, until there were ten males and eight females spread out around the sacred pool.

"Look! Children!" Alena said. A trio of half-grown Kaleen with twitching tails and bright, staring eyes peered through the *ploom* and the sturdy legs of their elders.

"We've never seen any of their children before," Liana said. "They always kept them hidden." She smiled at the nearest, and the solemn child smiled back.

"What do they want?" Alena whispered.

"Their sacred pool, probably," Rader said, buckling on the last of his equipment. He gestured toward the water, then pointed at them, and back to the water. He pointed at himself and his companions, then toward the head of the trail down the cliff. The Kaleen were expressionless.

Alena had her first opportunity to really study the *Homo lokiana,* closely, and it excited her. They had broad, muscular bodies, reddish-brown in color, with a thick mane of black hair that continued down their spinal column, with

tufts along their meter-long tails, ending in a large tuft
of coarse strands at the tip. They had two opposing
thumbs on each wide hand, and the two central fingers
were broad and strong. Their eyes were slitted like a cat's
and were golden green. The females had one broad breast
bulging at the apex of their chests, a lateral mound with
one nipple. They wore wide belts low on their hips, from
which hung several decorative pouches, and almost everyone had long knives in scabbards that were beaded in the
circle-and-square design typical of the Kaleen. Their
loins were covered with short loincloths of dappled soft
leather, but all the firm breasts were bare. Both sexes wore
headbands or earrings, or both, and often necklaces as
well—all of intricate, sophisticated craftsmanship, utilizing
polished sections of bones, beads of gemstones and carved
wood, and delicate beadwork.

Rader stepped toward the nearest Kaleen and raised both
his hands, palm out and open. "Greetings, fathers. Greetings, mothers. We meet on the Mountain of Destiny. In
peace," he added.

One of the females stepped forth. She had a quick, alert
manner, though obviously wary. While there had never
been any incident of animosity upon Destiny Mesa, the
meetings between *Homo sapien* and *Homo lokiana* had also
been rare on this sacred, neutral ground. The eyes of the
woman bore into Rader's, and he felt a strange discomfort.

Are they telepathic, really telepathic? he wondered. *Is
she reading my mind? Or is she picking up surface impressions, as many races can do?* He thought peace and
friendship, but he could not completely expunge the cautious thoughts that fear brought and which bubbled through
him involuntarily.

The female made a faint sound and turned toward her
companions. They started at once to unburden themselves
of the leather bags some of them carried. Spears were
thrust butt first into the ground. The children came in
from the purple fields, eyes on the humans, but doing their
chores of camp or ritual.

"Let's go," Rader said.

"No, wait," Liana said. She looked at her friends. "This
is such an opportunity . . ."

"But we might do something that—" Rader began, but Liana cut him off.

"We'll be all right if we don't *do* anything. Just stay out of their way, and if it looks like they don't want us, then we'll go."

Rader looked around at the Kaleen. They did seem to be oblivious of the humans, and it *was* a chance unheard of in the human-Kaleen association. "All right," he said, "but at the first sign that we're unwanted guests—"

Liana nodded, and they withdrew to the head of the trail that lead away toward the cliffs but still quite near the pool. Wind came across the fields of *ploom*, rustling the stalks and spreading more of the exotic pollen. The wind ruffled the spinal crests of the Kaleen as they emptied their sacks. Liana gasped with delight and astonishment as she saw the treasures brought forth.

There were more headdresses, delicate and ornate, strung with softly polished but uncut gemstones. Sitting in a niche was a statue of a Kaleen warrior, carved from a dark wood, with gems for eyes and a metal spear. Nearby, hung a cloak of long curling feathers taken from a huge bird Rader had never seen. And there was a GE-.2 laser of recent manufacture.

He stiffened at the sight, but the female handling it was not at all hostile. She simply set it out with the other items on a blanket upon a rock. Another female nearby took off all her clothes, her jewelry, weapons, and sturdy sandals as well, until she was quite naked. Rader saw that she, at least, had no pubic hair and that her female anatomy was different, but not too different, from women of Earth stock.

Then two females attended to the third, until she was regally dressed in crownlike headdress, bracelets and necklaces, wearing the feather cloak and carrying the laser negligently in one hand. She stepped onto the rock that overlooked the pool, and the others stepped close, until their feet were in the water. There was no sound except the sighing of the wind, the faint chink of jewelry as the ritually dressed female raised her arms to the sky, and the distant *tip-tip-tip* of a *ploom*-bug.

Liana looked at Rader, raising her eyebrows. The group was silent, yet Rader thought he could see a flicker of changing emotions cross the faces of the group of Kaleen, all at the same time. He put a finger to his lips to caution Liana to silence, then touched the fingertip to his forehead. She nodded. They *were* telepathic, at least among themselves.

Without warning the bedecked priestess—which Rader assumed she was—dove cleanly into the pool, sinking out of sight, to be gone quite a long time. Liana stepped forward but stopped at a gesture from Rader. Then the female burst up from the depths, gasping, her thick hair plastered darkly against her skin, and quite naked. She smiled at one of the males, who dived into the dark water to join her. Their faces, to Rader and his friends, seemed impassive as always, but their bodies betrayed their feelings. They climbed out, glistening and spotted with pollen, to quite calmly make love upon the rock, ignoring everyone.

The other Kaleen gathered up their leather bags and started away, toward the center of the mesa. Some of them looked at the humans, but most did not. Only the children still stared, and one lingered on, big-eyed, until his family, or clan or tribe, had moved on out of sight.

"Let's go," Rader said. Liana smiled and waved at the small child. The Kaleen were mostly small, about the size of Liana, but quite broad, and the children were very tiny, though they did not have the fragile, awkward look of human children. They looked more like models or miniatures of full-grown Kaleen.

They were almost in sight of the edge of the mesa when Rader, who was bringing up the rear, heard a sound. He whirled, hand on his laser, and saw the dark-eyed child behind them. The small male-child had tripped over a broken *ploom* stalk and was lying upon the ground looking both dazed and ashamed. He scrambled to his feet as Rader approached and backed away, looking afraid.

Rader felt bad for scaring the child, and he spoke softly, smiling in reassurance. "That's all right. You aren't hurt? You better go on back to your family, boy." He pointed down the trail and urged the child on with a wave of his other hand. The tiny Kaleen blinked and backed away. "Go on," Rader said, putting a little more sternness in his voice. The child whirled about, uttering a thin, high-pitched squeak, and instead of going down the trail, plunged into the thick *ploom* and was quickly lost to sight.

"Hey, I didn't mean to scare you—!" he called after the child, but it was too late. He could hear the rustle and swish of the *ploom* as the child battled his way through the growth. Rader shrugged. He felt too good to worry about it. *Maybe later, when the effects of the pollen wear off,* he thought.

Then he heard a roar and thought, *Oh, no—not a* shoka!

He heard the child's high-pitched squeak and another roar and the crashing of crushed stalks. "Stay here!" he shouted at the women as he drew his laser and ran into the *ploom* field. His passage broke more pods and purple dust half-blinded him. He became dizzy and dreamy, and the hallucinations came quickly. The sky went into purple, streaked with green; the stalks writhed and danced; the beams of sunlight through the purple dust were bars of twinkling lavender and blue. He fought the compelling ingestion of the *ploom,* fighting his urge to breathe it, swallow it, roll in it.

The *shoka* roared again, closer, and Rader turned in that direction. The stalks encircled him, the long grasses like vertical snakes, the bars of lavender light blinding him. He turned, again and again, confused, half-blinded by pollen dust and hallucination.

Rader saw Alena through the tall green-and-purple bars, a naked Alena, dusted with sunlight, lavender skinned—her hair, long strands of writhing red-violet. She beckoned, and he lurched toward her, tripping, falling, getting up, the *shoka*s roar like the bass notes of a thunderous opera, extenuating and ringing, the high-pitched notes of an alien horn splitting the images, fracturing them—

—a tipped world . . .

—purple, golden, blue, green, shafts of weaving light . . .

—Alena waving . . .

—the Kaleen child down . . .

—the *shoka,* a great furry beast, three meters high, clawed and fanged, dripping purple blood, snarling, smashing back the writhing vines . . .

Rader fired.

The ruby-beam slashed through purple stalks and the purpled *shoka,* death in ruler-line red, death that screamed, severed plants that screamed, *shoka*-Alena screaming, the Kaleen child, scrabbling, screaming . . .

Rader scooped up the child and fired again at the big *shoka,* on her hind feet, the luxurious fur, mottled and blotched with the pollen, the purple blood of chewed stalks dripping from her fangs. The creature staggered, and Rader was relentless—he fired again, and again. More plants weaved into the line of fire and were cut, screaming, and the *shoka* crashed back, twitching, crushing a great cup of *ploom* next to its wallowing place.

Rader clutched the child tightly and wiped pollen from his eyes with the heel of a hand that still held a ready laser. He squinted at the sun and lurched through the stalks toward the trail. The world was strange, bizarre; his senses were scrambled, the divisions between his senses crossing, blending switching. *Synesthesia,* some part of him said, quite calmly, but it went unheard in the maelstrom of impressions that flooded over him.

Sight became sound: the stalks were trills of a trumpet, rattling and spilling brass notes as he thrust them aside . . .

Taste became sight: the clogs of pollen, the dust and the fear and the coppery saliva became mottled blotches of primary color, shifting and running into each other . . .

Sound became taste: velvet apricot; minty orange; shivering, crystalline acid; chill burgundy. The child's whimper of fear was a shaft of sweet ice; the rattle of pods was microscopic dots of bitter lemon . . .

Touch became sound: the dry stalks were bells; the greener stalks were chimes; the warm body of the Kaleen child was the lower registers of a vast orchestra; the laser was a distant scream; the rub of equipment, a faraway thunder . . .

Odors became feeling: the dusty pollen was nubbins of cheese; the earth was furry; the child's skin was radiant heat . . .

The senses blurred, changed again and again. His own body didn't seem to work. He willed a foot to move, and he cried out; he inhaled, saw novas of flowers; he stared and tasted bile; he smelled the pollen and heard the whisper of angel's wings . . .

Great, blurred, grotesque shapes loomed up, and he aimed the laser in fear and tried to fire, but the butterflies and the clanging walls and the muffled rasps of fingernails prevented him. Someone, something, took the child from him, flooding his mind with a serenity like thick oil. He fought it, driving back the flutterbys and acolyte birds, forcing away the purple sprays of ice—still it flooded in. He screamed out a protest in clouds and rain and felt the touch of salt and silk; then the oil flowed over his defenses, and he stopped.

He stood, half-supported by a Kaleen male, quivering in every muscle. He gulped, gagged, spat up a soggy clog of pollen, then vomited without warning. The Kaleen stoically held him until it was finished; then Rader pulled himself free.

He looked around, saw the child being administered to by a male and two females. He was awake but wide-eyed and silent. They didn't seem to be doing much but wiping the wisps of pods and dust of pollen from his face, just staring at him. Rader saw the child start, then relax, then smile. Almost at once, he jumped and came over to Rader, to take his finger. Rader had to force his hand into stillness so the child could touch it.

The big Terran wiped his mouth and smiled apologetically at the upturned face. "Hey, son, I'm sorry I frightened you into running. I didn't know the *shokas* came up here, though I suppose I should have guessed." He smiled wanly. "Sorry." The child's wide, almost lipless mouth curved in what Rader assumed was a smile.

There was a crashing behind them, and he turned, his head blurring—green, blue, bitter, sparkles, burnt wood. . . . *Damn!*

From out of the *ploom* came five of the Kaleen, tugging at the carcass of a big *shoka*. They and the dead beast were mottled with pollen, though they did not seem to be mentally or physically disoriented as Rader had been. The *shoka* was dead, but when it had been alive, it had been three meters of walking death. The Kaleen looked from Rader to the *shoka* and back, and the Earthman felt good, as though bathed in a kind of milky warmth.

One of the females who had been attending the child came to Rader and was touching his head when Liana came running around a curve in the narrow trail, with Alena close behind, lasers at the ready, and breathing hard. They staggered to a halt to prevent overrunning the group, and Liana burst out in a string of harsh words in some language Rader didn't know.

"Easy, easy—hey!" he said, laughing.

"What the hell you laughing at, you garbled poltroon!" Liana snapped, but Alena stepped quickly to Rader.

"You all right?"

He nodded. "A little overdose there. Garbled me all right," he said, nodding at Liana. He grinned at both of them reassuringly. "Guess I came out someplace else, huh?"

Alena looked suddenly surprised and stepped back, though the Kaleen female had not said a thing. The small reddish-brown female reached up and pulled down Rader's head and examined the unhealed wound on his head. Several others came near, and Rader felt very sleepy. He spoke to his friends: "I guess that took more out of me than I thought. Just give me a few minutes to rest, and I'll be fine. I'll go over here and lie down—just a few minutes." He was asleep almost at once, lying in the shade of the tall *ploom* plants.

When Rader awoke, he felt fine. He looked up at the blue sky and saw the waving tops of the *ploom* blossoms. Sitting up, he saw Alena and Liana squatting nearby, looking at him in a strange manner.

"Why are you looking at me like that?" he asked, but before they could answer, he felt a twinge of guilt. "I'm sorry for going out like that, but—"

"You were put out," Alena said.

"Huh? No, I just got sleepy and—"

"They put you out, Rader," Liana said. She snapped her fingers. "Just like that. Then they operated on you."

"What?" He reached up and felt his head. It was bandaged. His face and neck were curiously clean. He felt fine.

He shook his head, very slightly, testing. He was surprised when it didn't feel as though he were shifting a load of stale blood and spikes behind his eyes. He shook again, a little harder. "Hey, I feel fine!" Looking at the women, he said, "Really. Just . . . excellent. What the hell did they *do?*"

"They operated," Liana said. "With their minds."

"They sat and stared at you, then cleaned you all off and . . . pushed a bit and . . ." Alena gulped. "Then they just stared for about an hour. Sometimes you'd twitch or make a sound or raise a hand or something. Once . . ." She hesitated. "Once you said my name. Then you . . . you just slept awhile."

Rader looked at the Kaleen. They had skinned the *shoka,* and a male and female were already preparing the hide, while others were filling their leather bags with the purple pollen. A tiny child came out of the stalks and dropped his small sack, then saw Rader and ran over. He stood a little distance off and looked solemnly at the big Earthman. Rader felt very good and smiled. "Hi, boy. What's your name?"

An image of *ploom* fields, unripe but lush, formed in Rader's mind. *"Ploom*-buds?" he asked. "Ploombud. Is that your name? Ploombud?" He felt a bright light within him, and he laughed. "All right, Little Ploombud, or whatever you call yourself." Rader felt around on his body for something, then found a small gemstone in a pocket on the back of his laser-belt. He had spent some time polishing it, then carving it into the head of a *shoka,* and had been planning to trade it in Shamrock, until other events intervened. He held it out to the child. "Take it. It's a present from Rader to Ploombud. All right?"

With great dignity the child stepped forward and took the stone and examined it at length. A feeling of warmth rose in Rader's mind, and he couldn't help smiling. Ploombud turned abruptly and ran to show one of the females the stone. Several of the Kaleen looked at Rader, and he couldn't diagnose the expressions on their faces, but he felt good.

"These are the people we've been fighting and killing?" he said aloud. All his previous experience with them had been on very formal occasions, with very rigid rules of conduct implied or stated. The wooden, secretive, hard-faced Kaleen of those early councils had become almost human now.

Almost human. Rader laughed at himself. The ultimate chauvinism. *Why, you people are almost good enough to be human! Almost.* Wryly, he got to his feet and gestured at Liana and Alena. "Let's go," he said. He stopped at a turning of the trail and looked back. Ploombud was standing down the trail, watching. Rader waved at him, and after a moment, Ploombud waved back.

Rader hesitated at the cliff trail, looking around. He felt strong and good. His headache was gone, like a boulder lifted from his head, spikes and all.

"Will there be any not so friendly ones on the trail?" Alena asked.

Rader shook his head. "I don't think they'll be trouble until we get well away from the mesa. I don't think they want any confusion about what is, or isn't, sacred ground."

They went down the trail quickly, refreshed and curiously shaken. From the trail's bendings, Rader looked over their route to the north. In the south he saw two dust trails, far away, hours off, but bearing in toward the mesa. They got to their horses, hidden within a temple tree, which was a smaller version of a cathedral tree, and mounted up. Without a word, they trotted out quickly and headed north.

The Kaleen stood at the edge of the sacred pool. They looked around at the footprints of human and Kaleen mingling, and at the crushed moss. They tasted the scent of the lovers and sensed the disturbance in the mud at the bottom. There was no anger, only a new and growing feeling. The child, Ploombud, stood nearby, fingering the gem, looking at the tiny face of the ferocious *shoka,* and thinking.

While Alena was exclaiming over the vast beauty of the maze of deep canyons below them, Rader watched their backtrail. The plumes of dust were gone, but they had disappeared before only to reappear. *Is it anyone from the mesa? Have they joined others? Is it finally a Startrade search party?*

They turned to ride north, along the rim, with the winding Marengo far below. There were rainbow trees along the top and spilling down the canyons toward the bottom, where the river flowed green and dark. There were groves of *pungi* and the blue-green *taba* bushes growing thickly. They smelled the fragrance of the rainbow trees as they rode under them, and the delicate pungency of the *dolce* flowers in the rocky edges of the cliffs. Flutterbys flew their erratic flight paths around them, and once, Rader caught a glimpse of a *kurri* sunning himself on a rainbow limb, before it slanted off and sailed out over the deep canyons.

Rader ceaselessly scanned the country around him, grateful for the concealment of the trees and annoyed that the same trees could also hide an ambush party.

Toward sunset, he lead them down into a draw, crossing over hard rock that would conceal the prints of their passage. He knew of a cave there, where he and Korda had camped before, just before the draw became a cliff that dropped to the river far below. He scouted the site on foot and found it empty, then signaled the women down.

They had little food left, but Alena and Liana foraged for berries and chimma roots while Rader built a fire. After they had finished eating and extinguished the fire, Rader went on guard at the mouth of the cave.

Alena joined him in the starry twilight. The Redflower nebula was disappearing over the western horizon, and The Sorcerer was just rising in the east.

"The Kaleen," Alena said. "They don't seem to be quite as primitive and savage as I thought . . ."

"Simple, yes. Primitive, no," Rader said. "They have a complex social structure that—as far as I know—no one understands as yet. Maybe the Moltari understand. They've been studying the Kaleen around Blackbull for quite a few years." He shook his head. "They are very religious, almost fanatic. But it isn't theistic, more like ancestor worship. Not that, only they . . . they evolve, during their lifetime. They never lie or steal from each other, although they used to fight between clans, between individuals."

He shrugged. "Kill, yes; lie or cheat, no. It's part of their religious purification rites, something like our 'survival of the fittest.'"

Rader laughed briefly. "They have replaced fighting dragons and their inter-tribal warfare with fighting us. They rate bravery and intelligence very high, and warfare is a test of these things as well as a spiritual and physical purification—for both sexes."

"Survival of the fittest," Alena said wearily. "Trial by fire. Death before dishonor." Her sigh was a condemnation.

"There's nothing wrong with that, if it's balanced across the spectrum of talent and endeavor," Rader said. "They have their standards. After they've undergone certain tasks . . . assignments, adventures, trials, whatever you want to call them . . . all set by their elders, they retire, and change. The ones that survive are allowed to breed. Fighting is a thing of youth and young adulthood. Breeding, the work of maturity. Then . . . well, we aren't quite certain what does happen. I've never seen a really *old* Kaleen. I get the feeling they hide out from strangers, the way the children are kept hidden," he said. "Except that, after they are mated, the mature Zikkalan lives rather like a monk."

Alena was amazed. "Those terrible fighters, the ones that all you starborn toughs fear—they become monks?"

"Well, students, learners, teachers, searchers—I'm not certain there is an exact word for it in Galactican. The Kaleen call it *mocklin,* but I don't think the word can be translated. It's just the way they are."

Rader again scanned the night. "I can't say it's a bad way. There is much about them I don't understand. They haven't let me, or anyone I know, in that close. It's almost as if they were guarding a fragile mystery."

Alena put her arms around him. "So are you." Rader was silent. "You are an undiscovered planet named Rader. I have no orbital geomaps to guide me, but I think I like it here."

Rader took a deep breath and let it out. "Get some sleep. It will be another long day tomorrow. We'll skirt the Redpaws and go up and down those deep canyons out there a couple of times."

Alena stepped away, trailing her fingers across Rader's

face. He kissed her fingers, and she scuffed her way back into the dark cave. Rader sat on the rock and thought. He'd wake Liana for guard duty when The Sorcerer set in the west, and she'd awaken Alena when Jörd set. It was going to be a long night, full of thoughts and distant *kurri* howls.

In the cavern they knelt before the shining ball of light and told it of the events that transpired. The voice spoke in their heads and felt their agreement. Then it spoke again of the inevitability of the cycle being completed. Not now perhaps, not for generations perhaps, but the cycle would be completed once again. Dim, racial memories stirred in the minds of the kneeling Kaleen, memories of a time when their race was less than now, before the disciplines, before the changing when the cycles changed them all.

The sphere of cold light sank into the rock and disappeared. It had been given much to consider. The Kaleen filed out, silent, thoughtful, determined. They picked up their weapons and trotted toward the surface.

It was just before noon when Rader led them down a steep valley filled with flowering meadows and tall rainbow trees. They came out on the bank of the Marengo flowing swiftly, green and dark. They turned northward, then crossed the river to start up the other side of the valley.

The Kaleen hit them in early afternoon, suddenly coming at them from a cleft in the rocks, running hard, red-brown and deadly. Rader thumbed off the safety and fired a sweeping volley of millisecond bursts that sent the survivors leaping for shelter. The Kaleen were brave, but not stupid.

"Ride!" Rader shouted, but Liana was already moving. A solid slap on the rump of Alena's horse sent her fleeing after the hard-galloping Liana. Rider shouted to Liana, "Watch out for a secondary!"

It was a standard Kaleen tactic to let a small force panic the enemy into running while a larger force waited in hiding to hit the demoralized targets further on, when they thought they had outdistanced the first ambushers. But there seemed to be no secondary attack, and after a couple of hard kilometers up the valley, Rader reined them to a halt.

"They're getting pretty far north, aren't they?" Liana asked.

"They might know something of the trouble back at Shamrock and are out seeing what they can pick off," Rader said, searching the canyon walls.

They made a cold camp that night and ate the last fragments of dried torg and redroot. Liana took the first watch as Rader said, "We'll be home tomorrow."

Early the next afternoon, they rode up onto the rim of a steep-sided canyon, with the beautiful hump of Miracle Mountain behind them, still snow covered in summer. Rader smiled at Alena and gestured toward a tumble of rocks downslope. "There it is," he said.

Alena looked at the wilderness, with the winding beauty of the deep and colorful canyons beyond, then back at Rader. "There's what?"

"Home."

Liana grinned, too, but she said, "Oh, stop teasing her, you showoff. So you guys did a good job of concealment." She kicked her mare and rode down over the hard black basalt that was the outer slope of an ancient volcano. She twisted and turned her way, first one direction, then another, as if following an invisible trail through a mine field.

Rader said, "Follow right behind me and keep that animal in my track. Watch closely and follow exactly. The rock is too hard to take tracks, but some places can get marked where dirt has drifted in."

They went on down, almost to the edge of the big dropoff into the deep canyon, then turned right toward a gnarled lump of lava rock, black with streaks and striated in red. From cracks and crevices grew nova grapes, deep purple and as big as thumbs, and falls of spiny, Zikkalan pea-pods.

Liana rode straight at the fold of rock, then around it to disappear where there seemed to be no place to go. Alena looked back at Rader with raised brows. He smiled and

followed Liana's trail. Alena followed and found a huge pothole, forty meters across and almost as deep. There was a shaded pool at one end, formed by seepage, and a wooden rick under an overhang of rock that held a mound of sweet-grass for the horses.

They dismounted, stripped off the saddles, and wiped down their animals, who whinnied and rolled on the grass. They put the saddles on posts near the rick, out of the weather, and Rader led them toward the southern side of the big pothole.

He stopped near a rock that was overgrown with a mass of juicy nova grapes and put his hand into the foliage. He withdrew his hand and said to Alena, "A little security system of our own, hidden among the vines. Don't try to go in without turning it off." He walked on ahead toward where another overhang of nova grapes fell off a rock. Pushing them aside, he revealed an opening.

Alena ducked under the vines and saw a smooth rock surface, then gasped as Rader pushed and it swung back. It was dark inside, but Rader and Liana walked through confidently. Liana tugged at Alena's hand, pulling her through onto a smooth hard surface; then Rader shoved the imitation stone door closed.

Lights came on, and Alena gasped. "My god, it *is* a home!" She stood on smoothed *pungi* planks that floored a spherical stone room. The walls were of black basalt, streaked with red as the lava was outside, and there were compartments cut into the walls and covered with decorative *pungi* wood panels. But it was the room beyond that caught Alena's eye. She stepped quickly to the circular opening and stood looking in with delight on her face.

The second room was floored with pink sand, raked into a pattern. There were three heavy doors set in thick wooden walls cut to fit irregular openings to other rooms. Part of the wall was a bas-relief of bright colors and swirling, abstract designs. It was almost completed, made of water-worn stones, semiprecious and precious gems, tumbler-polished, and bits of rich *pungi* bole, sliced and smoothed. The mural ran over the irregular surface of the wall, taking advantage of the terrain and becoming a part of the room in a most natural fashion.

"Did you do this?"

Rader nodded. "When I have time—like in the winter when we're snowed in. It's taken a long time, but I'm in no hurry. Every stone and piece is something I've found and enjoyed for its own sake." He ran his hand across the surface of the design so lovingly. "Some of these stones really only look good when they're wet . . ."

Alena ran her fingertips over a portion of the relief mural, and it made her shiver. "It's sensuous! It's really more like sculpture than a mural, Rader." She pointed at a nearby door. "What's in there, the treasure of Kublai Khan . . . or his pleasure dome?"

"Perhaps a bit of both." Liana had gone through the door earlier, and now Rader ushered Alena through. He smiled at her exclamation.

The next cave was the main one, a long cave on two levels. "There's a small valley in the mountain behind us, and a lake," Rader said. "Actually, it's the dead volcano that formed these caves with gas bubbling through lava. Water drips down through the caves, and that's what formed the stalactites and stalagmites."

Rader gestured at the rich, limestone drippings that formed fantastic curtains and pillars and forms. "The water wore through and diverted into a lower cavern, so it hasn't gone through here in centuries."

Alena was only half listening to him. She stood on the smooth *pungi* plank floor, the color of dark rosewood, pegged and carefully fit, and looked around in delight and amazement. Here were tape- and book-molecule cases, even some ancient-style books. There were readers, comfortable chairs that were fancifully designed, and homemade small sculptures sitting on smoothed rocks. These were all fitted neatly and pleasingly between the formations of limestone and the original lava rock.

"We raise crops up in the volcano valley," Rader said, "and breed some horses there. It's pretty well hidden . . . except from the air."

Alena walked down to the lower level, where a number of liquibeds were covered with the finest *shoka* furs Alena had ever seen. There was a Tetalla Musicmaster, with its quarter-million molecular recordings, sitting near a light-cellule from Varuna. Next to a thick pillar of intricately elaborate floor-to-ceiling limestone was a standing chest that contained a small armory of lasers, chemical-propellant weapons, and even some old fusors. On top of the darkwood chest was a delicate bird-carving by an anonymous Kaleen sculptor.

"You made all this?" Alena asked softly, her fingers running over the polished wood of the armory. "It's so . . . so unlike the rest of this planet! I thought I had a nice place at Shamrock, all things considered, but this—" Alena shook her head. "It must have cost a fortune to ship some of these things here."

Rader shrugged. "Why else do we desire wealth? We kill only the *shoka* who attack us, or the ones who are old and ill, yet their furs are worth much to people who have only seen the beasts on a screen. True, some hunters ask for the attacks, but we don't. We don't need to." He grinned wryly. "And there are gemstones, too, and other furs."

Rader gestured around them. "This is our home. We could leave it tomorrow without much regret, for these are only things. But no one will drive us from it." The tall hunter shrugged. "Some people want money for itself, or for the power it gives them. We only want it to make our life here better." Then he smiled abruptly. "Enough of that, let me show you the rest."

He strode to a wide *pungi* wood wall and touched a spot on the surface of the carved-bird mural. With a hum, the wall folded back and sunlight spilled in. With a gasp of delight, Alena walked out onto a ledge that overlooked the entire landscape of deep canyons.

The ledge was eight meters wide and four deep, a curving terrace shaded by an ancient rainbow tree growing at the lip. Far below, the twisting Marengo sparkled, and Alena could hear a splash of water as it fell somewhere nearby, cascading its way from pool to pool down the cliff.

"Korda and I smoothed this out a bit," Rader said, but we left it looking as natural as possible, for camouflage. You'll also note that when the door opened, the lights went out. We're careful here. Only a handful of trusted friends know where we live."

Alena breathed deeply of the scented wind blowing up from the groves of rainbow trees far below. Over her head, the gnarled old tree ran through a spectrum of colors, rustling and sighing. She spun toward Rader and flung her arms around him. "It's a palace! This is why you wanted to fight for Zikkala!"

"No," Rader corrected her. "I fight for the whole planet, for the Guild, for the Zikkalans, for you . . . for the idea of keeping Zikkala pure." He sighed. "We humans have already made enough of a scar on this world, but we'd like to keep it this way, we in the guilds. Oh, not stagnant—but calm, serene, living close to nature." He looked embarrassed. "I sound like some zongo, don't I? Or an ecologist or—" He stopped, grinning. "I'll fight for the two continents none of us have explored yet." He jerked his thumb over his shoulder. "If Startrade turned a laser on all that, it would be sad and a waste, but not worth one drop of Holtan's blood and certainly not Clem's life. That's why I'll fight, why Liana and Korda will fight, why we'll all fight. To be left alone. Perhaps that's why the native Zikkalans fight. Well, this 'naturalized' Zikkalan doesn't like to be pushed!"

Again, Rader's face broke into a smile. "Hey, we certainly seriqused up there! Let's go look at the rest of these holes!" He broke away and went into the cavern. Alena followed, her face thoughtful.

Alena was shown the three bedrooms, the kitchen bubble with its collection of cockbooks, spices, and well-used pots. She saw the workrooms with their clutter of tools and unfinished everything. Alena saw the gem-tumblers, the *rena* hides being tanned, the *pungi* trunks sliced into planks ready to be polished. She saw Liana's vibra-sew and her unfinished shimmercloth dress, as well as her design for a laser routing-tool.

With delight, the blonde beauty examined Korda's latest jewelry creation for Liana, a Cleopatra-style neckpiece, fringed with blue pearls from the Great Sea and done in the Moltari "royal" design motif. From a small chest with *shoka* bone panels, Rader took a golden necklace, bold and primitive, with pi-pearls strung on the metal and featuring a lustrous crimson stone. Rader explained the rare stone was formed when a silicate-type lava rock hit water and crystallized. "There's still a few left in the crevices back there," he said.

Rader held the piece toward Alena. "It's for you."

Alena took it in her hands and looked at it lovingly. "Isn't it shameful to like such pretty things?"

Rader shook his head. "We all like beauty. I made several pieces and just kept them until . . . until I found someone I wanted to give them to."

Alena's eyes turned mischievous. "Oh? Is this the last one?"

"No. It's the first one I've given away, except a couple to Liana." Before Alena could answer, Rader took her arm. "Come on, let's find her."

The fire, which had not been extinguished in the memory of the oldest of them, flickered shadows across the rock walls. Ka-morro-ma sat quietly on a rise of the cave floor, watching the young prepare their weapons. A young warrior, sharpening a blade, paused to look up at the teacher-of-the-way, finding it hard to believe this ancient person had once been a warrior that fought *shoka* or tested herself against the Miscos or Tambors.

I am Ka-morro-ma, came the voice in his mind, *and I survived. I proved my worthiness at the level of purification. But your greatest challenge is yourself, for ego is a formidable foe.*

Chastened, the young warrior bent again to the keen edge of the blade. His tools must be ready—the tools of the mind as well as those of the hand.

They went upward, past flanking storeroom caves, to a great hanging of *tangri* pelts and pushed it aside to find Liana in her bath. The tub was a small swimming pool fed by hot springs and a black basalt basin smoothed by several thousand years of flowing water. There were bottles of scent and lotion sitting on a low table nearby and a large goblet of chilled zumzum wine within Liana's reach. She lay naked in the shallow end of the pool, her ripe golden body glowing against the black stone.

"Hi! Come on in!" She kicked a foot and water splashed a bank of cave moss and dappled the tiny white flowers. The long-haired girl arched her wet body and laughed joyously, "Oh, I love it!"

Rader and Alena pulled off their sweat-stained clothes and threw them into a corner. Rader dived into the deeper end and surfaced in time to see Alena poised gracefully on the edge. She looked so beautiful and graceful that his heart thumped heavily against his ribs.

She dived into the warm water and curved up to meet him, her long blonde hair streaming back as she clung naked to him. She flung a long and happy cry at the dark dome of the cavern overhead, beyond the reach of the light spheres, and kissed Rader hard.

They splashed and washed and kissed and were finally clean. Then Liana rose, her body gleaming with a thousand water jewels. "Let's go dry off in the sun," Liana said, and Alena looked around the bubble of black stone, lit by the light spheres, and raised her eyebrows in puzzlement.

"This way!" Liana said and dived deeply. Alena went after her, and Rader followed. It was dark down there, but Alena could just see the flicker of Liana's legs and trusting her, followed. She felt the warm water flowing more swiftly, and she brushed against a smooth black stone wall. Then she was popping up, coming to the surface in the sunlight.

They lay in the sun until they were dry, and Alena touched the scars on Rader's body. They all wondered exactly what Korda was doing, but there was little they could do until all were rested and Rader's head wound fully healed. They went back into the cave complex through a secret door in a crevice, and Alena commented that they had made their home a fortress.

"Exactly," Rader said. "There are no safe suburbs on this planet, no slidewalks or police or air-conditioned play domes. So far, the Kaleen haven't found this place. If they do, well . . ."

None of them bothered to dress, and Liana went into the kitchen bubble to defrost some *rena* steaks. Rader checked the fusion plant in the innermost cavern, which they had made into their "secure room." Then he checked the alarm system and checked the four screens that fed pictures from the hidden video cameras.

Suddenly there was a scream from the main room and Rader started running. He snatched a laser from a secret compartment and went through the entrance to the main room at a jump, leaping to one side and going into a roll, coming up with his gun extended. He saw Alena's frightened eyes and swung the weapon in that direction and almost fired. Liana came through the entrance, holding a laser, and they both broke into laughter at the same moment.

Alena tore her eyes away from the terrifying sight and looked at Rader and Liana as if they were mad. "What the hell are you laughing at? What *is* that thing?"

"That's Moctezuma. He's a cavecat."

Alena stared at the enormous golden-red feline with a head as big as her own. "Montezuma?"

"No, Moctezuma," Liana said. "That's the correct name."

"He looks like a golden tiger, a pup maybe, but some kind of *beast!*"

Rader went down a level and walked up to Moctezuma, who had been sitting peacefully on a nubbin of limestone but was now on his feet and looking ferocious and making terrible growls. He hissed at Rader but did not bite or scratch as the tall lean man stroked his back and scratched behind his hairy ears.

"There were cavecats here before we were, and Moctezuma is the original tenant of these caves." To the golden-tawny beast he said, "She's a friend. It's all right." He gestured at Alena. "Come here and pet him."

"He'll eat me."

"No, you just scared him." He gestured her closer, and she cautiously moved to the big tawny animal. The cavecat looked at Rader, who spoke soothingly to him. He permitted Alena to caress him.

"Oh, his fur is *gorgeous!* My God, how soft!" Impulsively she buried her face in the ruff of his neck and made long sighs.

Rader smiled. "That will help. Cavecats are mildly telepathic. That's how he finds his prey in the dark. He was probably out prowling when we came home and sensed us."

"Oh, he's lovely," Alena said, hugging him. Moctezuma looked up at Rader, who made a thought at him. The cat arched his back and settled down.

Rader grinned and went off to check out the rest of the

cave. When he returned ten minutes later, Moctezuma and Alena, still quite nude, were curled up together on a liqui-bed, nestled into a pile of furs and pillows, and she was stroking his stomach lovingly. His purr sounded like a distant engine with something out of tune.

"Look! He likes me!" she said proudly.

"Who wouldn't like to have his stomach caressed by a beautiful nude woman?"

"Ohh . . ."

"Dinner is ready, milady."

"What's for Moctezuma?"

"He doesn't dine at the table *or* under it. He eats the live mice or whatever they are, back in the caverns."

"Urg," Alena said, looking down at the stretched-out cat.

"Cavecats never developed fire, you see, nor do they cultivate anything. But they don't eat their own kind."

"*Live* mice?"

"Sure. They're fresh, anyway. We're having defrosted *rena*. Come on, my love, dinner is hot."

As Alena rose, Rader told her the menu. "Rare *rena* steaks. Buttoneye, *pungi* berries, and something that's very much like Terran corn on the cob but isn't. A nice wine we make ourselves, from *pungi* berries and nova grapes. Chilled nova grapes with a wine sauce."

"And I thought you lived like a savage, eating raw lizard and slopping down tepid water with things floating in it."

"Well, thank you," Rader said, pulling back a homemade chair from a polished table. "And you came, anyway, despite these certain savage tendencies."

Liana came through from the kitchen carrying a big platter stacked with steaming steaks. "Oh," she said, scanning Alena's nudity. "I see we dressed for dinner."

Alena looked down at herself in surprise. "Oh, I forgot! It seemed so natural. Just a minute!" She jumped up and ran out. Rader and Liana exchanged smiles, and he helped her bring out the food. Alena was back in a few minutes, her hair combed and wearing only the gold necklace of pi-pearls with the crimson stone that Rader had given her.

"There!" she said firmly and sat down. She caught Li-ana's quick, wise look from her necklace to Rader, and she smiled.

"Let's eat!" she said happily. "I'm hungry and—oh, that looks very tempting!"

"So do you," Rader said.

Alena smiled at him. "I'll raise your blood sugar level."

"Liana says I like to live dangerously."

"Pass the butterbuds, please," Liana said. "And save that for dessert."

The fire, which had not been extinguished in the memory of the oldest of them, flickered shadows across the rock walls. Ka'morro'ma sat quietly on a rise of the cave floor, watching the young prepare their weapons. A young warrior, sharpening a blade, paused to look up at the teacher-of-the-way, finding it hard to believe this ancient person had once been a warrior that fought *shoka* or tested herself against the Miscos or Tambors.

I am Ka'morro'ma, came the voice in his mind, *and I survived. I proved my worthiness at the level of purification. But your greatest challenge is yourself, for ego is a formidable foe.*

Chastened, the young warrior bent again to the keen edge of the blade. His tools must be ready—the tools of the mind as well as those of the hand.

Rader pressed a hidden catch, and a panel swung out of a carved *pungi* wall. "There are several sets of controls like this at different places in the cave," he said to Alena. "I'll show you their location later." He pointed at the buttons, dials and small television screen. "There's a trap door beneath that pretty pink sand in the entrance. Drops unwanted visitors into the sewerage cavern below. This activates a remote control, laser-directed zapper that covers the main entrance. Here's another one for the waterfall area. This dial tells us if anything much bigger than Moctezuma is prowling the upper caves, toward the old volcano."

"I thought you had no radios on your pristine planet," Alena said.

Rader nodded. "We don't—but we do have a few guard monitors. Cost us dearly to trade for them, but what the hell, we each only risked our lives once each to take a *shoka* to pay for it."

"All the conveniences of civilization," Alena said with a mocking smile. "Guardian monitors, trap doors, proximity alarms. Some 'pure' planet you have here."

Rader shut the panel, and it seemed to disappear in the custom carving. "We have a certain contempt for the overly convenient conveniences of civilization, I do admit—but we aren't fools, either." He jerked his thumb back at the control panel as they walked into the main cavern. "If things like that make it safer—why not? Music molecules, lasers, certain additives to our diet, starship connections to other worlds—sure, they're nice."

Rader dropped onto a liquibed next to Alena. "But too much civilization can be debilitating." His face grew serious. "Civilization depends on man extending his mind and powers to the extreme. We can do that right here, without arcologs, subliminal advertising, and satellites beaming trash into our minds—and without having to live cheek to jowl with people you can't stand."

Alena laughed. "Just who do you mean—"

An alarm bell rang.

Rader rolled off the bed and was coming to his feet with a laser in his hand when the lights went out. Alena heard a scraping and a rustling, but she was too involved in trying to remember on which end of the liquibed she had left her own weapon.

"Hey—it's me!" A deep voice cut through the darkness, and she heard Rader swear. Then the lights came on as the front entrance closed, and Korda stood in the outer cave.

Rader grinned at his friend and shoved the laser back into its holster and draped the belt and holster over a chair. "That was close," he said.

Korda, dusty and obviously tired, said, "Aw, you couldn't hit me, anyway." He looked over at Alena and grinned. "Did I interrupt something? I hope."

Alena remembered her nudity and blushed slightly. "Hello, Korda. Where have you been?"

"Well, I've been riding the—"

Liana came down the levels at a dead run and threw herself into Korda's arms, kissing his dusty face all over. "Oh, you—you—stranger!"

Korda tried to talk, but Liana waved her arms and said, "No, unless the baddies are coming up the hill! No talk, no talk! Come on, you black *shoka,* let's get you clean enough to kiss all over!"

Korda grinned at Rader and Alena. "It's nice to feel wanted." He lost his smile. "Much to tell you, but nothing that won't hold."

Rader droped back onto the liquibed and snuggled into the luxurious furs next to Alena. "That's a load off my mind. There was always the chance he'd go back to Shamrock to blast me out and get himself zapped." He grinned at Alena. "Give them an hour or so, and then we'll get the latest news."

Korda was sitting up in bed, propped up by huge pillows, with Liana lying next to him in smug and sensual comradeship. He took a sip of wine and set the goblet down.

"I rode a circuit east to April Mountain, then north along the Marble. Met Juji Nakadai on his way into Neuvo Monterey, and he said he'd spread the word that way. So I went up toward Blackbull." He took another sip of wine. "That's a dusty trip. Saw Zachariah, then a pair of those Moltari." He peered at Rader curiously. "You think they're telepathic? Zach thinks so. Somewhat, anyway. Just for the hell of it, I told them I thought so, in my head, but they didn't answer me."

"They're supposed to stay pretty objective, not mix in. Guess that's why they're accepted on so many worlds. They'll fight Moks or Skrills, of course, but otherwise . . ." He shrugged. "So they are observers and keep the subject pretty well unsullied."

"Well," grumbled Korda, "we can use whatever help we can get, so maybe someone ought to check them out. So . . . what have you been up to?"

Briefly, Rader gave him a synopsis of their activities.

When Korda heard they had used a shockquizzer on Alena, his dark face went hard. "Those waste-eating wombats—!" But Rader hurried on past that, with only a quick look at Alena's face.

"So here we are," he concluded. "Mostly healed and ready to start doing something again."

"Oh, not so soon!" Alena groaned.

"I think he has to," Korda said. "The first working party has arrived."

"Oh, damn," Rader said softly.

"Worse than that," Korda continued. "They've already established a working camp on Tura—and *that* has got to be some chore! I got it from Nakadai who heard it from Waldstein. They landed two days ago, in the *Andrew Mellon,* a Startrade cruiser, and just took over Alena's."

The blonde madam made a wry face. "What's left of it, that is."

"They got two months' liberty. For them to get twice as much liberty as work time, Tura must be sheer hell," Korda said.

"A working camp already means they were setting it up even before Lockhart arrived here," Rader said angrily. "Setting up Zikkala was just a side issue of no great importance. Wreck a planet just to make a recreation area!"

"Take it easy," Alena said, touching his arm. Trying to change the subject, she asked about Tura. "What makes it such a terrible place?"

Korda laughed. "Ever see the survey tapes on that ball of waste? Goddamn, but that is the most annoying planet!" At Alena's expression, he began to enumerate the flora and fauna of the second planet in the Loki system.

"It's hot, for one thing. Average temperature in the high nineties, Celsius." Alena whistled. "There are a few big nasties—really evil things, all armor and claws—and a lot of medium and small nasties, but the worse thing is . . . it will annoy you to death!"

Korda laughed and looked at Rader. "Remember when Charlotte Calkins came in on the *Quigley?*" They both laughed. "She decided to try out Tura as a virgin territory, so to speak, before she landed here. Talked the captain into spending three days in orbit . . . but in less than two hours she wanted off!"

"Why?" Alena asked. "Too dangerous?"

"Too annoying. There's no native intelligent life, so everything's been named by the poor bastards that discovered whatever it was. Calkins ran into a bunch of meter-long frog like things with scabrous skin. They spit stinking gobs of digestive juices at their prey, then stick it with the coiled pointed tails and delicately nibble it off the spike. They hunt in frog packs." Korda laughed. "I can't help it. Frog packs are funny."

"Not to Calkins," Liana muttered. "She named them gorps."

"Then there's the Mother-in-Law," Korda went on. "That's a four-legged spiderlike thing more'n a meter wide that spurts spinning gunk on its prey, numbing it, and then it carries you off into a sort of honeycomb where you become living food for its young."

Alena shivered. "Let's see," Korda said with relish, taking a perverse joy in everyone's disgust. "There's Smelly Jelly, a kind of Portuguese man-of-war on land. There's squishees and white worms all over the place. The squishees like cool places—like your dome. The white worms have an incredibly fast breeding-cycle—which leaves dead, dying and very alive worms everywhere on and under the ground."

Korda sighed, as if he were describing Spectrum Valley or some beautiful vacation spot. "The Zips are interesting. They're fast little hard-shelled bugs that fly pretty much only in hereditary paths and hit you, even in protective suits, like a needle-gun. Then there are Floaters, big flying gauzy creatures that wrap around live objects and cling like glue. And the Trapdoor Skunk, which hides in holes and—"

"Korda, that's enough!" Liana objected.

"—rustcreepers, which rust almost anything they grow over. And some kind of airborne fungus. There's something that's part ant, part snake. Got an exoskeleton. They're all over."

"Korda," Liana said warningly. "I don't care!"

"But the real fun are these things like crocodiles—"

At that point, Liana began pounding on his arm, and Alena jumped in and began punching him in the stomach.

"Enough!" cried Liana.

"Save me, Rader!"

"Save yourself, you sadistic bastard. You asked for it.

Spiders and bugs and jellies—" He uttered a loud cry of disgust and jumped on the bed. But he snatched Alena away and began kissing her.

"Let me kiss away the horrids," he said.

"Toad packs?"

"Frog packs, and shut up."

They sat on the ledge overlooking the canyons. It was dark and Rader held Alena as they looked up at the stars. "That's the Iron Maiden," Liana said from another rock, nestled in Korda's arms. "See there, where those two bright stars are close together?"

"Um," Alena said.

"That's Renoir, Seurat, Velazquez over there, but the rest of The Painters are too dim. Where are the Sunjewels?"

"Can't see them from here," Korda said. "They're down in the Southern Hemisphere. Remember, we saw them in the Wizard Islands?"

"Um, yes."

There was a long silence as they watched the colorful parade of stars and the awesome bright swirl of The Wall of Stars spur. Then Rader sighed.

"I know that sigh," Alena said. "You're going to say or do something I won't like."

Rader smiled in the night. "Afraid so. It would be wonderful if we could stay like this—hiding in Paradise. But we can't. Tomorow we're going into Shamrock. Just Korda and me."

"Hey!" Liana said.

"Someone has to stay here and guard the fort."

"Who guarded it while we were gone?" Liana asked.

"But now they are certain to be tracking us with everything they've got. If they find this place, they'll slice it to trash."

"So? I want to be in on the fighting." Rader heard Liana sit up, struggling up through Korda's arms. "And you aren't keeping me out, big brother."

"Or me," Alena said.

"I—" Rader stopped, and he heard Korda chuckle.

"I told you it wouldn't work. None of that medieval protectivism, *num tok*."

"But Alena isn't—"

"Alena is." She poked him in the chest. "And don't you forget it."

Rader sighed. "All right, tomorrow we'll all head back to Shamrock and get everyone together. Full Guild meeting, both guilds."

"What about you two being wanted?" Liana said. "Me, too, probably."

Rader's voice was hard, and there was no lightness left. "Let that be *their* problem. Now we know what they're like."

They rode out early the next morning, fully armed, and anxious to get it over with. They took a shorter route going back than the big southwestern swing Rader had taken coming to the cave in the Redpaws. They went almost directly south and picked up two hunters, McAllister and Samuelson, and filled them in.

They lit a signal fire in the foothills north of Shamrock, and in little more than a day, they had a force of eleven. That night they went in, quiet and careful.

"They probably have infrared," Liana said, "but let's hope they're careless or dumb."

They weren't. The attack had been expected.

The ruby-beams winked into the black night, and Samuelson's animal screamed in pain, throwing his rider right through the cutting red light. Liana's mount had its legs cut off, and she lost some skin on a tumble. The night was black, filled with cries and commands. The survivors wheeled about and galloped away from the rays of red death, scattering into the hills.

Korda and Liana met at dawn, at the rendezvous.

"Where's Rader?" Liana said, looking around. "And Alena—?"

Korda gave her a dark look. "I thought they were with you. They were right next to me when the firing started. Her horse went down, and I thought I saw Rader stop to—oh, god."

"They'll turn up," Liana said.

Another trapper rode into the rendezvous and Liana ran over to him, but he had not seen the missing couple either. Liana ran back to her mount and swung into the saddle, but Korda's big hand grasped the bridle.

"Let go, dammit," Liana said savagely, but the huge black man shook his head. "Let me go! They have Rader and Alena—or they're hurt and hiding out somewhere!"

Korda reached up and pulled her from the saddle. She struggled against his hard muscles, then collapsed suddenly into his arms.

"Oh, my god, Korda—are they dead?"

He shook his head. "Takes a lot to kill a bastard like him. I know. We've been through a lot together."

Liana clung to him. "I don't know what I'd do if I lost you," she said. "I think I'd go crazy." Korda patted her back, his face drawn and hard in the dawning light. Nearby, two of the trappers exchanged looks and shook their heads.

Rader awoke in thunderous hurt. His head pulsed with almost blinding waves of pain. For a second he didn't know where he was. Metal walls, vacuum-welded seams, acceleration couches that also served as bunks. *A lander.*

Alena! Her horse had gone down and she had screamed, and he had jumped after her, pulling her into a gully. She was knocked out but not badly hurt. Then he had stood up, weapon in hand, to put the Shamrock turrets under fire, when a ruby-beam sliced into the rock near him, exploding it. Something had struck his head, showering him with dirt and a shapnel of granite. Then, darkness.

Now a lander. He listened for a moment to the hums

and clicks and other soft noises of a spaceworthy vessel and guessed they were still on the ground. Full Zikkalan gravity. He heard the muffled sounds of someone beyond a hatch and turned his head.

Wolf Briggs lay unmoving and crumpled in the adjoining bunk, as if he had been dumped as dead weight and strapped down. Rader started to sit up, dizzy, groaned with pain, and found he was bound to the bunk with multiple restraining straps, all lockdowns. He wiggled but couldn't get a hand free enough to unlock the straps.

"Now, now . . ." It was Lockhart, smiling and handsome, lifting a finger in mock caution as he stepped through the hatch. "You're all snugged in. Mustn't go wandering about —just about to lift." He glanced at Wolf, pursed his lips, then stood over Rader, smiling patronizingly. "A few minutes and the rest of the crew will be aboard. Then we are taking a tour of beautiful Tura."

Rader glared up at the Startrade executive. "Kidnapping me?"

An almost sweet smile crossed Lockhart's face. "You know we don't work that way—unless we really have to, of course." He waved a hand at the outside. "No, all perfectly legal, my interfering friend. You were unconscious, of course—both of you—and thought not to recover." He shrugged delicately. "You had legal counsel, which pleaded you guilty with extenuating circumstances; you had a judge, everything." He grinned like a fox. "At least, that's what the record shows."

Rader looked thoughtfully up at Lockhart, who had looked away as Wolf Briggs groaned. *A man's opinion of himself is very hard to hide,* he thought, and Lockhart's opinion of himself was a great flashing sign: Clever, devious, ambitious, victorious. *He thinks he's a planet-devourer,* Rader thought grimly; *and maybe he is.*

Rader had no intention of asking about Alena. Perhaps she had regained consciousness and gotten away or had been somehow missed in the after-battle clean-up. If she was still out there and they didn't know about her, the Startraders couldn't hurt her.

Lockhart turned back to Rader, his manner light and almost dainty, as though nothing Rader could say or do would stop him at all, and Rader had to admit, right then, it looked likely. "With you on Tura, your friends will act more carefully. No more stupid midnight charges . . ." He shook his head sadly. "Heroes have no sense of proportion,". he muttered. "They think courage is all. Well, it isn't. You . . . and your rather greasy little friends have been out here too long, Rader. You've forgotten the technological advances we of Startrade excel in." He shrugged again, almost comically, as if it were all a delicious joke. "You'll be on lovely, tropical Tura— and *not* a martyr!"

"A hostage, though," Rader said bitterly.

Lockhart waved his hand generously. "If you care to see it that way. Of course, neither of you will be coming back. Just can't have that. You friends won't know, not for certain." Again, a delicate shrug. "I'm sorry about that. Probably a nasty end, very nasty actually. We lose quite a few, really. I don't know firsthand, of course, because I plan never to go there if I can help it." He turned away, then stopped and looked back.

"Goodbye, Citizen Rader. For a short time you were an opponent almost worthy of respect, but . . ." He shrugged expressively and made an expression of mock sadness. "But you were out of your league, provincial."

Rader smiled faintly. "In other words, you have faults, but being wrong isn't one of them."

Lockhart's eyes flashed, but his grin barely wavered. "I think you could say that."

"Ah, vanity, vanity," Rader said. "But don't worry, Lockhart, things average out. When you think too much of yourself, others don't."

Lockhart flushed but quickly recovered. "Yes, brave words from a man packaged up for shipment out."

"I'll be back, Lockhart."

"Oh, Rader, my good fellow, don't be tiresome. How many judges have heard those words and how many criminals have carried out their threats. That's bravado, and your reputation is fast losing its luster." Lockhart looked very bored, but Rader suspected the expression on his face was exactly what he wanted it to be. "Oh, and don't suspect your friends will somehow rescue you. All ships are in our tight control, and we are hunting down the remnants of your criminal band right now."

Lockhart stepped to the side as men started coming in through the hatch and began getting into their couches, grumbling and half-drunk but respectful to Lockhart. They were all strangers, all Startrade hirelings. There was no one there that would release Rader or Briggs.

"Farewell, Rader. You really should have been a better champion, but I suppose the cards were stacked against you." He smiled in a self-satisfied manner and seemed about to leave but said, "Oh, by the way, the Petrovna bitch was scooped up along with you." Rader kept his face neutral, though it was an effort. "Yes, a little banged up, but the medics say she'll be fine in no time."

"Leave her alone, Lockhart," Rader said.

The Startrade executive smiled thinly. "You are so infantile, Rader. Your threats have no power." He looked thoughtfully toward the overhead. "I think she's just the one to try out something I've always wanted to do. This Jicron drug now. Gives you some mild telepathic powers, you know. We have a sensory recorder coming in—several in fact, to entertain the drones—and some very erotic tapes. I *think* if she were stoked with a bit of Jicron, fed some hot tapes and her own mental patterns fed back to her to reinforce the effect . . . hmmm . . . yes . . . biofeedback on such a basic level, she couldn't fight it. I do think I could turn the proud Citizen Petrovna into something of an insatiable nymphomaniac."

Rader felt his entire body tense, his face go flat and hard as he silently tested the restraints. Lockhart grinned. "Think of that, Rader, while you're over there. Alena and me, and her—quite, quite willing, I assure you . . ." The handsome Startrader laughed, a short, cruel, insulting laugh as he turned, going quickly out through the hatch, and Rader heard another sharp, echoing laugh in the passageway.

Rader forced a calmness on his mind and body. It was one of the most difficult things he had ever done in his life. He fought back fear and disgust, self-incrimination and a loathing that could blind him. He must be calm. Cold. Hard. *Somewhere they will make a mistake,* he thought. *And I will be watching. I will not show fear. I will not die on Tura. I cannot.*

He readied himself for the launch and for the destination. *Tura. The horror world.*

They lifted within the half-hour and were docked with the mothership two hours later. Wolf Briggs came awake during the transfer and looked at Rader with a shamefaced grin. They were transferred to a single small cell under the guns of two very tough-looking Startrade-sponsored "marshals." The fact that they even *had* cells was ominous to Rader. He had vaguely hoped for the openness of a regular starship.

"I really fouled it up," Wolfgang Briggs said sullenly. "I was feeling better and went out. I just wasn't a good enough actor, I guess. They pinned me for a partisan right away, when I saw them dragging you in. I . . ."

"Oh, never mind that," Rader said. "What's the news?"

"When I tried to, uh, save you, they banged me up some more and tossed me in a cell next to yours. You were out, and they kept zapping you with something to keep you that way." Rader made an impatient gesture, and Wolf gulped. "Yeah, uh, well, some of your friends were killed. I . . . I saw some of the . . . the bodies. I didn't know any of them, but none were Miss Liana or Korda or . . ." Wolf looked very nervous. "But . . . Miss . . . Miss Petrovna . . ."

"I know," Rader said. "Where did they take her? What condition was she in?"

"I saw her with a medic. She just had a little bandage on her head, but . . . but she's captured, all right." Wolf hurried on. "The company has some hunting parties out, trying to find stragglers. I heard some of them talking about wiping out the Kaleen, too."

"Why them?"

Wolf shrugged and put a hand to his head, wincing. "Well, one of the early parties was hit by the Kaleen, and a couple of the marshals—"

"They're not marshals."

"Yeah, well, a couple of the deputized Startrade men anyway—they were killed." He shrugged. "So they're going to wipe out all of them, or enough, anyway. I heard they planned to hit a whole cave complex with gas or something."

Rader tightened his fists into hard knots, and it took will power not to strike out at the steel walls in anger. "What else?"

Wolf shrugged. "Then they hauled us off. I tried to get away, but they zapped me, too. I woke up when they were getting me out of the bunk." He looked very sad. "I'm sorry, Rader; sorry I wasn't of more help."

"That's all right, Wolf. Look at all of us guilders. We didn't do too well, either. But we have to watch now, watch for a chance. There will be one. Maybe *only* one, but we must be prepared."

"Yessir."

"Just remember—when that moment comes, you've got to just *do* it, whatever it is. Watch my lead." Rader looked at the youth and smiled faintly. "And don't you worry about whether you have the courage to do what has to be done. You will."

"Yessir."

Rader was silent a moment, studying Wolf's downcast face. "Just remember this: wanting to live is not cowardly. It *is* cowardly to beg for it, to trade something vitally essential, something within you, for it. Oh, sure, fight to the very last second. Take as many of the bastards with you as you can. But when you *know* it's the end, the absolute, no-going-back-no-matter-what end—then, just let it go. But don't ever beg."

"Y-no sir."

Rader struck Wolf's shoulder lightly. "Don't think I'm psyching you up to be a hero, boy, because I'm not. It's hard to find the right words . . . harder still to find just the right path, Wolf. You should be brave but not so brave that it goes too far and becomes bravado. A man once said, one cannot always be a hero, but one can always be a man."

"Yessir. I think . . . I think I understand."

"Courage, compassion, conscience," Rader said softly. "If you do not have them, you have nothing."

Wolf looked up, and a smile came to his lips, shy and indistinct. "Yessir. I'll try to remember. And, uh . . . thanks."

"No need. I'm scared, too."

Wolfgang looked startled. "You?"

"Sure, me. But a little fear is all right. It kind of gets you ready, you know? Just as long as you don't panic. Fear can breed a kind of unreal, or unnatural, courage. The anxiety you're feeling, that's just fear unvisualized; you don't know what's coming. Hell," he shrugged, "I always approach breakfast cautiously. After all, chances are someday it will eat *me,* statistically speaking."

Wolf grinned and nodded. "All right. I'm all right."

"Just remember *one* more thing, if I'm not overloading your memory banks—anyone who says he isn't scared when he damned well ought to be is either lying, stupid or so inexperienced he's dangerous."

"Like me, huh?"

"You must start someplace. You're not doing so badly. You're still alive, and you took on the Kaleen and the Startraders, both."

Wolf was silent a few moments, and they felt the faint thrum of the ship around them. "Why are you telling me all this? I'm just as liable to be a bother to you as—"

"Cut that. There are two kinds of people that really scare me, much more than just the greedy and the teacherous. That's the crazy and the scared. You never know what they're going to do." Rader shrugged and grinned reassuringly. "You aren't crazy, and I don't want you scared."

"You think I can help you? Really?"

"Hell, yes. You are Wolfgang Amadeus Mozart Briggs, aren't you? Notorious Kaleen fighter and daring pioneer type."

Wolf grinned and ducked his head in embarrassment. "Ah, hey, come on . . ." But Rader could see he was pleased.

They came down onto Tura in the lander. Everyone was nervous. The landing officer told them he was lifting in twenty minutes after touchdown, so they had better have everything and everyone off in that time.

Rader and Wolf were taken out by the same two marshals

and escorted to the airlock. Rader saw they had stretched a tube of impervium flex from the airlock down to the dome airlock below. It still didn't stop the bugs and worms, which were squeezing in around the seals. Two crewmen stood at each end of the tube, a club in one hand and a big pressure can of Deathspray in the other, stoically and methodically clubbing and spraying the invaders. Rader and Wolf stepped over the sticky writhing mess on the deck and jumped into the tube and slid down to the airlock.

At the bottom, another set of men were inside the airlock, spraying and clubbing. All of the men were in light armor. Rader and Wolf tried not to breathe as they passed through the clouds of potent insecticide, but their eyes stung and watered. Once inside, the corridors were relatively clean, though there were innumerable blotches and stains on the walls, ceilings, and especially on the impervium floors.

They were escorted along the curving outer corridor of the dome to a cramped, claustrophobic office. The escort knocked, entered, saluted and offered two dossiers to the beefy, florid-faced man behind the desk.

The officer had a bad rash; there were several red bites with swollen white centers on his face, and a tic contorted his features about every eight seconds. The name on the deskplate said COL. NORRIS GARFIELD, COMMANDER, STAR-TRADER'S TERRITORIAL SECURITY FORCE.

He stared at Rader with undisguised malevolence as he dropped the dossier cubes into a reader. He thumbed the screen switch, glanced at the record for a few moments, then put in the other cube and spent even less time. Rader amused himself by counting the exact seconds between tics. Then Colonel Garfield raised his eyes slowly to stare bitterly at Rader, a leer twisting his face in grotesque satisfaction.

"Remember me, Rader?"

Rader frowned. He honestly couldn't remember the fat Startrade security man. At his lack of recognition, a look of venomous fury crossed Garfield's face. "Goddamn you, it was you that got me busted out of the Merks, you son-of-a-bitch! On Seurat, in The Painters, you holy bastard!"

Rader remembered. They hadn't been able to prove anything, but Garfield had been accused of selling Mercenary Guild weapons to the Wachatta, a race of intelligent antlike creatures almost as big as horses. So he had been given a "For the Good of the Service" discharge without honor, and Rader hadn't thought of Garfield since. The age difference between the youthful Garfield and the embittered, middle-aged sourball confused Rader; but with the n-jump a man could become older than his father by staying on a planet, while the father starhopped.

"I remember now. The lasers you sold those bugs were used on the Holy Cross school and killed Candy Harding. You remember her, Garfield—she was your captain."

"*Colonel* Garfield!" he snapped, his face going red. One of the marshals rapped Rader in the ribs with the butt of his laser. Rader gave him a dark look, and the man stepped back, ready to fire.

"Easy, Stevens. We don't want this crudball checking out *too* soon." Colonel Garfield sat back in his chair, his blotched face fatuously smug. "Well, Prisoner Rader, the duly-legalized marshal of Zikkala has given over your contract to the Startrade corporation for execution, as per the Treaty of Centauri." He smiled meanly, enjoying himself. "As they have no suitable prison on Zikkala, it was decided . . . legally, of course . . . to transfer you to Tura, Base One."

"Forced labor is illegal!" Wolf said, and Garfield glared at him, the smug satisfaction wiped away.

"Forced labor, *sir.*"

Rader looked at the two marshals as he saw them step toward Wolf. Rader locked eyes with the nearest, the one that had struck him earlier, and the man stopped. His hand dropped, but he arranged his face in a sullen scowl.

"I accept your prisoners," Garfield said, handing one of the marshals a signed slip. He pressed a button, and almost at once a very large muscular man came in, followed by a short stocky man with a face and neck scabbed and blotched with some kind of blue paste. They both had been bitten badly by insects, and the larger man had a nasty fungus growth on his left hand, which was suppurating.

"Yes, sir?"

"Take Rader here and this pup and—"

"Okay we leave Colonel?" one of the marshals asked. Garfield looked at him with annoyance and then nodded. The two men left quickly, and Stevens rapped Rader again as he passed.

"Watch this one, Meyers."

"What you want me to do with 'im, Colonel?" the big man asked, aiming a thumb at Rader, his other hand resting on the butt of a laser.

Garfield sat back again and looked into Rader's eyes from his little mean marbles. "Well, Meyers, I think Prisoner Rader would make a first rate Xorno-teaser."

The big, broad-shouldered man nodded, scratching at his chest. "Uh-huh. I give him a lesson, then we—"

"No," Garfield said, cutting in. "No. Just take him out and give him a Xorno to talk with." He started to laugh.

"With or without a suit?" Rader asked wryly. He was certain Garfield had orders to see that Rader died in working conditions that could later pass any Guild inspection.

"Oh, my, yes, by all means, Meyers, give Prisioner Rader a suit. But don't waste a new suit on him." He started to laugh and choked, growing very red. He bent over the edge of the desk and spat something into a wastebasket, looked at it angrily while wiping his running eyes, then back to Rader and Wolf.

"Give the kid, Wolf, some work on the Jicron line."

"Yessir." Meyers took Rader's elbow and guided him out. He was almost a head bigger and quite a few kilograms heavier. Rader gave Wolf a faint smile and shook his head. Wolf nodded back. This was not the time. Find out more about the place, the traps and routes and possibles.

Meyers grunted at the short, blue-faced guard. "Take the cleanboot punk down ta D-2. Give 'im ta Pinky." The short, bullet-headed man took Wolf's arm and yanked him away. Meyers grunted and poked at Rader to precede him along the curving corridor, away from the airlock. Rader looked around, memorizing, inspecting, evaluating, maintaining his sense of direction and orientation.

Meyers grunted again. "No think escape. No good. Stay and work, eh?" He cackled. "You do good, maybe we give you leave on Zikkala?" He laughed some more, until he choked, coughed and spit phlegm.

They arrived at the protective-suit robing room. Rader saw at once the suits were better than any he had seen before. He found a patched but serviceable suit and donned it, then was directed to get into a suit of light armor. He raised his eyebrows at that but started fastening it on as Meyers also suited up.

The armor Rader had was strong enough to stop micrometeorites, even though it might knock him down, and had superb joint-sealing. The armor atop an excellent pro-suit told him the surface of Tura was not going to be a picnic.

The airlock hissed open, and the cylindrical room was immediately invaded by swarms of insects. A curious, blue spider as big as a hatch wheel started over the edge, but Meyers casually squashed it with one of the hardwood clubs he carried. He handed Rader one, and they stepped out.

The landscape was in motion. Everywhere he looked things wiggled, crawled, flopped, jumped, leaped, dropped, rose, and flew. Despite the swarms of insects there were still plants growing, although some of their tough leaves were ragged and chewed. The ground was covered with writhing worms, and paths of squashed goo led off in several directions from the airlock.

Something pinged off the airlock door as it started to swing shut. Rader slapped at some large buzzing insects and immediately regretted it as he squashed them against the faceplate of his armored helmet.

"Come. Xorno this way." Meyers waved at him and started along one of the paths, not looking back.

He has the airlock release-mechanism. I can't get back in without him, Rader thought. He shrugged and followed. *I'll have to let them get used to me before I try something.*

Rader saw Meyers take a grip on his hardwood club as they approached a thicket of dark green plants. "Watch for Mother-in-Law," Meyers said. Almost at once, he struck out at a leaf. The leaf curled and changed color, becoming a huge insect with flapping, broken wings. *"Uh,"* Meyers said. *"Don't touch. Corrosive."*

Rader had no intention of touching. Out of the corner of his eye he saw a large dark shape move. He turned his entire body to get a better look and caught a huge glob of sticky stuff on his chest. At once a huge four-legged spider, more than a meter across, waddled out of the shadows toward him.

"Goddamn," grunted Meyers as he stepped between. Without emotion he clubbed the spider into broken parts and kicked it back from the trail. Then he turned to Rader, still cursing, and unclipped a can of spray from his belt and sprayed Rader's chest. Steam rose from the glob, which Meyers used his club to scrape off. *"Watch, damn you,"* he reprimanded. *"Ain't got no time to clean you up."*

"Then why did you?"

The big man grunted again. *"Huh. Glop gets hard, you can't move, armor fucked up, you no good for anything."*

"Thank you, mother," Rader said. Meyers looked at him with a dark, speculative glare before he turned and continued up the path.

They skirted sink holes, quicksand, a nest of one-biters that broke teeth on their armor and passed a stream of ugly-looking fluid that Rader was certain would stink if he were breathing the same air.

Rader saw Meyers duck down and cross a little glen, bent over. There didn't seem to be a reason, but he followed in the same manner. He felt two pings off his suit and realized they were crossing the hereditary paths of the Zips, the hard-shelled insects that hit like bullets.

The gravity was almost a third more than Zikkala, and Rader was getting tired by the time they reached the small valley. His armor was blotched with suiciding insects, scratched by a dive-bombing clawing bird and stained by the blood and entrails of things that had tried to eat him.

Rader paused and looked at the graceful, beautiful Xorno trees. Beneath the first one was some rust-protection armor —with a partially dissolved bit of human hipbone protruding through a cracked joint. Insects swarmed over it all, fighting for morsels.

I want to go home to Zikkala, he thought. *I will kill to go home to Zikkala.* He paused for a moment, then sighed. *I will have to kill to go home.*

The time for prayer was over. The two glowing spheres of light that were Kaleen-ka and Shir-ka-kaloon sank into the rock floor as the warriors left the chamber, hurrying lithely toward the surface and their personal and racial destiny. The cavern was silent again.

It was the time of final testing.

The Xorno trees were spread out along a wide, low valley less than a kilometer from the Startrade base. They were four or five meters high, very wide, with thick, tapering limbs that branched out from a knobby, stubby trunk, arching to the ground all around and apparently reattaching themselves to the soil. The first one Rader saw had been sliced in two by a laser and was lying in a blackened patch of sterilized soil, rotting. The next one had been drilled from a distance, but the laser beams had killed it, too.

Here and there, Rader saw ruined trees, great pale green fleshy growths with blue-tinged edges to the thick leaves, barely alive, looking wasted. But most of the trees were alive; a few were blossoming with pale lumps that swarmed with insects.

By the time Meyers and Rader stopped at the first work team, the smash-and-spray technique had become automatic. Someone was routinely walking a perimeter around the group, spraying the air and ground from a bulbous backpack and keeping much, but not all, of the deadly insect life back so the team could work.

"Rader, you watch Mullins. When he finish, you try. But first, take red pill." Meyers pointed inside his helmet, and Rader pulled back his head to look down and see a standard stim-tab helmet-dispenser loaded with red capsules. At his frown, Meyers grunted in annoyance. *"Jicron-5; give you telepathic connection to Xorno. Tell 'im, Mullins."*

Another voice came on, speaking very slowly, almost dreamily. Rader saw one of the three-man team look at him, then turn back to an Alpha-wave projector on a tripod. *"Hullo, cleanboot . . . I'm . . . Mullins . . . Take . . . the pill . . . ya gotta get into . . . the plant's . . . reference pattern . . . see?"*

Rader shrugged within his armor and reached out with his tongue, loosened a pill and sucked it in. He went over to the projector. Mullins pointed at it. *"Alpha . . . irritates the . . . hell . . . outta the plants, see? But ya gotta . . . be in tune . . . cause if ya don't . . . and it gets too mad . . . it'll spoil the iridium pearls . . . ya unnerstan?"*

"I think so. Are these things intelligent? I mean, how high on the scale?"

"Ohh . . . 'bout like a cat . . . maybe a jooska. Got roots that go down . . . spread out . . . hundreds a meters . . . we think. Sucks up the iridium . . . pumps it up . . . makes these pearl things."

Mullins seemed to be speaking a little faster now, but Rader realized he was somehow slowing down. He was getting impressions from the men around him . . . vague shapes and pale colors . . . but there was a kind of almost-visible wind coming from the Xorno tree. A sort of blue sunlight or grayish fog or . . .

The mind of the plant. It was annoyed, disturbed . . .

The impressions of the humans faded, or were disregarded, as Rader focused on the plant. The thick, fleshy leaves seemed to wiggle, to quiver. There were a few bone fragments within the cagelike construction of the limbs, and Rader noticed that behind many of the leaves were curving, flexible thorns, incurving to trap anything that got inside.

Carnivorous. Telepathic. Deadly. Surviving on a death world of murderous life forms. And rich.

The Jicron drug was surging through him now. He glanced around and blinked, for the virulent plant and insect life seemed speeded up, boiling and surging against their targets. Rader felt a swift pang of fear. *I'm slowed down—they'll get me!*

But the perimeter guard was doing a good job, and

Rader realized that the other two members of the team were guards, nothing more. With calm, unhurried efficiency, they batted and sprayed any that got through and used other cans of spray to blister off the gobs of matter that would come flying at them, sticking to their armor.

Rader turned again to the Xorno, fascinated by the delicate manner in which Mullins raised and lowered the Alpha-wave impulses, sensing the feelings of the plant.

"How long does this take?" he asked.

"A day, usually. The trick is to get the big pearls, see? Ya hit one too soon or not at the right angle and ya get one a them minis. No good. Well, good—but not as good, see?" He pointed at a bulbous swelling on the near side of the knobby trunk. *"Right there; that's the spot. These trees, they're making pearls alla time—three, four, six, eight, all in different stages a developin, see? But the pucker-spot with the bluest edges, them's the one to aim at."*

"Mullins, ya got Rader now. Bring 'im in with ya," Meyers said. He seemed to be speaking with almost inhuman speed, barely comprehensible. *If they keep me on this Jicron,* Rader thought, *I'm in trouble, too slowed down, mentally and physically.*

"Yah," Mullins said, waving at Meyers, who immediately walked off very swiftly to investigate the other teams.

An eight-legged insect with a mottled-gray carapace fell out of the sky and seized one of the guards around the helmet. Rader heard him cursing in a steady stream as he batted at the creature, which was the size of a trunk. The other guard nonchalantly batted away the huge insect from his companion's head, crushed it with several brutal blows of his hardwood club and kicked the dripping mess beyond the circle of sterilized ground. Then he sprayed the other man's head with something that sent up clouds of steam, and in moments the first man was back crushing and spraying bugs.

"Are these things dangerous?" Rader asked, pointing at the tree.

"Uh-huh." He turned and pointed at a nearby tree. There, hidden in the undergrowth, half in and half out of the ring of limbs, was a rusting suit of armor. The helmet was cracked, but there was nothing within but a few shards of bleached bones. *"They got two, three defenses. They*

*encapsulate other junk, too—mostly copper and salts 'n'
stuff. They can pop those things out like old time cannon
balls. Pop!"* He made a gesture like a fighter striking an
opponent. *"Or ya see them little-bitty pods up underneath
the top, where the branches come outta the trunk? A buncha
pollen, almost like gas. That don't bother us none, though.
Then there's the pitfalls. Right under the branches there.
Looks like solid ground, huh? Ain't. Not always. Opens
up—gulp!—ya gone."* Mullins seemed to take great satisfaction in the deadly qualities of the Xorno.

"How far can they fire those copper balls?"

*"About . . . to here. When the Xorno spits out a pearl,
the surface is soft; vulnerable, the big brains call it. Ya gotta
get ahold of it fast, afore it gets acted on by the air, the
bugs—stuff like that. And the hooks will mark 'em up."*
He pointed at a bag at his waist. *"Get 'em in there, seal 'em
up fast."* He jiggled a line in a reel behind his waist, one
with a metal ring hanging from the end. He turned toward
Rader, unfastening it awkwardly and gestured for Rader to
turn around. Mullins fastened the retrieval reel to his waist,
then handed him the bag.

*"It'll spit it out 'bout a meter out from the trunk. That
gives ya 'bout two meters to go. Now ya can't blast ya way
in, 'cause the plant'll get ruined. Startrade will have ya
stern for that. So go in and come out the same place, between the same thorn-bars, see? Domingo and Brownie will
have the line—pull ya out if ya get stuck or drop inta a
trap, see?"*

Rader saw, and didn't like.

*"If the pit opens up . . . there be maybe three, four
'round each tree, and we ain't spotted 'em here, 'cause this
is a new tree . . . and if ya fall in, don't panic. Long as the
line ain't cut we can probably pull ya out."*

"Probably—?"

Mullins made a palms-up gesture. *"Edges a them pits got
sawtooths, with a kinda acid er sumpin. Eats right through
this fancy high-test line in about ten, twenty seconds. We
ain't got nothing better, though."* He made some minor ad-
justments on the Alpha projector and turned back to Rader.
"Glad ta have ya help out."

"My pleasure," Rader said mockingly. "But what if I
don't go?"

Mullins was unperturbed. *"I'll go, then we tell Security and ol' bottom-face'll declare ya beyond the protection a the Startrade Company, 'n' toss ya out. De-clared an incorrible uh sumpin."* He gestured again.

"Without a suit, I suppose."

Mullins didn't answer. He was suddenly very alert. *"Hey, Domingo, pay attention."* One of the club-wielding guards dropped the club and turned quickly to grab Rader's back ring. The other guard sped up his efforts to control the invading insect life. *"Get ready, sucker,"* Mullins said.

A minute passed, and the flood of blue sunshine from the planet seemed to deepen and come in waves rather than a pulsating steadiness. *"Maddern hell,"* Mullins muttered. *"Good . . . Good . . ."*

The trunk of the plant seemed to writhe. Around the puckered swelling, tiny hairlike cilla wavered; then suddenly the puckering opened and a steaming sphere was ejected. It hit and rolled to a halt on the matted, decaying vegetable-matter carpet under the tree, and Mullins was screaming at him. *"Get it, ya cleanboot sucker—get it!"*

Rader ran at the tree and took both hands to wrench open the curving limbs. He felt the thorns beneath the leaves spring erect and harden in some strange way. He shouldered through and heard Mullins call out to him, *"Watch it! Gonna fire!"*

Rader threw himself toward the ground as he saw a small puckered swelling near eye level open. An object flew at him, and he felt a blow on his right shoulder. It flipped him onto his side and deadened the left arm. He saw a steaming coppery lump rolling away; then he was reaching for the gleaming pearlloid.

"Scoop it inna bag, you scum-brain! Toldja it was delicate! Don't touch it, ya tank-thief!"

Rader put the mouth of the sack around the still steaming ball, barely noticing it had a dull beauty, and collected the sphere of iridium. He turned back, starting to go through the way he had made through the thorny limbs, so as not to entangle his backline—and the ground fell away beneath him.

"Pull, Domingo, ya knob! Pull!"

Rader dropped into darkness, a great irregular pit that was filled with some kind of dust. The air filled with bits of falling crud from the surface as he landed heavily on the sticky bottom of the pit. He caught a glimpse of the sides of the pit, where the curving limbs went into the ground, spreading out, enmeshing themselves into a fiber cage of great strength. Then the saw-toothed edges of the trapdoors—eight-sided sections that overlapped—started to close. He leaped up, but the sticky stuff on the floor of the pit clung to him, slowing him down. He didn't make it up before the panels swung inexorably closed.

It was at once dark, but with faint dots of light where the panels came together. Rader made certain the sack was firmly attached to his belt and leaped for the walls. He dug his fingers into the soil around the sturdy roots as he felt the backline tighten. He was drawn up and helped pull by grasping the roots. He reached upward, feeling for the edges of the pit covers. One of the lines broke and he almost fell back into the pit. His injured arm, barely functioning, was screaming in pain as his fingers dug into the dirt and grasped desperately onto the roots. With all his strength he pulled down at the edge of one panel. He saw the metallized gloves being scratched, then etched by the secretions of the sharp edges. Drops fell onto his helmet and sizzled, etching the hard plastic. Suddenly the panel he was pulling at broke, almost dropping him back down into the pit again.

Rader reached up, grasped the lower part of a root where it entered the ground and pulled himself halfway out of the pit. *"Keep ya head down!"* Mullins cried. Another coppery ball crashed through the leaves over Rader's head. His left arm was still almost useless, and throbbed painfully, but he pulled himself out and slithered through the thorn-bars. Domingo and Mullins were taking in the slack, helping him across the few meters of raw, almost animate, Turan soil.

He got a good close-up look at the fertile soil: worms in every stage of life and decay, eating each other, set upon by insects from the size of mites to fist-sized, hard-shelled, eight-legged horrors with endless appetites. *The whole damned planet feeds on itself,* he thought as he got to his feet slowly. Domingo sprayed him with different cans held in each gloved paw.

Mullins took the sack and looked in. *"Good. Good."* He clipped the sack to his belt and peered in at Rader. *"Ya*

*better go on back. Another half hour 'n' those spores'll
eat right through that good Startrade armor. Ya did a good
job. Domingo, ya take 'im back."*

Domingo set a fast pace, and Rader felt the effects of
the Jicron wearing off. The blue sunlight of the Xorno
faded away, and then the dull red glow of Domingo's mind
seemed to fade into the background. The writhings of the
plant and insect life seemed to slow, too, as Rader's per-
ceptions caught up with it all.

He heard Domingo grunt a warning just in time to see
a creature like a sectioned worm in blotched-green armor
rise up from a thicket of thorny blue-gray plants. Clouds
of insects flew up at the creature's sudden rise. Domingo
started to run along the trail, but Rader was cut off as the
green thing crashed across the path. It turned toward Rader,
thick pale antennae twitching at him and two large faceted
eyes glittering. The length of it curled and uncurled in a
jerky way, as though it were a snake with its back broken in
several places. But it was a huge worm, a meter thick and
five or six meters long, and not a snake.

Rader backed up slowly, looking from right to left. The
thick underbrush was alive with things. He couldn't out-
wait the worm; there wasn't time. The creature, having
moved suddenly into his path, now moved sluggishly, weaving it's head, inching toward him, not in inches but in meter-
long advances. Rader retreated before it, and called out to
Domingo.

"Hey, Domingo, what is this thing?" Domingo didn't
answer. "Mullins? Hey, Mullins, there's a big green worm
here. Mullins?" No answer. *Goddamn bastards,* he thought.
*Every man for himself, huh? Only reason they pulled me
out of the pit was the pearl, and maybe the suit.*

Angry, Rader looked for a weapon. When he found it, it
was living. Or rather, when *it* found Rader.

There was a rustle of leaves, and Rader turned to see a
spiny thing that looked more like a plant than an animal
or insect move into the path. He was caught between two
Tura horrors, the smallest of which was twice his size. The
spiny thing rolled, with its long spines acting as legs when
on the bottom and as flexible, spike weapons when up. It
rolled toward Rader, and he saw that several of the spines
already had impaled creatures upon them—insects, a still-

writhing snake in brilliant colors, something that looked like a watermelon with hair—and it came at him as though it were absolutely confident that Rader was next.

Rader looked from spiny ball to approaching worm and around at the hostile jungle. He backed away from the rolling spiny sphere and tried to study both of the things that menaced him. As if it were a porcupine, there seemed to be no way for a weaponless man—or someone armed with anything less than a laser—to get to the creature. The worm was different. It was slower, with no obvious weaponry except size and weight, but the nightmare creatures of Tura had surprising attributes, as he was finding out.

Rader chose the worm. Not only was Base One in that direction, but the creature moved far more sluggishly. Rader timed himself, hoping that neither of the monsters would make a last-minute rush. When he had almost backed into the worm and the spiny menace was almost upon him, Rader turned and dove at the worm, striking at its hard shell with his fists and grasping the edges of the carapace sections. He pulled himself over the worm and dropped to the other side just as it turned toward him. At that moment the spiny creature moved to attack. There was a high-pitched squeal and the worm reared, knocking Rader into the brush with a whip of his long body. Rader jumped out quickly, brushing away at the things that clung to him and started running down the trail.

A red light went on in his helmet and a tiny Integrity Alarm went off. He was leaking air. Or worse, the air of Tura was getting in.

Domingo was standing by the airlock, methodically crushing bugs as Rader ran up. Without a word he thumbed the closure as Rader staggered inside. He hit the decon switch as the lock closed, and the small chamber filled with gas, then that was sucked away and they were bathed in several kinds of rays, emitting from the ceiling, walls, and lamps set flush in the floor. Domingo raised his arms and spread his legs to be certain the decontamination procedures got to every part of his suit's exterior. Rader followed his example, and in a few minutes they were admitted to the dome by the sullen watch officer.

Domingo sprayed foam all over Rader's armor, then it was flushed away, and Rader returned the favor. They stumped into the warding room and took off the heavy suits. Once they were both unencumbered, Rader said, "Domingo," and hit him on the jaw.

The stocky Startrader slammed back against the suit lockers and fell heavily to the floor. He looked at Rader with dazed eyes and a hurt expression. "Whatcha do that for; huh? Goddamn." He waggled his jaw, then his ferret's eyes darted warily at Rader as the big man stepped closer. "Hey, no kicking, no kicking!"

"Why did you leave me out there, you son-of-a-bitch?"

Domingo looked sullen.

"Aw, hell . . ." He made a vague gesture then almost rolled himself into a ball as Rader reached for him. "*Hey!* C'mon, man, it's the Colonel. Hell, ya gotta know that! I wunt leave no real buddy, ya gotta believe that, but the Colonel he said . . ."

"Let me die, huh? A convenient example of Tura flora or fauna hits at me—look the other way, right?"

Domingo glanced up at him and nodded. "Nothing personal," he said. "Startrade's got us by the *cojones,* man. We gotta buy at the company store. You know how that is. A man's credit goes or his records get lost—hell. Ya can starve t'death if the Colonel gets bony about ya."

Rader straightened up, nodding. He looked down at the man, who was cowering and trying to look like he just happened to like it down there. "Get up. I won't hit you again."

"Hell, man, they own our soul. I got a wife . . . no, really, a real fine woman from Tookamorga, back in The Painters. She's supposed to be along the ship after next. I screw it up and they'll nullify the goddamn contract and skip her right by here." He sat down on a bench and put both hands palm up. "Listen, ya gotta believe me."

The flood of words embarrassed Rader. He no longer felt anger at the short, stocky man; instead, he felt pity. Whipsawed by fate and a greedy industrial complex, he was destined for doom. "Skip out on them," he said. "Hide

out some place until they go on by. You don't owe the
blood-suckers anything."

"Yeah, like where, man? Ya gotta have papers in any
place big enough to disappear in. On some pioneer world,
they find ya easy, if they wanta. Or it's too damned dangerous—like Tura here. So you go along, hoping for a bonus
hit, something special, and ya can bargain ya way out. It
happens. Sometimes. Just often enough so ya don't give up
hope. The bastards."

Rader turned to him. "Maybe we can help each other.
Zikkala is a beautiful place. You could make it there. The
guilds would help you . . . if you help them . . . and me."

Domingo looked confused, then puzzled. "No guild's
gonna help a nuthing like me. That's for the fancy dudes,
with money and punch."

"I'm Tiger Guild starbuck on Zikkala. If I say so, it happens. Help me . . . and I'll help you. I'm going to live
through this; I'm going back and I'm going to kill Lockhart."

Domingo's eyes grew big. *"Lockhart?* Oh, now, hey—
that's a whole different . . . ah . . . look, Lockhart's as
mean a mutha as ever came along."

"So am I. And Lockhart is a dead man."

Domingo looked at Rader, and for a moment he didn't
breathe. "Look, we better get inta the showers, huh? I
stink like a Lacterian outhouse and you ain't any better."

Rader followed him into the shower room just as Mullins
and Brownie came in, dripping foam from their steaming
suits. Rader stood under the sonic beams and felt the crud
and sweat and skin irritations slough off. "What about it,
Domingo?"

"I dunno. I gotta think on it, Rader." He was silent
a moment, head hanging, turning this way and that under
the beams. "Ya mean it about the Guild?"

"Yes."

"I . . ." He stopped as Mullins and Brownie came in.

Out of his armor, Mullins was a pale-skinned, freckled
man with rusty hair and a number of skin eruptions.
Brownie was dark-skinned and sullen and gave Rader a
baleful eye. They were joined by a third man, thin and
wiry, with hooded dead eyes and lank hair, who Rader
assumed was the perimeter guard.

"Well, well, Rader, so ya got past ol' Greenie, huh?"

Mullins laughed. "That bugger's been hanging around all week. Now we'll have a stinkin mess on the trail for a while."

"The spikey get it?" Domingo asked, and Mullins nodded.

"The carrion bugs had it stripped down ta the shell by the time we got passed," Mullins said. "The shelter-crawlies will have the pieces hauled off ta build their little forts, but for a day or so we'll halfta go easy. Them greenies have mates."

As Rader stepped out of the sonic beams and began to don a fresh tunic, Mullins eyed him from the shower pads. "Hey, you, Rader." Rader looked at him but went on dressing. "What has Garfield got against you, anyway?"

"He and I were in the Mercenaries together." He glanced at Domingo. "In The Painters. He got kicked out."

"You did it?"

"He did it himself. Sold energy weapons to a bunch of big arthropods, and they wiped out a children's school." He shrugged. "Couldn't prove it, not legally, so he was discharged."

"Sounds like him," Mullins said. "That all?"

Rader looked into his eyes. "And Lockhart sent me here."

Mullins nodded as if that was no news. "Yeah, I heard. You're lucky, inna way. I've seen Lockhart gut a coupla fancies—right nice-looking females, not no used-up dogs—jist because they annoyed him."

"He's playing it a bit more legally now. I'm Tiger Guild starbuck for Zikkala. Joint guild, really, with the Dragon. I need help and I can offer *our* help, the Guild's help, when this is over."

Mullins looked suspicious, and Brownie and the perimeter guard seemed to be acting as though they weren't there. *And probably run to tattle,* Rader thought. *But Mullins will know that, and if he bites, he'll stop them. If he can.*

Mullins didn't say much, and none of the Startrade men looked at each other as they finished the sonic showers and dressed in worn but clean clothing. "Ya better get back to ya cell, Rader," Mullins said. "At least till mess time."

Domingo passed close to Rader and gave him a quick, impassive look. *I've planted a seed,* Rader thought. Mullins took him along to a small, bare room that seemed no different from the rest in that corridor. They passed a number of sullen, rather introverted-looking men en route, but none of them paid much attention.

Rader inspected the room, saw the blotches on the walls and floor and in the corner, the short hardwood club, stained and nicked. There were story blocks in the table's drawer, mostly porn from Triska and New Africa and a documentary on xerophytic farming on dry planets. *Did he want to retire to some sunny world, after he made his score?*

Rader sat down on one of the two bunks and reviewed what he knew of the base and of their security procedures. He knew he had to escape soon, before chance or error or Garfield's instructions got him. He couldn't leave until a ship was there to leave in. Guards. Airlock. Exterior flora and fauna. Lander guards. Ship guards. No warning could be sent from the base, or it was all over. That meant destroying or controlling communications. He flexed his arm, which was feeling better, and massaged it. *And speed, lots of speed,* he thought.

Wolf Briggs came in, escorted by a white-coated, brutal-faced man who reminded Rader of a mole. The youth flopped into a sprawl upon the other bunk and grinned weakly at Rader. "We're dead, and this is hell."

Rader nodded rueful agreement.

Wolf looked up. "I thought they'd guard us better. That door isn't locked. There are no guards at the end of the hall." He shrugged.

"Where are we going to go? Not outside. I imagine the security tightens up when a ship comes in. And that's when we have to make our break. In fact, it's the only time, as I see it."

"What about breaking out at minimum security times and stealing their armored traveler? It's a big thing, equipped for long distance explorations—flame guns, laser turrets, waldoes, everything."

"And do what? They warn the lander and we never get off-planet."

"Uh, maybe I could steal it, and they'd think you were in it, too. And while they're out chasing me, you hide out and zap the lander crew." He looked hopefully at Rader, who sighed inwardly. *Every young boy wants to grow up to*

*be a hero. Those who try that once too often don't always
live to enjoy the reputation.*

"Good idea, Wolf, but I'd like to get us both out of here."
His eyes bore into Wolf. "Don't you try anything until we're
ready, understand?"

"Yes, sir."

The tiny speaker over the door buzzed and announced
a meal about to be served. Rader slapped Wolf's knee and
suggested they eat.

The mess hall was a big room, the biggest Rader had
seen in the Base One dome. The walls were lined with
electronic games of chance, with food and drink dispensers,
a few wallscreens with tape-block libraries next to them,
and a large framed notice of COMPANY RULES.

Men in worn jumpers and stained tunics were edging
past a long dispensary table where irritable cooks ladled
out various kinds of glop. Rader got in line, and Wolf fell
in behind. They took trays and heaping bowls of various
kinds of food, without knowing what any of it was.

"I pass on that," Wolf said, indicating a great steaming
tray of blackened lobsterlike creatures. "It looks too local."

"Can I have your share?" the man behind Wolf said at
once. When the youth nodded the man speared two of the
insectile things and grinned at Wolf as though he had put
something over. "Only thing worth eating here, practically.
Tastes like Terran lobster crossed with Debussy worm gall."
He smacked his lips and hurried away, looking down happily. He was almost the only one smiling in the room.

Rader saw Mullins at a table, beckoning to him, and
they went over. Rader introduced Wolf, who sat looking
suspiciously at the bowls of various vegetable matter and
stewlike mush.

"That iridium pearl weighed in at three point one kilos,
Rader. Some high arc dandy will have it on a pedestal back
inna Inner Worlds, telling lies about how the brave, frontier
Startrade em-ploy-ees wrestled it from the jaws uh a terrible
monster plant." He chuckled and scooped up some of his
mush, tasted it and made a face. "Certainly keeps ya guess-

ing. Is it crawly worms, stompers, or some kinda capsuled crap from Company stores?"

Wolf gulped and shoved the food away. "Ya gonna eat that?" the man to Wolf's left said at once, reaching.

"Leave it alone," Rader said. To Wolf he said, "Eat it."

"But . . ."

"Eat. Like the man said, where are you going to go?"

Wolf nodded and pulled the tray back, then lifted a spoonful of mush and peered at it closely, which caused Mullins to almost giggle. "Don't look too closely, boy—it might look back."

"Eat," Rader said and followed his own advice. The mush tasted bitter, with an aftertaste of sour milk. The brown lumps under a pinkish sauce tasted like overripe banana. The meat was like burnt toast. Their mugs of greenish drink tasted like flat beer, but was spicy hot.

Rader turned to Mullins. "Say, how often do ships land here, anyway?"

The freckled man opened his eyes slightly and looked at Rader, his pale lips curving in a smile. "Why ya wanna know?" he asked slyly. "Ya got some place ta go?"

Rader shrugged. "Want to know everything, of course. I don't plan on staying here. Maybe I can grab one and run."

Wolf blinked at Rader's casual announcement of their plans, but Mullins only grinned. " 'Bout every week, from Zikkala; every eight, nine days, anyway. We're just getting set up, so nothing is worked out real tight yet." His voice was soft and almost lost in the noise of the relaxing Startrade crews. He leaned toward Rader. "Ya ain't gonna get off, man, I'm tellin ya. Too smart for ya. They done all this before. With Garfield on ya stern, ya ain't got a chance a making it another week."

Rader ignored that. "How many men are here?" he asked.

" 'Bout four hunnerd here," a man down the table said. " 'Bout three hunnerd each at the other two bases." Rader shifted his attention to the thin, sallow-skinned man he recognized as the perimeter guard.

"More coming in?"

The man shrugged, his eyes hooded and restless. "They never tella ya." He hesitated and licked his dark lips. "Ya really gonna try to bust off?" Rader nodded. "Aren't you afraid I'll leak onya?"

Rader shrugged. "So what? If they didn't think I was going to try, they'd find *that* strange. Garfield knows me."

The thin man nodded judiciously, then jerked his head faintly toward the sleeping quarters. He got up, stretched, picked up his tray and slumped toward the garbage containers. He scraped in the leftovers and tossed the dirty tray onto a stack and gave Rader a look over his shoulder, then shuffled off.

Rader got up and grinned at Wolf. "You want dessert?"

"My god, what might it be—frozen bug-eye or spider pie?"

Rader laughed and took his tray to the garbage, then walked on after the thin man, with Wolf following.

"My name is Deft," the thin man said in the corridor as he turned. "I'd like to get outta here, too—except there ain't no way in ten worlds I'm gonna get free of the Company, not legally. I know that now; dint before." He eyed Rader suspiciously. "You mean it, 'bout some a use being able t'settle on Zikkala?"

"If you help me, yes. There's room. Two-thirds hasn't even been explored yet."

The man was silent a long time, searching Rader's face, then looking at Wolf as well. "All right," he said. "I'll help ya. Talk ta Domingo and Brownie, too. Mullins . . . well, I dunno. He's . . . odd sometimes. One time he's cussin out the Company, the next he's kissin stern. But he's no dropped core. He's smart enough, even if he ain't got no edu-cation."

"We'll need to move fast, without alerting the starship," Rader said. "That means we either control or destroy the communications here." Deft nodded. "Some . . . some of us may have to stay behind and hold the fort." Deft nodded again.

"Yeah," he said. "Figures." He shrugged his thin shoulders. "Well, why not?" He shuffled away, and Rader went back toward the mess hall with Wolf, stopping just outside.

"They're desperate men, all of them," he said, "but they'll need to be constantly reassured. They've been lied to all their lives, and they're suspicious."

"Anything's better than baked bug for dinner," Wolf said, making a face. "Even getting zapped."

Rader grinned and said, "Let's circulate. Sound out the people you've been working with, find out what you can."

"We better hurry. Look at the way they're popping pills."

All the wallscreens were on, and all were showing flesh. Beautiful naked women in flashy shows and erotic spectacles; a diamond dancer from Centauri; cloned look-alikes in dazzling graphic choreography from Xolotl; a raw, unsophisticated porno from Gottlieb, with a cocaine-belching *trierotiphile* mating with a panting human female who was tattooed with flowers. Wall dispensers belched out a variety of pills; the men leered and hooted at the screens while downing the pills of their choice.

Rader found Mullins half-asleep, with his head in his arms, and lifted him up. He'd taken some kind of striped pill. "Where's your quarters?" Rader asked over the din.

The laughter and crude jibes of the Startrade crews diminished as Rader helped Mullins down the passage and into room 304. He set him down on the couch, and Mullins mumbled something unintelligible. Rader swung Mullins' feet up and pulled off his boots.

He straightened up and looked down at the pale, freckled man. *Poor bastard. Legal slave.* Rader looked around the room, which was slightly more decorated than Rader's Spartan cell. A tri-dee of a middle-aged woman, with what looked like fern trees in the background. A big box of Mind-Mover pills. The empty shell of some kind of animal or bug with an intricate and quite lovely swirl of colors on the curving back. A plastic box of video cubes and a battered and much-mended reader. Rader picked up the box and looked at the titles. *Scenic Tchaikovsky III, Triton —the Underwater Paradise of Terra, The Women of Murlo.* A few had hand-written labels: *Meg on Piranesi, Picnic on Grayhorn Is., Peggy's First Birthday, Bobby's 2nd.*

Rader put down the box and looked again at the freckled man. He was surprised to see that the man's eyes were open —and studying him. Mullins's voice was slurred and slow, but he smiled as he spoke. "I been thinkin . . . you . . . me . . . that kid . . . my crew . . . maybe a coupla others. We bust outta here, huh?" He hesitated a long time, his eyes wet and glistening. "You ain't bulling us 'bout being able to . . . to set on Zikkala with no trouble? No reprisals?"

"No," Rader said. "We'll find a place. A good place."

"All right," Mullins said, closing his eyes. "I'm with ya. And if I say so, m'crew, too. Satisfied?"

"Not until I get to Zikkala."

Mullins smiled, and his eyelids fluttered. "Yeah . . ."

"Mullins?" The pale, freckled face twitched, but he didn't open his eyes. "Where's your family?"

An expression of great sadness came over his face as Mullins spoke softly and with a choke in his voice. "Dead. Company took 'em. Took 'em on, ahead. Never caught up. They've been dead a century a more. Goddamn n-drive."

Rader took a deep breath and let it out slowly. "All right, Mullins. We'll do it."

"Bugger the Company?"

"Yes. And more."

Mullins smiled. "Yeah," he said dreamily. "And more."

Rader went out and slid the door closed. *Startrade is not very smart,* he thought. *They should build, not destroy; maybe then their own men wouldn't be so quick to turn on them.*

Rader was deep into a conversation with a couple of garrulous and old—for Startrade employees—utility men who had made the triangle trip to Bases Two and Three several times. They were telling him about the pit spiders that could almost trap a twelve-meter traveler and the dog-sized beetles that were smart enough to roll rocks down on their enemies.

Then Colonel Garfield came in. Rader saw him at once. He stopped near the entrance, backed by six burly men with dead eyes and sullen, mean faces. Rader saw him scan the gathering of workers, then find Rader and come toward him. Rader swung around slightly, to disengage himself from the two old men and keep them out of trouble; he gave the impression he was eavesdropping and the two Startraders caught on at once.

"So then Johnson 'n' Willard *bought* the first born a this Pyrancton, see—this on Pyramus, remember—then they . . . oh, there's the Colonel. Good evenin, sir," the speaker said deferentially.

Garfield ignored the man. His eyes looked scornfully at Rader. "So you got back." Rader just looked at him. "You won't always be so lucky, Prisoner Rader." His eyes gleamed with fanaticism, and for the first time Rader considered that he might be quite mad, as well as bitter and mean. "The odds are against you, *Captain* Rader." Garfield seemed to take pleasure in that. "Yes, the odds are very much against you," he repeated.

Rader shrugged. "One day at a time, Colonel. 'Course here the days are, what, eighteen hours. But still, a day at a time."

"That greenie'll have a mate, Rader. Always do. Squirt acid, you know. Powerful stuff. Attacks helmet plastic like it was rotten paper." He smiled brightly, his face flushing. "Like paper, Spores get in, you're blinded; they eat out your eyes, stop your breathing—you're dead in two, three minutes . . . but they are very nasty minutes, Rader."

The men in their immediate vicinity had fallen silent. They didn't look at Rader or the Colonel, but they were listening. Rader stood up slowly so as not to alarm the colonel's guards. He stretched and yawned, almost in Garfield's face. "Been a long day, Colonel; think I'll just go on to bed."

Garfield flushed, this time with anger. He obviously didn't like Rader standing, for the lean dark man was taller. "Not so quick, Prisoner Rader! You still have some duties. You are not going to live the easy, high-paying life these other turtles do. No, not you! Schelling, show Prisoner Rader his second-shift duties."

Rader shrugged and went out after the guard, passing along through the tables filled with men falling silent. He felt the fear and the resentment around him and noted it. How many could he count on to help, come the crunch?

Schelling crooked a finger and took Rader through the kitchens and to a cargo airlock. He handed Rader a hook with a handle, a lance about two meters long, and a belt knife, then pointed at the lock. "No suit?" Rader asked narrowly.

"Ya don't need one. Blister dome outside. Just go out there, kill one of the rollers, tear off the shell and skin 'im. Spray the meat down good—there's a hose with a Decon-2 nozzle—and bring the hunks in ta the cooks." He jerked a thumb at the kitchen where helpers were spraying sonic hoses over the dishes, their heads in protective respirators.

"What's the catch?"

The guard shrugged. "You can handle it. Just don't let one a them bastids corner you, though."

"Oh. Big enough to hurt, huh?"

"Uh-huh," the guard said stoically. He gave Rader a gentle push toward the airlock and began thumbing the controls. The hatch swung back, and Rader went in. The first lock swung shut, then the other lock swung open. Almost at once, a gray-shelled lump, taller than he was, struck at the hatch. It bounded away, and Rader got a look at what was out there.

The airlock opened into another dome, much smaller, with stained floors and walls, and an exterior airlock beyond. Inside were three monsters, a meter high with many sturdy, stubby legs. As he watched, one of them had a convulsion and bucked into a ring, propelling itself at the airlock with great speed. Rader dodged to one side and jabbed at it with a spear, which skittered off the gray plates of armor. Another of the rollers bucked up and came at him, spinning, propelled by the sturdy legs, careening off the dome wall and almost falling as it writhed around into a flat slug almost six meters long.

They seemed very muscular, but Rader saw they had only one attack: become a huge rolling ball, crush what was there, and drop back flat. They had a trapdoor mouth, lined with hundreds of little teeth, eyes with hard-shelled lids, and one stubby horn. Rader was already tired, his left arm still weak, and his reflexes slowed. The beasts were obviously trapped, kept handy for a supply of fresh meat, and another of Garfield's ways to reduce Rader's chances a swiftly as possible. *After all,* he thought, *how many of these monsters can I evade in any one day?*

The third gray creature moved slower, as if older or sick, but it, too, hurled itself at Rader. He ducked behind the airlock door to escape it, then became aware that the lock was closing. "Hey!" he shouted. The hatch was his edge, something to duck behind. But the thick door was swinging closed—remorselessly.

"Just one, Rader; you need only kill one," Garfield said over a speaker. Rader looked up, saw a camera and a

speaker high above the airlock. *"And shell it, of course. And get the meat in—while you watch out for the others."* The security chief laughed, and there was a maniac edge to it. *"Go right ahead. You have an appreciative audience of one, at least."*

Rader did not reply. The first creature charged again, and Rader evaded it, quickly studying it for patterns. He saw almost at once that the gray-shelled "roller" came straight from whatever direction it was pointing when it was flat. It rolled until it hit something or lost momentum, then disconnected and flattened out. Sometimes the roller hit the dome and unrolled on its side or back, then writhed muscularly around onto its eight legs again. Once the pattern was discerned it was not difficult to keep clear of the creatures. Rader simply waited until one unrolled on his back; then he plunged the two-meter spear into its soft underbelly. The roller convulsed, curling up, snapping the spear, and went into a writhing death dance.

Rader kept clear, watched the other creatures, and waited for the thing to die. The dome was filled with the smell of sweat and ichor, a burnt-wool and too-sweet perfumy odor that was suffocating. The other two rollers lost interest and flattened out to lie near the outer airlock, their eyes hooded with the hard-shell lids.

There was nothing from Garfield, and Rader noted that the camera had stopped turning after the action. He squatted, waiting, until he was certain the roller was dead. Then he spent a long hour with the hook and knife ripping off the shell. The dead carcass smelled like excrement and cheap perfume, but Rader stayed doggedly at it. He was throwing the big curving shell-sections to the side, exposing the meaty slabs of yellowish pale flesh when the airlock opened again and a cook and two thin, lank-haired helpers came out. They kept an eye on the two live rollers as they sank hooks into the carcass and tugged it inside the lock.

"That's enough," the cook said to Rader. "Go clean up, ya stink." As Rader turned to exit through the interior hatch, the cook called quietly after him. "Ya did a good job. I take 'em down with a stunner or a laser, myself." He looked embarrassed and took it out on his helpers. "All right, you miserable gluttons—watch what you're doing!"

Rader paused and looked back. The cook looked over at him and raised his chin in a silent question. "Hey, cookie," Rader said, "what sort of wine do you serve with roast bug?" The cook made a face, and Rader went back to his room.

Wolf Briggs heaved a sigh of relief when Rader came in. "I was just about to go recruit a suicide squad to save you, but Domingo said you could handle the rollers—whatever they are."

"Tomorrow's dinner, but I think I'll pass. What did you find out?

"Ship in eight, nine days—at least it's on schedule; there might be one sooner, but we can't count on it."

"Let's get some sleep." Rader undressed and went to the showers—stained plastic cubicles that sprayed gray water reeking of disinfectant. When he returned Wolf was still not asleep. Rader slipped into his bunk and turned off the light. He lay thinking, but no plans crystallized, only vague fragments of unrelated ideas, which did more to frustrate him than anything else.

Sleep came at last, and with it came dreams. Dreams of Alena . . . and of Lockhart. Lockhart's face on some giant spider creature, and Alena going to it . . .

In the morning Rader would have been much happier if he had not dreamed at all.

Rader did survive the next eight days, but just barely. He continued working on Mullins' Xorno team, extracting, so far, twelve iridium pearls with a combined weight of more than sixty kilograms, plus another seventy or so kilograms in dented cannon balls of different types of metal, mostly copper. It was not a great harvest, but enough to keep Garfield and the Company happy.

Rader had proved quite good at pearl retrieval and at recognizing the pitfalls under the spreading limbs. He fell only twice, but both times got out before the eight-sided trap-leaves closed over him. With Mullins and his crew reacting quicker, there was less chance of him getting caught below ground.

The trips to and from the Xorno "orchards" were still very dangerous. Mullins banded with the other crew chiefs to demand they be transported in the Company's armored traveler, two tightly-packed crews at a time. The "bus service" to the work site gave Rader a chance to study the functioning of the tank—he knew he could operate it in an emergency.

"Ship's due in orbit—oh, nine twenty tomorra," Deft whispered to Rader in the mess hall. He made a gesture with his spoon. "Fella in communicashuns told me. Lander down 'bout eleven." He looked around. "But lifting 'fore we get back at night, I hear."

Rader stared into his brown stew. "I'll have to come back early . . . sick or wounded," he said quietly. Mullins looked at him from across the table, chewing stoically.

"Need a couple men bring ya back, you hurt that bad."

"Maybe it shouldn't be Rader," Wolf said. "Garfield might just refuse entrance." He looked at Mullins, who nodded.

"Boy's right. *I* get hurt, muh crew brings me back, alla ya." He nodded with satisfaction and spooned in more stew. "Always wanted ta be a holo-actor, y'know? Carryin on 'n' all." He grinned and winked at Wolf.

"All right," Rader said quietly, "here's what we do . . ."

Morning brought surprises. Colonel Garfield appeared himself at their cell and ordered Rader out. "Got a new job for you, Rader." He was grinning, and it was a mean, vicious smile. "You're going to Base Two for a little more training."

Rader felt his stomach sink. Their carefully worked out plan was ruined, and it was as if Norris Garfield knew that he had wrecked it. For the first time, Rader thought seriously about the possibility of a traitor in their group.

"Get along that way," Garfield ordered. He was backed by three burly guards. Wolf looked sick as they brushed him aside. Rader wouldn't give Garfield the satisfaction of asking where he was being taken, or why. Probably because he really knew why: Garfield had his orders to get Rader killed in a "legitimate" way and keeping him in new situations would do it, at least on Tura.

They went through a dome-skin lock into the transportation blister and climbed into one of the big transporters that was housed there. At least two of the guards kept an eye on Rader all the time, so he just belted himself into a padded seat and watched things through the nearest port.

The transporter went out through the stained airlock and rolled into the jungle. Rader began to pay more attention to the interior workings of the transporter. A map was projected on a screen, and a series of lights marked a route. He saw the gap in the line as Garfield did. "Damn! Shaw, get a marker replacement ready."

The assistant driver got up and opened a locker, then pulled out a bright red pole about as thick as his arm and two meters long. He started to get into a suit, but Garfield stopped him. "No, let Rader do it."

With an expression of relief the assistant handed Rader the armor, helped him get into it and adjust it to his larger size. Rader said nothing and kept his face expressionless.

"Got to keep the marker line working," Garfield said with great amusement, his eyes bright. "With the sunspot activity bumming up our communications, these markers only work for about a kilometer or so, in each direction. If one goes, we can always get to the next, but if two go out, well . . ." He grinned. "Damn jungle grows so fast we can't keep a trail open."

"Do I get a weapon or do I use my dazzling personality?" Rader asked.

"Ohh . . . I don't think a weapon is necessary. Just be quick. If you can't find the old marker, just plant the tube somewhere out of the track."

Rader fastened the faceplate and walked into the airlock, stooping to avoid the low ceiling. The transporter stopped, and the outer hatch opened. The bugs came at once, and Rader picked up a stained and splintered club and whacked at a few of the bigger ones. He dropped down to the ground, kicked free from the vine that wrapped itself sluggishly around his leg and looked around for the old marker.

He saw a glimpse of red in a nearby clump of haze plants and walked toward it. Then he realized that the red was just the empty carapace of some insect as big as his head. He shrugged and drove the pointed end of the marker into the ground. He flipped the switch on top. "You getting that?" he asked.

"Loud and clear," the driver said.

Rader started back to the transporter. Something long and lithe, like a snake with legs, raced at him, biting him on an armored ankle. He clubbed it and kept on. Some sort of insect or bird dive-bombed him, splashing his head with a green goo. He had only a small patch of clear helmet, on the right side, and blotchy vision through the rest of his faceplate.

Then he saw the transporter moving off.

"Hey!" he said without thinking.

"Just keep looking for that ruined marker, Rader," Garfield said. *"We'll pick you up on the way back—in a few days. But don't you worry none—we'll give you a real nice burial, with holographics going back to the Guild and everything. Providing, of course, there's anything to bury."*

The big cylindrical transporter was moving off through the jungle, making it's own path. A laser spat out, from the domed turret, cutting through some smoke vines, which exploded, spurting a pale yellowish mist into which the transporter disappeared. Without thinking Rader started running after it.

The smoke vines were still puffing out their last lethal clouds as he ran through. He stopped on the upwind side, saw the path of crushed vegetation left by the vehicle. He checked his air supply. Nine minutes at normal breathing rate; much less while running. He ran.

He caught a glimpse of the transporter as it felled a tall, swaying tree, which crashed like a tufted whip. Then something struck Rader in the side, toppling him into a carpet of catch'em, a thorny low bush with powerful thorn-claws. He ripped himself free and peered around awkwardly through the tiny cleared spot in his faceplate. A creature something like a spider, half as tall as he, with eight smooth heavy-muscled legs and a face like a mad parrot, was recovering from its leap at Rader. It advanced on him swiftly, and Rader dodged away, kicking at it. He didn't have time to fight it. He started running after the transporter, but the spider-thing came after him.

Rader fell again, entangled by the long thin tendrils of some half-plant, half-animal that had been crushed by the transporter's passage. Again he ripped loose just in time to get away from the drooling spider-thing's grasp but not before it spewed liquid over his back. Within seconds his equipment-belt was partially dissolved and it had slipped down to his knees. He tore away at the goo-covered straps, flinging them into the face of the eight-legged horror lumbering after him.

Damn thing is dissolving high-tension plastic! he thought in rising fear. *What will it do to my faceplate or the armor joints and seals?*

There was no time to think about that. Rader put on a burst of speed and caught sight of the metal crawler ahead, going slower, down a hill toward a sluggish, muddy stream. The forward laser turrets were firing at armored creatures that were half-hidden in the dark waters.

Rader ran hard, hoping that all their attention was on the river and the large whatevers in it. The rear laser turret seemed unoccupied, but Rader couldn't be certain. He ran a zig-zag path after the crawler and threw himself at its rear airlock hatch. He took hold of the manual controls, but they seemed to be locked.

Silently swearing, Rader pulled himself up onto the traveler itself and risked a peek into the slits of the laser turret. There was no one there, but he could see into the twelve-meter vehicle. Garfield was standing between the two drivers, pointing and gesturing as they went into the water slowly. The three guards were at the two front-side laser turrets and up in the flame-gun turret.

Rader was starting to crawl toward the top turret when something landed heavily upon him. Four-fingered hands clawed at him, and thirty-two knifelike hooks tore at his armor and faceplate as the eight-legged spider sought to pry him loose from the traveler's rear end.

He struck at the creature with balled fists, but it seemed impervious to the blows. Rader struggled around to the side of the vehicle, where he braced his feet on the metal rungs of a ladder and hooked one arm through an exterior tank brace. He kicked at the spider until he could get his feet up. Then with great effort, he hammered away at the thing until it released him and he could kick it into the water. The spider-thing struck the water and was instantly seized by an armored black creature with bulging, hooded eyes and gleaming teeth and dragged below the surface.

Rader pulled himself up the ladder as the traveler pulled out into the water. Other shapes wiggled through the dark liquid, and Rader heard a hollow boom and scraping sounds as something attacked the traveler below the water line. He also began to smell something and knew that his suit was beginning to leak.

He spread himself flat on the curving roof, hoping that the flame-gun turret wouldn't turn in his direction and the guards see him. He unlocked the emergency-hatch controls, flipped open the lid and reached for the over-ride switch. He popped the hatch and dove headlong through it.

He struck the floor of the traveler with a bone-shaking blow made worse by the heavy armor. Garfield was turning toward him, an expression of fear on his face. The guard in the right laser turret stared with wide-eyed fear at the hatch, opening right into the deadly Turan sky. Insects already had found the opening and were homing in on warm flesh.

Rader was still on the floor when he kicked at the open-mouthed guard, toppling the unarmored man, who screamed. Rader rolled over and blindly threw himself at the guard turning from the left-hand turret, smashing him back against the wall. Before the man could recover, Rader struck him in the mouth, knocking him out. Garfield was pulling his weapon when Rader lurched into him, thrown off balance by the traveler rising up on the far bank. The drivers were screaming, but Rader couldn't hear any of it—they weren't using the radio. The driver was slapping at switches to close the hatch as a swarm of small red insects filled the interior of the transporter.

Garfield was batting at them, his eyes wild and mad. The sting of the insects raised instant welts. Rader wrestled the laser out of Garfield's hand and turned toward the guard who was dropping down from the topside flame-gun turret. But he had nothing to fear, because the unprotected guard was in the throes of a spastic seizure, his face and hands covered with green insects and small armored flying slugs. The first guard was struggling up, his face welted, his eyes wild. He screamed soundlessly and clawed at his face, ripping away at the flying centipods that were sucking his blood. He fell back, writhed and went limp.

The driver was slumped over the controls, his assistant still batting at the swarm of insects, but he, too, fell. Garfield brushed past Rader and ran toward the airlock, bellowing incoherently. Rader made a grab for him but slipped in a slime of crushed insects and fell heavily, striking his helmeted head sharply.

Rader blacked out for only a second or two, but Garfield, still screaming horribly, was pulling open the interior hatch. He pulled it closed behind him, and Rader's dazed eyes went to the control panel. There, under the bulging, sightless eyes of the bloody-faced driver, the light for the opening of the outer hatch came on.

Rader felt sick. He reached over, thumbed the emergency hatch shut, then closed the exterior airlock door. He staggered to a locker and pulled out two cans of Deathspray and killed everything left alive in the interior of the vehicle. Then he dragged the already bloating bodies into the airlock, closed the interior door and opened the outside. Minutes later he felt something heavy get in, and the traveler shook for a bit. Then he started up the vehicle quickly, hoping to dump out or frighten off whatever had come to scavenge the airlock; then he closed the outer hatch and sat down wearily. The fear he had been suppressing washed over him—his hands trembled and his stomach quavered.

Rader was afraid to change into a clean, unruptured suit, not knowing what lingering effects might be left in the stained and corpse-clotted interior. He used several cans of disinfectant and cleaner to cleanse his suit and patched all of the suspected spots where his suit might be leaking. It left him unable to move too freely, but he wasn't smelling anything bad.

Then he turned the traveler around and started back toward Base One.

"Base One, this is Traveler Four, approaching the east airlock."

"Gotcha, Tee-Four. Back early, huh? What happened?"

"Long story," Rader said curtly, keeping the words to a minimum. "Tell ya later, huh?"

"Ah, another story of desperate adventure on exotic Tura," the person in Control said. *"Outer lock opening now. Don't take too long. You know how they hate to waste Deathspray cleaning out the lock every time."*

"Right. Rolling in now."

Rader stopped the traveler within the cavernous dome after navigating the long lock. Deliberately he had not cleaned up the front port, hoping to keep visual detection down as long as possible. He waited at the airlock with a laser in each hand.

"Okay, Four, you can come out now."

Rader went into the lock, closed it, then opened the outer hatch. He dropped to the rock-melt floor and looked around. Two stocky men in decon suits blinked at him. He waved a laser at them with a finger to his lips. They nodded and carefully set down the spray nozzles they held. They preceded Rader to the lock to the main dome, and they all entered the decon chamber together.

Washed clean and smelling of the disinfectant, Rader popped his faceplate. "All right, boys, now let's you and me start changing things around here."

Wolfgang Briggs grinned. "I knew you could do it!"

"No, you didn't," Rader grinned back, "you *hoped* I would. But come on, we've got a date with a lander."

Surrounded by eleven men, Rader and Wolf swept through the dome, immobilizing the security forces and herding the gloomy-eyed workers into the mess hall, where they could keep an eye on them. Meyers, the big supervisor, glowered at him but said nothing.

Mullins, Domingo, Deft, and some others—all of them with unaccustomed lasers in their hands—put everyone together. Wolf took Rader aside. He looked nervous. "I'm not *certain* of this, but I think . . ."

"I think Brownie's a snitch."

Rader nodded. "Someone was; that's almost certain. A

bit too neat, me being taken out when I was." He glanced over at Brownie, who was helping to guard the workers and security men. He looked nervous, his eyes, slippery and quick. "Well, keep an eye on him. If you get a chance, swap him this laser for the one he has."

"Why?"

"Because I found out this one's busted. I went to pop Garfield's safe, and the damn thing wouldn't heat up. Must've been busted in the fight. Just give him this, you know, in case he gets some idea."

"How? Oh, I'll pretend to be checking loads. This one is charged."

Rader nodded. "Now . . . let's get things ready for the lander crew."

The young officer heading up the lander detail blinked at Rader's laser aimed right at his head. "Easy," Rader said. "Reach up and turn off your radio. The rest of you the same," he said softly.

Standing just inside the decon chamber, the four men did as they were told. Wolf checked them over, then put a drop of fast-fix on every switch but the officer's.

"I know we are not the legal navy of any United System world," the officer said in an attempt at sensible conversation. "But we *are* a legally franchised space force on contract to the Startrade corporation and thereby—"

"Shut up," Domingo said menacingly. He started forward, his fist balled, but Rader stopped him with a curt command. "None of that!" Then he smiled at Domingo. "He needs to be as unmarked as possible when we go back to the lander and up to the ship, understand?" Then his eyes swung to the officer's. "But I wouldn't mind too much if you were bleeding into your boot, you follow me?"

The officer gulped and said, "Y-yessir."

"All right. Wolf, Brownie, Deft, Domingo—suit up." He turned to Mullins. "We've got to keep the planet-to-ship channels silent, or rather, looking normal. Who do you have for that?"

"Easy," grunted Mullins. "One a my boys has been relief onna thing for a coupla weeks. Goddamned crackle'll driva ya nuts. I'll have him report the set's going down for repairs a sumpin, right after ya take off, all right?"

Rader nodded. "I'm depending on you."

Mullins peered at him narrowly. "Yeah? Well, don't you garp this up, mudballer, y'hear? Screw it up, and it'll be our ass. We'll be on penalty service for the rest of our stupid lives."

Rader nodded and reached for a suit of armor. "Watch Meyers," he cautioned Mullins. "That man is dangerous."

"Takes one to know one," Mullins said, grinning.

"Why Brownie?" Wolf asked quietly. Getting aboard the lander had been no problem, with Allen, the young officer, fronting for them.

"I want him where I can see him," Rader replied. He was watching the approach to the starship on the screens. They were still well out of visual range.

The docking symbols popped onto a screen and started blipping out information. Rader glanced back into the lander's cargo hold. The four Startrade men were tied up. Everything was ready.

"Docking in four minutes," the co-pilot said.

Taking the ship was ridiculously easy. The *E. A. Lynn* was operating on a skeleton crew during the simple run from Zikkala to Tura and back. They found only three crewmen on the way; the sleeping one they let sleep; the others they shoved into a cabin and smashed the intercom and welded the door shut with a quick blaze of laser fire.

The captain turned as they entered, and the words died in his throat. "Who the hell are you?" he snapped, staring haughtily at the three men in their stained and tattered mudballer's clothing.

"The new owners of this ship," Wolf said, waving his weapon at the startled crewmen. "Up . . ."

"Your ship is a prize of war," Rader said evenly and smiled widely. "I take it in the name of the combined guilds of the free planet Zikkala."

The captain opened and closed his mouth. One by one the rest of the crew were brought to the bridge, captured and, in some cases, disarmed. Quickly, all nineteen crewmembers were in detention.

Rader nodded to Wolf Briggs, who thumbed a stud on a console. "Navigation computer *on*."

The ship's bridge came alive as screen after screen lit up and men began talking into microphones and computer terminals. The big starship swung gracefully out of orbit and started for Zikkala. After a few minutes Rader looked around, then frowned. "Where's Brownie?"

Wolf looked around. "He was here a second ago."

Rader jumped up, then caught himself in the almost absent gravity. He kicked off and rocketed out of the bridge and down the passageway. There were only a couple of places he might be if he was indeed up to trouble: the auxiliary communications room or the ship's other lander, where there was a com console.

The communications room was empty, and Rader twisted, heading back for the cross passage to the opposite side of the ship, where a lander bay held the *E. A. Lynn*'s other lander.

". . . calling Zikkala, calling a Startrade ship, this is Brown— Brownie, in the *Lizzy Lynn*, out of Tura . . . goddamn it—answer!"

Rader came through the still open hatch and slammed into Brownie, smashing him in the face with a hard fist. The man screamed and fell away, and Rader slapped the switches off before he yanked him to his feet. "You're the one!" he snarled and took him by the tunic front and smashed him against the wall by the airlock. Rader ignored his frantic protests and yanked him out into the passageway just as Mullins arrived, his dark brows meeting in a bull-like fury.

"Ya slimeball! You're the fribbin' ear for the Company,

huh?" He grasped Brownie's arm and glared at Rader. "I'll take charge a this scrote!"

Rader hesitated, not liking the dull hatred in Mullins' eyes. "Seal him up in a cabin, Mullins. We'll judge him later."

"Sure." Mullins gave him a shove along the passage as Rader headed back toward the bridge.

"He get through?" Domingo asked when Rader returned to the bridge.

"I didn't hear an answer, but they might have heard him." He frowned at the computer-readout graphics on the navigation screen. "Do we have an estimate on arrival in orbit?"

Wolf's fingers touched a few buttons, and the figures raced across an auxiliary screen. "One hundred two hours and change," Wolf said, looking around at Rader.

The big dark-haired man sat down and slapped a restraining strap across his lap. "Plenty of time for them to prepare something."

"And for us to prepare countermeasures," Wolf said seriously. Then he smiled. "Hey, are we really gonna take this ship as a prize of war?"

Rader shrugged. "Oh, that sort of thing can take forever in courts. But we have it when we need it."

"What do you think the other guys have been doing while we've been gone?" Wolf asked.

"Harassing them, keeping them off balance. Hit and run. Guerilla stuff."

"Uh, Captain . . . uh, Rader . . ." Domingo pointed at a light that had just come on. "Someone just opened the dorsal airlock and . . . uh-oh . . . they speed-cycled it . . ."

"Whatever's in there has gotten out!" Wolf said, reaching for a control.

"Hey, bridge!" It was the voice of Mullins, in a rough good humor. *"Just wanted to report me anna boys had a trial and sentence was jist passed on Theodore Brown, Company ear."*

There was silence, then Rader's voice cut through like a sword. "In the future, Mullins, all trials will be held before a joint Guild committee, until we can create a legal government of Zikkala."

"Yeah?" Mullins answered sulkily. *"Me anna boys ain't*

in your fribbin' guild, Rader. But we do know howta handle ears."

"Mullins," Rader said, and Wolf glanced at him. The ice in his voice gave the boy a scare. "I am Guild starbuck and the guilds are the nearest thing we have to government or law out here. Either you obey Guild law or you answer to me."

There was a silence, then Mullins said, almost inaudibly. *"Yeah, right, I unnerstan. Ya gotta have rules. Yeah, fine, Rader, only me anna boys are gonna have a say come election time."*

"Of course." Rader snapped off and sat back in the control chair, his face gloomy.

Domingo flicked his eyes at him several times over the next few minutes. "You sure you want that buncha scrotes on Zikkala, Cap'n?"

"If they fight for freedom, they deserve a share."

The starship raced on, at sub-light speeds, in normal space, in the long arc of interplanetary flight.

There was a big Startrade ship in orbit around Zikkala as the *E. A. Lynn* came in. Almost instantly it established communications.

"E. A. Lynn, *this is Captain Marcus Digby of the* Éleuthère Irénée Du Pont, *Startrade ship NC-845, come in, please."*

Rader pressed a stud, and Wolf's eyes widened in surprise. *"Du Pont, this is Captain Otto Kahn of the E. A. Lynn,* Startrade Ship NC-4682. Welcome to our little outpost of civilization. Did you bring any *bhang* with you, Captain?" Rader spoke conversationally but politely.

"Lynn, *we have an unconfirmed report about some difficulty on Tura. What do you know about this?"*

"Oh, a little of the usual discontent. Tura *is* a nasty place, after all. You know these mudballers, they want every convenience. Some kind of big reptile—ugly thing really—knocked out their main com disc. They should have it repaired any moment now."

"Captain, uh, Captain Kahn—?" This was a new voice,

also uncertain but sounding even more suspicious. *"Go into standard orbit, please, and prepare to receive a decontamination party."*

"But we're thoroughly deconned—who are you, anyway?"

"I'm Zikkala Command. My name is Fulcher, and I issue all landing permits."

"Landing permits?" Rader's voice was incredulous. "What has happened here? You guys turning into bureaucrats? Who else is out here but us? I have a schedule to meet, cargo to offload and—"

"Captain!" Fulcher's voice snapped angrily. *"We have a definite problem here. Since communications ceased from Tura, we are on full alert. We wish to board and debrief you for—"*

"All right, all right," Rader said, his voice annoyed and sulky, as though he had been unjustly accused. "We'll reach standard orbit in . . . about an hour. Send up your inspectors or whatever."

"Thank you, Captain."

Rader clicked off and Wolf said, "Who is Captain Kahn?"

Rader jerked his thumb back toward Tura. "I thought I might get away with it, impersonating the exskipper of this tub to a newcomer ship, especially while we are still out of video range and with the Startrade power plants punching through the sunspot interference. But this ground control may have met him. Almost certain to, unless this Fulcher came in later on, on the *Du Pont,* maybe."

"Lots of ifs and maybes there," Wolf observed.

"Too many. Domingo, you know what to do." Rader unstrapped and started to get up, then stopped Wolf, who was doing the same. "Maybe you better stay here . . ."

"The hell. Deft can back Domingo. I'm going with you."

"All right, hero. Let's get ready."

Domingo called out to Rader. "Hey, Cap'n! What about all the, you know—?" He aimed his thumb at the rear of the ship.

"Tell them to hold on for a rough trip," Rader said. "You're in charge, Domingo. Don't let Mullins bluff you."

"Don't worry, Cap'n," Domingo said, his face lighting up as he straightened in the control seat. "I'll take care a them scrotes." But Rader and Wolf were already gone, hand over hand, pulling themselves down the passages, flying through the faint gravity like arrows.

In their suit radios, Rader and Wolf could hear Zikkala Control querying the ship. "E. A. Lynn, *you are below standard, parking orbit. Please adjust.*"

"*According to shipboard computer we are well out still, Zikkala Control,*" Domingo said, a puzzlement in his voice. "*Please recheck your responder radar.*"

"*Check your own, Lynn,*" Zikkala control snapped. "*You are much too low. Please adjust.*"

"*Your transmission is breaking up, Zikkala Control. Say again, please,*" Domingo requested.

Rader's gaze swept over the lander's controls. "You ready?" he asked Wolf.

"*E. A. Lynn, we are ordering you to ascend to standard parking orbit. You are entering the atmosphere, you moron!*"

"*Say again, Control. I got about every third word. You want us to enter the atmosphere? What the hell for? You guys crazy down there?*"

"*Just about there,*" came Deft's voice, quietly, on the other circuit.

"*No, you cloned moron! I said not to enter the atmosphere! Oh, for—Captain Digby! Digby! Du Pont, come in, please!*"

"*Captain Digby here, sir.*"

"*We can't take any chances, Captain—fire on the Lynn!*"

"*But that's a Startrade ship—!*"

"*Shut up and do as you are told, Captain!*"

"Deft, plug me into intership on line two," Rader ordered. He heard the click, then the carrier wave and thought to throw more confusion into the matter. "*Zikkala Control, our navigation computer is malfunctioning! Quick, feed us the orbit data from your control—!*"

"*Hey, Lynn, what the hell's going on here?*"

"*Captain, this is the Du Pont! How can we help?*"

Rader grinned at Wolf and said, "*Thank god! Listen,*

*there's something the matter with—oh, no! It must be sabo-
tage! No, it's—"*

Rader snapped off for a moment, then started talking
and cut the intership com line in and out. *"Abandon ship!
This is Captain Kahn! Abandon ship, abandon ship! Zikkala Control, this is the* E. A. Lynn, *we are abandoning
ship! The—"* He snapped off the final time and gestured at
Wolf.

The lander dropped away, scattering thousands of metal
chips and streamers of foil and a cloud of metal dust. The
starship veered away and the lander plummeted through
the thickening air.

The lander was heating up beyond the capability of the
ship to handle the heat. Gently, Rader began to level the
ship off, but they still fell toward the rugged mountains
below at a terrifying rate. He slapped at the executive
switch; the lander banked sharply to avoid a high peak.
Rader brought it into a valley, still rocketing at much too
high a speed. The valley was not long, and he sought to
bring it above the peaks.

"We're not going to make it!" Rader yelled and, in des-
peration, he sent the ship into an almost vertical climb.
The gray-stone cliffs of the mountains loomed before them,
a blur in Wolf's mind; then there was only blue sky in the
screens. Something metallic snapped; then they heard it
ripping loose from the fuselage and falling, and both men
passed out from the gravity stresses. Uncontrolled, the ship
wobbled, then abruptly fell off, swept around in its stubby
wings and sheered one off against a granite mountain. The
vessel tumbled, end over end along the cliff face, then fell
away, ripped and torn, to crash into the valley floor.

Rader came awake first as the blood returned to his
head. He was trapped beneath a fallen screen that had
ripped loose from the side of the ship. He heaved on it and
cried out with pain. His left arm seemed broken, but the
screen clattered away.

"Wolf!"

Rader looked through the dust and smoke of the ruined

lander and saw Wolf Briggs in a crumpled heap against the bridge bulkhead, his seat strap still holding him into a crushed and splintered molded seat. Rader pulled himself to Wolf and unlatched him from the seat. He dragged the dead weight of the boy's body toward the bridge hatch leading to the airlock; then he saw that the whole side of the ship had been crushed in—it totally blocked their way. Groaning, Rader pulled at the limp body, and they slipped and slid toward the great rend in the metal on the starboard side.

After an eternity he managed to get Wolf out of the lander. They lay together on a shelf of rock, while Rader fought back the waves of nausea and pain. At last he was able to raise himself up and start stripping away his spacesuit so he could check Wolf for damage. He knew Lockhart would send a search party for them, but first things first. To avoid awkwardness and passing out from pain, Rader made a crude splint from a shred of metal conduit and strapped his arm down with bits of wire and torn fabric. He injected himself with pain killer, but only locally, as he wanted to keep a clear head.

He examined Wolf's head injury, hoping there was no concussion. He stripped off the youth's spacesuit and bandaged up the other cuts, then did the same to himself. Awkwardly, he got to his feet and pulled Wolf up, too. His head was swimming, and he felt very weak.

Then he heard the ship coming. It was a starship lander and it came swiftly up the valley. There was no place for him to hide, but Rader groped for his laser, only to find it broken. He sat back, fatalistically accepting that they would be taken. If there was no resistance, there would be no firing. Alive, he was still a threat, still able to function and to escape. He made Wolf more comfortable and watched the ship come down, ready to take advantage of any opening.

Four men in bulky armor got out of the lander and spread out quickly. They carried heavy bull lasers expertly, and Rader knew the pros had arrived. One of them had a camera, and he kept it aimed at Rader like a weapon. The first voice Rader heard was not that of any of the armored quartet, but Lockhart's voice, coming from an external speaker on the fist-sized camera.

"Dear, dear, dear," he mocked. *"Citizen Rader and . . . yes, the Briggs lad. A rather undignified return to Zikkala, is it not, Convict Rader?"*

"Wolf is hurt. He may have a concussion."

"Yes, yes, I'm sure. I watched the crash from the monitors on the Du Pont. *Really quite a rash idea, Citizen Rader, I—oh, I forgot, that's right—you are no longer a citizen."* His voice was positively glowing with warmth.

Cocky bastard, Rader thought.

"Emery, I'm afraid these escapees did not survive the crash."

"Yessir," the armored man with the camera said, unemotionally.

"Dispose of them and log it as killed by misadventure during an ill-advised escape attempt."

"In cold blood, Lockhart?" Rader said.

"Does it matter to a dead man how he died? Really, Rader, you have such romantic ideas. Should I patch you up and we have a face to face duel?" He laughed, quite charmingly and with delight. *"Really, now. I do wonder what sort of nonsense you were brought up on. And you a Mercenary, too."*

"The Mercenary Legions have rules, Lockhart, and we stick by them. One of them is that unarmed prisoners are not shot!"

"You put too much importance upon yourself, your guilds, and your precious backward planet. You are nothing to me, Rader. A momentary annoyance at best. Zikkala is nothing to me, except as a stepping stone. The Federation of Sovereign Systems is corrupt and old, Rader, ripe for the plucking. And it shall be I who does the plucking, my mudballer friend. I am building a power base unlike any in history—a grand alliance, a new galactic empire!"

To his own surprise, Rader started laughing. He winced with pain but still he laughed. One of the armored men stepped toward him, but Emery stopped him with a grunt. There was nothing from Lockhart, safely in Shamrock.

"You are so . . . so banal, Lockhart! Pedestrian dreams of galactic glory! How many before you, dreamer? You are a cliché, Lockhart!"

"Kill them," Lockhart said flatly.

The armored fists raised heavy lasers and fingers tightened upon firing studs. Rader's thoughts were dark, chaotic, angry. His only gladness was that Wolfgang Amadeus Mozart Briggs would not know.

Then the ground burst into light, and a great ball of fiery cold light rose into the air.

Rader stared at it dumbly. A sphere of light, two meters or more in diameter, floated between him and the four armed men. One of them shrieked and fired. The sphere absorbed the ruby-beam, and it did not penetrate to Rader and Briggs.

"Kill them!" cried Lockhart. But Emery had dropped the camera and was pouring energy into the sphere. All four bull lasers were firing; then one of the men on the end started running to flank the sudden sphere of cold light, firing past it at Rader. But the sphere expanded, and into all their minds came a pressure, a numbing presence that brought all to immobility.

I am Kaleen-ka, Mother of broods, Father of the nest. These entities are under the protection of my people, for you have violated the convenant.

"Emery! What the hell is going on? Are they dead? Emery?" Everyone ignored Lockhart's scratchy voice as the camera lay battered upon the stone shelf.

"—who the hell are you?" Emery growled.

I am Kaleen-ka. I am your judge.

"Like hell you are, puffball, you—"

Emery fell, his words unfinished. He lay still, without moving, and the others gaped.

I am Kaleen-ka. I have judged. Go.

The three remaining Startrade toughs did not argue. They ran, and in moments the lander made a rapid ascent and screamed away into the distance, making a reckless dip through a pass to put a mountain between them and the glowing sphere that could rise up through solid rock.

"Kaleen-ka!" Rader said. "Help us."

The sphere of light did not respond.

"All right, you *did* help us—but why? What are you?"

I am Kaleen-ka. They were violators of the covenant.

"What covenant?"

The covenant that has existed since your species arrived upon this world. The covenant of the testing.

"The testing?" Rader felt stupid, as if something very obvious was being overlooked.

Mine are tested by yours. It is the greatest testing we have ever faced, and we are grateful to you. We mourn those who fail, but we glory in the new levels to which the greater testing has brought us.

"You? Who? The Kaleen?" Sudden comprehension dawned. "*You* are a Kaleen—of course!" Rader struck his forehead, then regretted the blow for it brought pain and dizziness. "You *do* evolve, not racially, over generations, over millions of years, but *individuallly*, through . . . the testing?"

Yes.

"And you saved us because the contest was not even?"

Yes. They were of your species, but they are not like you. Their minds were stunted and warped from what we have perceived to be your norm. Their minds were closed, as if within a rock. They were of your species, but they were violators.

"I'll make no excuses for those thugs, but you . . . you Kaleen, this is your fight, too. They want to rape Zikkala, to change it and gut it!"

They are adversaries. Their ruthlessness makes them testers.

"This isn't a game! When they control Zikkala they will hunt your people down! They have starships, long-range lasers, bombs and sensors, probably biological warfare! They'll kill every one of you if you resist!"

You resist.

"And they are doing their best to kill me, too, and my friends. As soon as they think you are an enemy, they will kill you, too!"

That will not be a simple task.

"Not you, maybe, but what of your flesh-and-blood brothers? Your children? *They* are vulnerable! I have killed them myself—when they were trying to kill me."

Yes.

"They will be slaughtered in ways you know nothing of! Ultrasonics, germ warfare, tailored viruses, genetically sculptured predators, missiles, air attacks, death sprays—"

The ball of light did not speak in his mind, and Rader

turned as he heard Wolf Briggs stir. The boy moaned and brought his hand to his head.

Your companion awakens.

"But he may die if nothing is done!" Rader snapped, wadding up some grasses to make a pillow.

Move away.

"What? What is it you—"

Move back.

Rader struggled to his feet and moved back. The sphere of light floated over him, and as it descended, Wolf awoke. He stared up at the light, but he did not seem frightened as it closed over him. The sphere sank halfway into the rock without effort, completely enclosing Wolf's form. Rader stared, wondering if what was happening was something he should try to prevent or to encourage.

After a long moment the sphere rose again and drifted a little distance away. Rader went quickly to Wolf's side. The boy seemed awake but dazed. The blood had clotted. Wolf looked around and saw Rader. "Wow—that was some crash! Are you all right? Oh, your arm!"

"Never mind that." He looked up, and Wolf followed his gaze.

"Kaleen-ka," Wolf whispered.

"You know who that is?"

"I had a . . . a dream. It was all white . . . no, all colors, no . . . I don't know. Kaleen-ka was there. He's very old . . . very . . ." Wolf's words drifted off, and he stared at the sphere.

He is healing.

"Thank you . . ." Rader said softly.

You are injured. Do you desire healing?

"No, I . . ." A primordial fear came over Rader. To be absorbed by an alien creature—!

You need not fear. I do not touch the essential you. Only your body, which is transient.

"I'd like not to make it too transient," Rader said, but Wolf interrupted.

"Let him, Rader. It's . . . it's all right."

Rader took a deep breath, then let it out slowly. In his mind, and not with his mouth, he said, *Yes.* The sphere floated toward him, and there was a quiver of fear. The unknown. *Nothing is more feared than the unknown,* he thought bleakly. Then he smiled, wanly, as the light flowed over him, covering him, absorbing him. A line from the ancients came to him, words from the very dawn of technology, when the universe must have seemed very strange and terrifying, and almost totally unknown. *Any sufficiently advanced technology may be indistinguishable from magic.*

The light was everything. It was white. It was all colors, merging, blending, alive . . .

His body was filled with a tingling, a penetrating trembling. Fear shot through him in little distant thrills, like a bird bursting from the brush.

The mystic is a scientist in a hurry. Another string of words from the beginning of the atomic age. *All great discoveries are made by men whose feelings run ahead of their thinking.* The tingling persisted, but there was no pain; none at all.

Then it was over.

The light receded, and Rader stood swaying on the rocky shelf. There was no pain. His arm was still bound to the improvised splint, but he was refreshed and alert.

"Thank you . . ."

Your body chemistry required some adjustment. The procedures on Tura are not as stringent as they believe. There are many antibodies that escape decontamination. They are eliminated now. The physiognomy is faulty but adequate. There could be some genetic changes made. Your descendants could be superior to you.

"I hope they are, but . . . no offense . . . let's just let things happen naturally, huh?"

As you wish. Your race has never been one that was attracted to self-improvement.

"How do you know us?" Wolf asked. There was respect in his voice but curiosity as well.

I know what you know. But my perspective is different. I believe the word is objective. You have many admirable qualities and many despicable ones, with much gradation between. You as an individual and as a species. There are more individual differences among you than between members of the Kaleen.

"You know everything we know?" Rader asked, his voice tight.

"Yes. As I absorbed your memories, I stored them in a way to give a vastly higher retrieval rate. I could show you how. It is much more efficient. Information that cannot be wholly retrieved is useless, even dangerous."

"Uh . . . no thanks," Rader said. "Let's leave my memories where they are."

I perceive your fear. Your memories are you. You do not perceive them as information but as experiences. Intriguing. Faulty but interesting. There was a pause, and Rader and Wolf exchanged looks as Rader massaged his arm. With a start he realized the bones were no longer broken, yet they were still not healed—but somewhere in between. Yes, interesting, Kaleen-ka continued. You have a practiced illogic you call emotion. You perceive it in the thalamus and hypothalamus, what you call your old brain. A totally alien experience to me. I cherish the opportunity and have communicated it to my brethren, to those who have returned to the nest for the final meditations.

"The final—" Wolf gulped. "You can die, then?"

All things die, who do not change. Those who cannot ascend to the levels above them all die.

"Good god," Wolf said breathlessly. "What can be more than a ball of energy?"

When I know, I shall transmute. If I cannot know, I shall not, and eventually I shall dissipate.

Rader perceived an unusual hesitation in Kaleen-ka's manner. Then the words and images formed again in his head. I am undergoing change now. Perhaps it is death, I do not know.

"Those laser bolts—" began Wolf.

No. That is welcome energy, like light from the sun. I feel my life energy might be terminating. I must consult with my brothers, my sisters. Shir-ka-kaloon, Brother to the Spirit. Tula-ka-shula, Mother of the Ascendants. Tupa-ka. Skree-aboo. My children, my ancestors, my siblings.

"There are more like you?" Wolf asked anxiously.

Yes. All newer to the ascendancy than I. But I must consult. The energy flow is changing. Toward matter. Is it to be thus?

"Maybe you—"

Rader brought Wolf back to the present and the now with a sharp command. "But first we must survive! With the lander wrecked, we are half a world away from Shamrock!" *And from Alena,* he thought. *I pray we are not too late!*

They heard a laugh, faint and tinny.

"The camera!" Rader searched for it in the rock and found it in a crevice, hidden in the tough grasses that filled it.

"What sort of playlet are you putting on, Rader?" Lockhart sneered. *"I'm not surprised you took Emery, but why did you let the others go? A stupid move, Rader. Was it prompted by some sort of chivalry?"* The final word was heavily accented with scorn. *"But thank you for showing me that these natives aren't quite so primitive as we thought. As soon as the lander returns, I shall begin elimination."*

"Lockhart—! Alena, where is she?"

"Goodbye, Rader. Come visit us, won't you? I shall look forward to your arrival." He gave a short, harsh laugh. *"It looks as though you and I are destined to meet in some outrageously primitive fashion. Well, so be it."*

The transmitter was dead. With a growl Rader turned toward the glowing sphere of light. "Help us! You heard him. He's going to kill your people!"

"They'll be slaughtered!" Wolf said.

The sphere floated toward them. *I shall help you.* The light flowed around them and their bodies tingled.

"Oh, my god!" Wolf cried out. "It's lifting us—!"

Then there was nothing but light. No sensation, no sound, no sight, nothing.

The timelessness ceased, and they were there.

The light dimmed around them, and night came. Rader staggered weakly as he regained his balance, and Wolf Briggs fell against him with a gasp. They stared around and saw that it was near dawn; the splash of stars across the heavens was dimming to the east. They were behind a hillock, and to the west were the rock-melt walls and dimly-seen domes of the trader outpost of Shamrock. As they adjusted to the new situation, they heard faint cries, and the ball of cold light that was Kaleen-ka drifted away to the north, bobbing and dipping.

"What's—what's happening?" Wolf asked in a quavering voice.

Before Rader could answer, there was a ruler-straight red line that split the sky, straight into the moving ball of light. Another and another joined it, blinking on and off, but with deadly accuracy, every shot a hit on the fiery sphere.

"It's drawing fire away from us," Rader muttered, looking around to discover a way to take advantage of the situation. But they were weaponless and dawn was coming; they were certain to be discovered.

A strong visible light beam came on, swept across the sunbleached soil and pinned Kaleen-ka. Two more lasers joined in the firing, and there was a steady blinking of millisecond pulses dead-ending at the sphere of light. But nothing seemed to hurt the Kaleen; it made its erratic way north, absorbing all the hits without apparent harm. Another light came on, from another wall, swept around quickly, then back, and Rader tugged Wolf lower behind the hillock. He cursed silently, knowing that in all probability infrared detectors were also covering the same ground. From this wall and that, single laser bolts probed the plain around the city, furrowing the hard-packed sand into glass and setting a scrub *scrit* bush on fire.

Then Kaleen-ka disappeared, sinking silently into the earth. The beams still swept across the plain erratically; then one by one they cut off. But still Rader kept down, cautioning Wolf not to look over the hillock. They waited for the furor to die down.

It took almost half an hour, and by then the predawn light was blotting out the eastern stars, but the desert plain before Shamrock was still dark. Silently, Rader gestured to Wolf and they slipped away to the east, found a gully and took it south until they felt safe.

Wolf fell back against the bank and slid to the bottom

with a sigh. "How the hell was *that* supposed to help us?" he grumbled.

Rader squatted and picked up a stick, staring at a flat piece of bare sand before him. "He got us half way around the world in less than a day," he replied absently.

"Yeah, but . . ." Wolf shrugged helplessly.

Rader stared at the patch of sand as if it would reveal a hidden plan; then he squinted at the eastern horizon. Dawn was almost here, and with it—what?

Then without warning there was movement, the cascade of sand into the gully, bodies dropping with almost silent thuds into the sand around them. Rader leapt to his feet at the first sound but stopped.

Kaleen warriors.

More were slipping into the gully up and down the wash. Wolf stared, half-rising, frozen into astonishment. Their near-naked bodies gleamed in the dawning light, their knives and spears glinting.

Rader raised both hands in a gesture of peace, and the nearest warrior mirrored his movements, but there was a spear in his hand. Rader saw that there were females among them, their single broad breast bare, their loins hung with knives and slings, and their leather bags heavy with their burdens. The earrings, pendants, and other jewelry the humans had seen them wear on Destiny Mesa were gone. Their slitted cat's eyes were unreadable in the dim light, but their tufted tails twitched with nervous energy.

One of the females looked familiar, and Rader wondered if she were the one who had "operated" on his head. He smiled and said, "Kaleen-ka brought us to—"

At his mention of the name, there was a sighing along the line of warriors. The female that Rader thought familiar stepped toward him and raised her hands. Clearly, Rader saw the double-opposing thumbs, the wide, center fingers, the musculature as she reached up toward his head. He bowed down to her, and her fingers touched him: it was like a rush of warm water over his head, and he quivered involuntarily. Then the feeling passed and his head grew clearer.

What he heard was more felt than heard; what he felt was more memory than message.

. . . they were there to help.

. . . they were allies.

. . . more were coming.

. . . the other testers were arriving from their hiding place.

. . . a great testing was about to happen.

. . . Kaleen-ka had promised them a great challenge.

. . . an even greater test was beyond, away from the home world.

. . . all was good.

. . . all was right.

. . . the cycle continues.

Rader straightened and looked down at the much shorter Kaleen. Her name was Healer With The Touch Of Light, and she was the mother of Cliff Spider and of Spearlike Lightning, who was now dead. Rader smiled and she smiled back, a solemn happening across her serious face.

"Rader . . ." Wolf asked in a choked voice, "what the hell is going on?"

"Friends, Wolf, and fellow warriors."

They seemed to be waiting; then from a long way off they heard scuffling and a soft grunt as something heavy fell into the gully. Rader estimated the time until the first light and knew they did not have much time. Then, bewildered humans were coming up the gully, staring tensely at the gauntlet of reddish-brown Kaleen. Korda was in the lead, big and black, towering over the Kaleen, his face hard, his eyes wary.

"Korda," Rader said softly, and the big black cursed.

"Rader—!"

Liana was there, too, her dark eyes flicking around, her long black hair tied back, her graceful body draped with weapons. "Rader, you tough old bastard—you came through!"

"Where does he have Alena?" he asked roughly.

Liana bit at her lip and shot a glance at Korda. "We don't know. Shamrock probably, but we don't have any sources of information, no snitches, nothing." She touched his arm lightly. "We . . ."

"Never mind. I'll find her."

"What the *hell* is going *on*?" Korda rumbled. "We were camped out near the North Trail, hoping to ambush a patrol that's been searching for us, and right out of nowhere this Kaleen appears. Damn near got herself drilled! Stark naked she was—no weapons—which I guess is the only thing that kept Liana from—"

"She put her hands to my forehead," Liana said, "and damned if I didn't get a message. Like it was something I remembered, and—"

"We started down here right off!" Korda grumbled. "Goddamn all-night run. My blasted shins are all banged up with the—"

"The Kaleen are on our side," Liana said, hugging Rader's arm tightly. "They're going to attack with us and—"

"Against that fort?" Wolf asked in astonishment.

"The power plant is going to be sabotaged," Liana said. "Don't ask me how, but I got the picture that a ball of light was going to do it—crazy, huh?"

"No, not crazy," Rader said softly. "That's Kaleen-ka . . . or one like him. It. Her. It can go through rock like you go through water. It would probably just hit the fusion plant from underneath, or . . ." He wiped his hand across his face. "God only knows." He turned to Healer With The Touch of Light and bent his head. She reached up and cupped his head in her small hands.

How and when is this to be done? Rader asked in his mind.

. . . as it is needed.

. . . when the test begins.

. . . it shall be as Kaleen-ka, Mother of broods, Father of the nest, wills.

There will still be the charges in the hand weapons. Many will die.

. . . as it is willed.

. . . as it shall be.

. . . the great test is upon us all.

. . . the cycle must be completed.

What cycle?

. . . the meaning, the elevation.

. . . the ancient cycle.

There were images, figures that shaped and reshaped themselves, all misty and blurred in his mind, figures that changed to spheres of cold, pulsating light like Kaleen-ka, then became solid figures again, cycling, changing, evolving.

He had the impression of caves or darkened rooms that were meditation chambers or—what?

... the testing begins.

The little Kaleen's hands dropped from his head, and the reality of dawning Zikkala returned. The Kaleen began trotting away, up the serpentine twists of the gully, running silently, with only the faintest scrunch of sand under their feet. Korda held out a laser to Rader.

"C'mon," Rader said quickly.

There were other humans down the line, grim-faced trappers and hunters, and they ran along with the Kaleen, mixing in, single file. Rader wasn't certain how many humans and Kaleen there were, but there must have been fifty at least.

At a bend in the gully, they found another half-dozen Kaleen, waiting, and further on another eight or ten came trotting out of the desert and dropped into line. They spread out in the gully almost directly east of the fort of Shamrock, the first rays of dawn sending long shadows across the flat plain. *Scrit* bushes and the tubular cacti caled *tingle* made purple finger marks across the ground. Every rock and sandy stretch was heavily textured by the slanting light.

Rader watched a glow on the side of a dome within the fortress; it was the light from the guard house windows, which was powered by the main fusion plant. When it went out, it was time.

"I can think of better times to attack," grumbled Korda, staring over the edge of the gully, his breath blowing little grains of sand. "What kind of plan is this, anyway?" he asked, looking at Rader.

"I don't know if it's a plan at all," he replied softly. "But it *seems* right."

"All these," Korda said, gesturing up and down the gully at the silent Kaleen. "Enemies one minute, big friends the next—?"

"They're allies now—against Startrade." He turned the other way, to Liana Chang. "You stay here and be our backup."

"There you go again," Liana said nastily.

"You can fire a lot steadier from here," Rader said. "Pick off the gunners. But for God's sake, keep moving along the gully. Don't shoot twice from the same spot if you can help it."

"You're just trying to protect me," she grumbled. "I'm going with you."

"Like hell you are," Rader snapped, then lowered his voice. "Liana, are you a good shot or not?"

"Better'n you."

"Right. Then you stay here *as you are ordered.*"

She made a growling noise and looked hard at the dark walls of Shamrock. "Just keep their heads down." Rader insisted. "With the fusion plant out, they can't control their weaponry by linking it into radar or heat-trackers. Their computers won't function, they'll have no contact with any ship. They'll have to fire by eye, line-of-sight; to do that they need to look over and see us. We can't fire very accurately while running. You just keep their heads down—all right?"

"Goddamn protectivist bastard," Liana began.

"That's an order," Rader said. He pointed down the gully at another trapper. Zachariah, too. He's better than either of us. Go tell him."

Liana glared at Rader for a long moment, her slanted eyes fiery. "You sentimental goon, you—"

"Sentimental, my butt. Standard military tactics. You and Zachariah are the best shots." He shrugged. "Best use of peoplepower available."

Liana look disgusted. "Uh-huh." She rose to a crouch and said, "You're doing this to protect me. I don't need that kind of protection, Rader." Then she grinned quickly. "But I *am* the best shot." She scampered off down the gully.

Rader smiled grimly as he squinted at the reflected light on the dome. It was becoming more difficult to see as the sun rose. Then the light went out.

He waited a second, just to be certain, but he knew it was still too dark within the walls for the guard light to be extinguished by the coming of dawn. He raised his hand, hesitated, wondering where Lockhart might be keeping Alena, then swept his hand toward the trade outpost. He scrambled up the crumbling sides of the wash and started running in a weaving, erratic route toward the walls ahead. Liana called out something to him in a low voice, but he didn't catch it.

He ran in long-legged strides, his eyes flicking from the stony ground ahead of him to the walls. They were a third of the way there when they heard the first shouts. A ruby-beam struck out at them, furrowing the ground ahead, then overshot when the gunner overcompensated. An answering shot came from behind the charging line, rainbowing off the lip of the rock-melt wall, then silencing the gunner. There were more shouts, more ruby-beams cutting at them. A Kaleen went down, tumbling, a leg severed, blood spurting. A long groove of bubbling glass appeared close to Rader, and he jumped high, then changed direction as he landed. His own laser spoke twice, but his running threw off his aim, and his shots only flared along the absorbing rock wall.

The air was laced with scarlet lines, blinking on and off, a cat's cradle of death. One of the running humans screamed and fell, rolling. Rainbows of laser fire rippled along the rock-melt walls as the attackers kept up their barrage. Chips of overheated rock-melt cascaded from the strike points. Rader noted with satisfaction that none of the turrets moved; their power was definitely off.

Then the walls loomed over them, and the main gate was only a little distance along. The Kaleen mixed with the panting, wild-eyed humans as they gained the shelter. Rader ordered two of the men to keep a watch on the tops of the walls; any defender would have to lean over to fire.

Unless they had grenades.

But it was the Kaleen who turned up with grenades. Almost as soon as they hit the wall, the Kaleen began untying the thongs that held the leather pouches to their bodies. Using the thongs as a sling, they twirled the sacks, then shot them over the walls. Rader saw a dark liquid spill from them, then heard screams from beyond the walls.

Rader ran to the gate and emptied his laser at the split between the massive halves of the panels, where he knew the crossbar to be. The thick *pungi* slabs burned with an oily smoke; then Rader heard the dull thumps of the cross-bar fragments falling to the ground. They threw themselves against the gate, and the heavy sections swung inward. Laser fire splattered off the gate and off the walls as they charged through. Rader threw away his depleted weapon as a screaming human ran at him. There was a dark oil on his flesh, and he was crying out in horrible pain, blind to where he was running. One of the Kaleen cut his throat as he ran by, and the unfortunate human collapsed, his skin already purpling and distorting like something in a fire.

A scarlet beam downed a Kaleen at one side, then blinked death into another just ahead. Rader jumped into an open doorway as laser fire from down the street cut spattering slots in the wall. His eyes swept the dark room and saw a dying Startrade tough lying on the floor. The man tried to raise the laser in his hand to fire, but Rader kicked it away, then scooped it up. It had a quarter-charge left.

The Startrader cursed him in a voice bubbling with blood, but Rader ran out again. He saw Korda shooting left-handed around a wall, picking off the wall gunners as they scrambled for safety.

"Korda! Where's Lockhart!"

The black marksman shrugged, burned the leg of a scrabbling defender, then ran on up the street. Rader followed, his eyes swinging back and forth, searching. The firing from the walls had all but stopped, and there were screams and cries echoing through the domes.

"Lockhart!" Rader heard Korda's bellow and turned to his right. There Korda stood, and up the street, in the entrance to the Dragon Guild dome, stood Lockhart. Rader leaped back as someone fired from between the warehouses, bubbling a trail across the wall over his head. He fired back as he threw himself down. A ruby-beam drilled an erratic pattern through the hard foam of the Tiger Guild Hall, just where Rader had been standing, and he triggered a sweeping figure-eight death-sweep into the dim recess. He heard a choked cry—and the firing ceased.

Rader got to his feet in a crouch and edged out. Korda was still standing, just beyond the edge of the wall that had protected him, but he was softening, his legs bending, his arms dropping. His laser fell from his hand, and the great black giant started to fall.

"Korda!"

Rader blinked as his friend fell sideways into the dirt, twisting to show the terrible raw hole in his stomach. Rader screamed in anger and fired a long burst at Lockhart. But the Startrade leader was no longer in the Tiger Guild entrance. Rader's laser stopped, it's ready-light going out as he set the doors afire with a long, futile burst of energy.

Running, Rader came up to Korda in a flurry of dust, dropping down beside him. The big man's face was ashen, a ghastly gray. His life was trickling out of the immense gut wound, and Rader knew with a sickened heart that his friend was dying. No medic, no Kaleen healer was going to save him.

"You bastard!" he snarled at his friend as he cradled his head. "You son-of-a-bitch, why didn't you save him for me?"

The faintest of smiles came to Korda's lips. "You . . . you got . . . him . . . all to . . . to yourself now . . ."

"I'll get him," vowed Rader, looking around. The outpost was misty, blurred with his tears, but the rage within him was a fiery furnace of hate and revenge.

"*Korda!*"

Liana was screaming as she ran up to them, staring in horror at the blood-soaked body. Korda tried to speak, but only a foam of blood came up. The black-haired woman let out a cry of rage and grief, her face a twisted mask of anger and fear. "Don't die, you big *shoka!*" she said fiercely, kneeling to gather him in her arms. "I haven't used you up yet!" She bent over him, her tears falling like crystals. Her head came up abruptly as she looked around. "Somebody— *do something!*"

Korda struggled to speak, and she bent close to him. "Guh . . . get away," Korda said, the blood glistening on his cheeks and chin.

"No, darling, I'll . . . I'll—"

"Get away," Rader said. He rose and then bent to pull Liana away, but she resisted, staring at him in stunned disbelief.

"No . . . a medic . . . that Kaleen healer woman . . . *something*. There must be *something* we can do, you bastard!"

Rader shook his head and pulled her up. Blinking and uncertain, she set Korda's head back in the dust. "It's too late," Rader said. He put his arm around her and tried to turn her. "He doesn't want you to see him die," Rader said softly. With a moan of horror, she turned toward Korda.

The Kaleen healer ran up and without hesitation knelt at Korda's head. The small reddish-brown female spread her finger tips across his forehead. Liana moaned and tried to turn back, but Rader stopped her. "No," he said softly. "Leave him this."

The Kaleen healer's face was slack with pain, but Korda sighed deeply. There was a vast emptiness in Rader, but he turned Liana away from the sight of her lover. "Let him die alone, as he wants."

Liana looked at Rader, her face twisted and mad. She staggered away, then broke into a run and disappeared up the street. Rader beckoned to the gray-faced Wolf, and they went between the Guild domes.

"That Kaleen—" Wolf began, but Rader stopped him.

"She'll . . ." He couldn't finish, but somehow he knew Healer With The Touch Of Light would ease Korda's final moments.

"It's horrible!" Wolf said, shivering.

"No," said Rader softly, "only sudden." Wolf stared at him in disbelief. "It's better than dying a piece at a time, better than dying bitter or of disappointment. He died *for* something, at least." And in his mind Rader added—*after so long a pursuit, he finally overtook death.*

"Alena," Rader said. He started toward her pleasure dome, where he imagined Lockhart set up his headquarters, for Alena's dome-top apartment was the most luxurious in the outpost. Then he stopped, looked at his weapon and asked Wolf if his was charged. The sweating youth nodded, and they exchanged weapons. Rader took it and started running.

Rader found three Kaleen dead in the dust before the pleasure dome entrance. One of them was a female, cut almost in two by a bull laser. But two of Startrade's tame marshals lay with Kaleen spears in their chests. Rader listened at the partially open door, then went through fast, rolling then leaping behind Hayim's lectern. There was no enemy fire, and the whole dome seemed silent. Then, as his ears adjusted to the interior, he heard muffled moans and the whimper of a woman. He crept toward the carved *pungi* panels that lead into the dome's main room, and the noises grew louder. He heard some muffled words, then the silence grew.

"Hayim?" Rader called out, and at once a laser's red lance spat through the partially open doors. *"Hayim!"*

There was a silence, then a cautious question. "Who is it?"

"Rader."

There was a soft curse in some liquid tongue, then a scrape of some kind and some muffled words. "I am coming," Hayim said.

The thin dark man appeared in the door and Rader gasped. He was badly wounded, and a large bloody lump of a bandage ended where his right hand had been. A charged laser was in his left and a wild, half-mad gleam in his eye. He stared at Rader with such vehemence that Rader thought for a second he was going to be gunned down. But the swarthy Arab clamped his lips in a hard line.

"He took her. Miss Petrovna. He and Gossett, the marshal."

"Took her? Where?"

Hayim gestured up with his thumb. "Space. He came . . . just a few minutes ago . . . I had been pretending to be with them . . . protecting Miss Petrovna . . . they . . ." He swayed on his feet, and Rader stepped to him, grabbing him. The hasty bandage was darker now. "Gossett did this to me, but I . . . I stopped two of their men . . . inside . . . the other women . . ."

"Have they left yet? Where's their lander?" Rader said harshly.

"North side . . ."

Rader started to help the sagging man into a comfortable position, but the Arab protested. "You must do something for me . . . stop the bleeding . . . I can . . . always go back . . . grow another . . . but . . ." His dark liquid eyes pleaded with him in a proud way, and Rader nodded. He set the man down on the steps and quickly unwrapped the bandage, which he found to be some woman's fancy blouse.

"Ahh . . ." Hayim sighed. "Once we might have met and . . . and let Allah decide who would possess the prize . . ."

"Alena?"

The Arab nodded, his face pasty beneath his dark skin.

The stump was raw, ending halfway down his forearm. The cutting laser had not seared all the arteries, and blood pumped forth alarmingly. Rader thumbed his weapon to a wide, low-intensity beam and glanced at the Arab. "Hold on." Hayim's hand dug into Rader's biceps, and the ruby-beam played across the raw meat. Hayim screamed and passed out. But the wound was seared. There would be no more bleeding. Some ship would take him back, his DNA processes would be stimulated and a new forearm would eventually grow, slowly and agonizingly.

Rader called out into the darkened main room for someone to come and help. Then he ran out of the dome and turned north. He saw Wolf running toward him, yelling, but he couldn't make out the words. He seized the youth, who gasped out terrible news.

"Liana—! There's some Startraders against the east wall and, god almighty, Liana won't let them surrender! She's going to get herself killed!"

Rader started running, with Wolf after him.

Liana was slaughtering the remaining Startraders like an avenging angel. They were barricaded behind crates, some of which were burning and others were slashed and hacked with laser beams. They were firing at Liana and at several Kaleen and traders, but Liana seemed impervious. The hot beams shot passed her like a red net, but she stood calmly, in full view, firing with a cold precision that was as startling as it was deadly. With each one of her millisecond pulses a man died or fell back, horribly wounded. Men cried out that they surrendered, but Liana ignored them. Rader ran toward Liana, but a blast of fire rainbowing off a dome splattered him with foam dust and he dodged back.

"Liana!"

He saw that she had a seared cut across her bare golden thigh but was otherwise unhurt. *But her mind and heart are wounded,* he thought as he cried out to her again. Wolf dropped down beside him. A desperate Startrader rose up, leveled a weapon, and Liana fired at him coldly. The man's face dissolved in a splatter of blood and he fell back, dead.

There were cries from beyond the barricade but no more shooting. Rader ran out and grabbed Liana. Her eyes were wide, staring, horrible. A dead man's leg twitched as he protruded from behind a crate, and Liana fired past Rader's hip, depleting her laser in a final burst at the corpse. Then her arm dropped. Rader put his arm around her, looking her over again for injury, but she was just a stiff, golden statue of hatred and remorse.

And inside, there was ice on fire.

"They're dead, Liana, all of them, or surrendered."

"Not Lockhart," she said in a small voice. She gestured to the north, and Rader saw that a new small gate had been lasercut in the rock-melt wall. As he looked, a starship's lander rose up rapidly, glowing as the sunlight struck it. In seconds it was out of range, a dot in the dawn sky, and gone.

Liana swayed, her face dead, her eyes bleak. She turned away from Rader, staggered, and Wolf caught her. She clung to him, and he looked with a stricken face at Rader, who motioned him on. The youth took the stumbling woman into the shadows, to sit on a crate.

Rader looked around: wounded and dead. Kaleen and human. Those that were alive and victorious moved aimlessly, the shock of combat over. They searched listlessly, with blank-eyed aftershock, rounding up the prisoners. Rader saw Liana hunched into Wolf's shoulder, her shoulders moving in anguish as the flood of tears came at last.

"He got away," Rader said softly, looking up. *If he gets to a starship and that ship has weapons . . .*

Rader turned and yelled down the street. "They had a laser with long-range capabilities! Does anyone know where it is?"

A bearded trapper stepped out from between some buildings and shouted back. "Heard about one put in at Black-bull, 'nother being built over near Nuevo Monterey!"

Too far, too far. "You!" he said, shouting back. "Take some men and go to Blackbull and take that battery. Gastoni? Gastoni here?" Rader heard a faint shout. "Take some men and go to Nuevo Monterey—we'll need those laser batteries if we get in a fight with a starship!"

"Yo!"

"We're sitting on Target One," Rader said, thinking

aloud. *No ship, no lander, no way to protect ourselves except by scattering. To be hunted down, one by one, from space, from the air, with reinforcements arriving regularly.*

"All right, everyone!" he shouted. "We've got to disperse! Lockhart's gotten away! If the *Du Pont* didn't follow the *Lynn* into null-space, it will be back! Or another ship can come along on the chain from Startrade headquarters!"

Several of the men cursed and began moving about purposefully. "Get what you can from stores and spread out! You Kaleen—you better get out, too, I think we—"

A sphere of light rose from the ground at his feet, and Kaleen-ka spoke in his mind.

I will help you.

"How?" Rader pointed at the sky. "He's out there, with Alena and that marshal—must be in parking orbit by now . . ."

I will take you.

The sphere floated toward Rader, but he backed off. "Wait a minute! Up *there?* Into space?"

I will take you.

Rader looked around as he spoke, "Not that I doubt you, but . . ." He broke off to run to the nearest laser-carrying human. "I need your charge."

"Take it."

Rader ran from man to man, bleeding off the power. It was an expensive way to charge a laser, for much was lost, but the fusion plant was in operation again and Rader told them to get charged up before they left Shamrock. He stepped to Wolf and Liana. "I'm going after Lockhart."

For a second Liana's grief-stricken face hardened, and she said with a terrible low intensity, "Don't let him die easy."

"Rader, I—" But Rader stopped Wolf's words.

"You watch out for her. Take care of Korda. I know you want to go along, but this . . . this is something personal."

"All right. I understand," Wolf said, though he didn't.

"I'm ready," Rader said to Kaleen-ka.

The sphere of light drifted toward him . . . around him . . . he felt weightlessness lighten him and a tingling over his whole body.

You are a warrior.

"Yes." His voice sounded strange and muffled, and Rader

was not even certain he had spoken. Everything was white, featureless, even, without form.

And more than a warrior.

"I hope so."

The Kaleen are also more than warriors.

"We're finding that out. Just what *are* you?"

The Kaleen. The people. Different from you, but not so different. We evolve, you evolve. Your evolution is slow, and no one entity is much different from another, yet you constantly change. You adapt.

"There are only two things to dread—change . . . and not changing."

Yes. The strangeness I felt earlier is gone. I have consulted with the others. We agree. A cycle is closing. We are evolving.

"You're . . . evolving . . . now?"

Yes. You do not fear change?

"Yes, but it is necessary. We cannot survive without changing."

Do you fear death?

"Yes, because it leaves me incomplete, but we all die incomplete . . ."

You mourn your friend.

"Yes."

You desire reunification with your mate?

"Yes . . . I'd guess you'd call it that."

You will kill these other humans you pursue?

"Yes. Definitely. I must."

Is killing so much a part of you?

"It is right now. We who live all kill—to eat, to survive."

You humans are testers unlike any we have encountered.

"Oh, we're fine killers, all right—but are we good?"

You survive.

"Is that all of it? Just survival?"

Zikkala means Treasure, a benign glory.

It's that, all right. But can we live together now? Do your people plan to always . . . test us?

We test ourselves. But I believe we have found an even finer test. The world called Tura.

"Oh, that's a test, all right!"

We will need your help.

"Our help? What can we do?"

Transport us. Even those at my level of development cannot go so far. Your ships of metal and plastic—they can take my people for the testing.

"Why? No one in their right mind would want to go there voluntarily!"

Greater testing means greater achievement. Already I am perceiving that the cycle is being completed. I told you earlier that even I did not know the next level of my evolution. Now I do. It is to complete the ancient cycle, a cycle so old only the ritual is left, the ritual of change, of completion. The myths are re-established, and the cycle begins anew.

"What cycle?"

I shall return to a form not unlike those of my people. Before I could not do it, for I did not know the way. Now I do. It is the proper time. My genetic change shall lift the whole race. I understand the cycle now and what must be done. We rise to the challenge of Tura.

"And after you have conquered Tura?"

We shall not conquer Tura, but live with it, learn from it. I have seen the images in your mind, and it shall be a glorious test.

"But after Tura is no longer a challenge?"

Then the cycle will begin again. The proper stimulus will be at hand. We shall complete the cycle and evolve.

"We'll do what we can . . . if Lockhart is defeated."

We are almost there. Your testing is upon you.

Rader felt the glow dissipate even before he saw the whiteness recede into the efficient gray of the lander's pressurized cargo deck. Kaleen-ka had brought him to the speeding lander. He felt the faint gravity of a ship under drive and gripped his laser tightly. The hold was empty, and he made his way toward the bridge. Once there, he put his ear to the closed hatch leading to the small control room. Faintly, he could hear a voice calling over and over again.

"*Du Pont*, this is Lockhart in Lander Three, come in please. *Du Pont*, this is Lander Three, goddamn you, come in. If you've gone off chasing that decoy into null-space,

I'll leave orders to have your ears fed to you! *Du Pont,* dammit, this is Lockhart!"

"Give it up, Lockhart!" Rader recognized Gossett's voice. "That damn fool went off into null-space chasing that decoy. What we gotta decide is what to do next? Can we stay up here until the next ship pops out? Can we make it to Tura? How about going down to Blackbull and holing up until the next Startrade ship comes in?"

Rader slipped closer and carefully edged the hatch open a bit. The slice of control room he could see was empty. No Alena, no men.

Lockhart uttered a string of oaths, and there was a clatter that sounded like equipment being tossed down. "We can't go to Tura. There's been no answer from there—"

"Could just be those blasted sunspots," Gossett said.

"No, no, I think Rader fixed things there. We can't take a chance. These landers aren't made to be interplanetary shuttles, you know."

"Why don't you just surrender?" It was Alena's voice, clear and composed, and Rader's heart leaped.

"Shut up, you cleo!" snapped Gossett.

"Surrender to what?" Lockhart growled. "A prejudiced and very illegal court? Or maybe get shot trying to escape?"

"Don't judge everyone by yourself, Citizen Lockhart," Alena said.

"I told you to shut your hatch!" Gossett said, and Rader heard a slap and a soft moan from Alena. He gripped his laser and fought to keep from charging in. But he needed better information. *Where are they, in what position, is Alena in position to be a shield for them—?*

Rader squatted down and carefully eased the hatch open further. Gossett and Lockhart were arguing, then they suddenly stopped. There was a whisper, then Lockhart called out? "Who's that? Who's back there?" Rader swore to himself; there must have been some betraying motion of the hatch, some reflection.

"This is Marshal Gossett! Who's back there?"

Rader did not answer, but swung the hatch open, keeping well back. A laser bolt rainbowed off the metal, and for a moment the manual controls glowed red. "Goddammit, who's there!" Lockhart snarled.

"The name is Rader and I'm going to kill you, slimeball!"

"Rader!" There was a moment of panic in Lockhart's voice, and it gave Rader a deep sense of pleasure.

"I want you to know who is killing you, Lockhart. You'll die and your galactic empire will die with you!"

"There are Startrade ships coming along, Rader," he called out. "They'll take you and—"

"No, they won't. They aren't real warships—they're cargo ships, and we have a way of putting men aboard."

"How did you get aboard? I left you with that black's body." Lockhart spoke deliberately, and Rader knew he was trying to get him angry.

"The Kaleen, Lockhart. They're a fantastic race. One of them floated through bedrock to disable your fusion plant, then he just brought me up here."

"How interesting." Another scarlet blast struck the metal hatch, and Rader heard a sound. Lockhart was changing locations. Rader heard whispers and knew they were working out a plan. To keep them from coming up with the obvious solution—Alena—Rader kept talking.

"You never understood the Kaleen, Lockhart, any more than you understood the humans on Zikkala. Anyone in your way is automatically to be eliminated, isn't that right?" As he talked, Rader looked around for something to use as a distraction. He saw a bundle of second-rate *shoka* furs left in a corner, along with some discarded food cartons. He went to the corner and scooped them up as Lockhart tried soothing words.

"We can reach some kind of compromise, you and I, Rader. You'll do all right. You can stay on Zikkala as my representative. Say ten percent of the take? Full pardon from the United System? I can arrange that, easily."

"Crawl, Lockhart!"

His voice came back indignantly. "I'm not crawling, you ignorant mudballer! I'm *negotiating!* Everything can be settled to the satisfaction of all concerned—"

"To Korda's satisfaction? To Alena in the shockquizzer? To *mine?*" Rader thumbed his laser down and fired into the bundle of furs, setting them afire. He catapulted the roll through the hatch and dived after it. Landers were much alike, and he knew the basic layout. His laser criss-crossed the control room with the first figure to fire—Gossett—but the tame Startrader marshal was firing at the burning, flopping roll of furs. Rader did not miss. Gossett jerked as if invisible strings were constricting him. His fingers tightened on the firing stud and he made a melting scar down the control room wall as he fell.

Alena screamed as Lockhart rose up behind her, a triumphant expression on his face. Shielded by Alena, counting on Rader's instinctive resistance to fire at his lover, Lockhart took deliberate aim. Lashed to a control chair, Alena used the only weapon she had, a primitive but still effective tool: her teeth. She bit into Lockhart's wrist and hand, drawing blood and jerking his hand toward her. His laser beam exploded the communicator, but before he could tear his bleeding hand from the woman's savage grasp, Rader shot.

Lockhart stared at the burning slot in his tunic, staring incredulously. "No," he croaked, "no, that's not the way it's supposed to be—!"

His eyes came up to Rader's, his attractive face drawn with shock, a membrane stretched over death, a mockery of the handsome man he had once been.

"No," Rader said softly, "it *is* the way it's supposed to be."

Lockhart stared at him, swaying, then fell forward, crumpling to the deck. His laser clattered among the navigation instruments and everything was still.

Rader stared at the corpse, the tension draining out of him, the sickness rising in his stomach. Alena and Rader stared at each other for a long moment. "Are you all right?" he asked huskily.

She nodded. "He thought you'd . . . that you'd not come after him if he had me."

Rader nodded as he went to her and started unfastening her bonds. "A fatal mistake for a careful man." Rader looked at her in the eyes. "You knew I'd come after you, didn't you?"

She nodded, pulling her arms free and putting them around his neck. "Yes. I just didn't know how." She smiled and kissed him. "Were you kidding him about a Kaleen bringing you up, or did you stow away?"

Rader smiled tiredly. He had a lot to tell her. He slumped into a control seat and bypassed the ruined communicator into the backup system. Then he punched in the screens and read their position. "No," he said slowly, "the Kaleen helped us, and . . . I guess . . . we help the Kaleen."

He began punching in a return orbit.

Back to Shamrock.

Back to burying Korda.

Back to Zikkala.

The lander sat upon a finger of rust-red rock almost three hundred meters high that stood out from the sheer carved cliffs of a nameless canyon. Far below, a green river wandered in serpentine curves through the rainbow trees at the bottom. The wind was gentle, the sun warm, and the crypt that had been carved in the top of the rock column was precise and rectangular. The carefully cut slab that was to seal it rested next to the grave.

Wolf Briggs helped Rader lower the coffin of *pungi* wood into the stone slot and manage the bulky weight into position. Wolf raised his sweating face and looked at the impassive Rader, who nodded. The boy heaved himself out and stood brushing off his clothes self-consciously, while Rader climbed out more slowly. The big man ignored the stains of red dust upon his black clothes, his face bleak, his manner slow and deliberate.

Alena and Liana stood nearby, as did Gastoni, one-footed Konstantin, and several of the others. There had been burials all over Zikkala, but Rader wanted his friend buried here, atop an unscalable spire of rock that Korda had once said he'd like someday to climb.

Gastoni and Wolf moved the slab into position; then Gastoni looked at Rader. No one said anything, and Rader made an abrupt gesture. They lowered the slab, and Gastoni fused the rock around the edge with a flaring laser.

Rader looked out over the wide, winding valley. *What a beautiful view. You'll like it up here, Korda. The hawks fly below, and you can just see our home, over there on that cliff. Wolf is all set to be pilot, running the Kaleen over to Tura in the lander. We have it all set how we're going to take the next Startrade ship that comes out of null-space.*

The Kaleen will evolve. The shoka will breed. Alena and I will live in the bubble cave. Rader looked at Liana.

The slant-eyed woman stepped forward, looking down, her face empty. She sighed and said something under her breath that no one caught. A bluehawk swept up from the canyon, banking with spread wingtip feathers, and sailed higher on the updraft. Liana raised her head and a faint smile came to her lips. The wind ruffled the long black strands of her hair and swept them around her face. She pulled them back and turned to Rader, nodding slightly.

Rader gestured toward the lander, and they all trooped aboard, silent, somber. It was done.

Wolf lifted the lander with a growing expertise, rising up from the column of rock, and made a wide, banking, unnecessary turn around it while they all looked through the ports. The lander leveled off for a run to Shamrock, and Liana said, "I'm leaving Zikkala."

"Liana!" said Alena. "No, don't go!"

The black-haired beauty smiled. "Too many memories here. As soon as Zikkala gets herself a little defensive fleet, courtesy of Startrade, then I'll be moving on with the first ship out."

"Aw, hell, Liana," Konstantin muttered. She smiled and patted his cheek.

"Got to, old friend. You know I can't come back, at least not in your lifetime, but I'll be thinking of you." She looked at Rader and Alena and smiled. "Maybe I'll come back and see your great-grandchildren, huh?"

"Or Wolf's," the blonde woman said, smiling at the young man's sudden embarrassment.

"Well, uh . . ." Wolf stuttered. "I'm still learning how to handle women."

Rader smiled wryly. "The experience a man needs is how to *be* handled!"

Gastoni cackled, and Alena punched Rader lightly on the arm. He put his arm around her, and they watched the deep, color-banded canyons pass below them.

The war for Zikkala was almost over. The *Du Pont* had chased the *E. A. Lynn* into null-space. The men on Tura could be taken off just as soon as they got themselves a new prize of war from the Startrade company. They'd be sent on, the ones that wanted to go, with all the treasure taken from Tura. The Kaleen were active, beginning a new cycle, eager to test themselves on Tura. The thought of going, without armor, from Base One to Two to Three and back, was terrifying to Rader. But the Kaleen were determined.

Rader sighed. Liana was going off into the stars, into the future, toward new adventures. But Rader felt he was beginning the greatest adventure of all: love.

The lander streaked through the afternoon light. Far below, a wind passed across a grove of rainbow trees, creating an undulating dance of colors. In the eastern sky a bright dot glowed: Tura, the testing ground of the new cycle of Kaleen.

Everything changes but change, Rader thought and held his woman close.

In the deepest and most sacred cavern, five spheres of cold light floated up through the smoothed rock, illuminating the assembled Kaleen. The sphere in the center pulsed, rippling with sudden color, and the words came into the minds of the Kaleen.

The cycle has finished and another has begun. It is the time of changing.

The other spheres now pulsed with color—surging, spreading, circling bands of brighter and richer colors.

We who have transcended return to the flesh. We return as males, to spread the mutated seed, to charge the generations with new life. Another cycle has begun. Another time of testing is upon us, a greater challenge, a higher reward.

The spheres of light shrank, still pulsing with the blood-beat of life, until the staring Kaleen could see the figures emerging from the chrysalis of throbbing light. New figures, shining and naked, different yet the same, changed but familiar.

I was Kaleen-ka.

The mind-voice was new and stronger.

I begin the new cycle with a new name and a new des-

tiny. We shall rise together, my brothers, my sisters, my children. We shall learn from the humans and learn from our new selves.

There was a brief moment of light in their minds.

Then we shall grow again.

PLAYBOY PRESS PAPERBACKS SCIENCE FICTION

A SUPERB SELECTION
OF THE BEST IN
SCIENCE FICTION NOVELS
FOR YOUR READING PLEASURE

"A BOOK TO HAUNT
YOUR MEMORY AND YOUR DREAMS."
—ROBERT BLOCH,
AUTHOR OF *PSYCHO*

The Sibling

By Adam Hall

An absolutely gripping psychic thriller about a brother and sister whose fierce love and murderous hate would terrify the world for all time.

Drawn together by a mysterious passion, pulled apart by strange forces from beyond the grave, both are condemned to relive the rites of a long-forgotten past and must answer the voices of ancient gods demanding sacrifices that can end only in death.

16522 $2.50